LEFTOVER GIRL

Leftover Girl Book 1

C.C. Bolick

LEFTOVER GIRL

Dirt Road Books

ISBN 978-1-946-08901-4

Cover Design by EbookEditingPro

Books by C.C. Bolick:

Leftover Girl Series:
Leftover Girl
Secrets Return
Prison of Lies
Illusion of Truth
Fate of War

The Agency Series:
Run Don't Think
Love Don't Wait
Fight Don't Fear

For Moses and Bucky

No one knows the reasons, but I have faith we'll meet again

CHAPTER ONE

Another Move

"Twenty minutes," Dad said from the doorway. "Pack whatever will fit in your bags."

For once I didn't feel angry at his words. Instead of looking up, I stared at the art table before me as he sighed and disappeared back down the hall. Twenty minutes was an eternity when my whole wardrobe consisted of a single drawer and a dozen or so hangers. Besides, the cat needed more shadow beneath his ears. Charcoal that bled to my hands formed the sharp V above his eyes and the fierce twist of a bobbed tail.

A door slammed and I closed the book. Probably better to pack before the boys busted in.

I pulled two suitcases from under the bed, a roller covered with glow stars that no longer lit at night and a striped bag handed down from Mom. Since the bag was still packed, I only opened the roller. As I stood to grab the entirety of my wardrobe, Danny charged through the door with Collin close behind.

"Why are we leaving this time?" Danny asked.

Stupid question, I thought, as he crossed his arms. I didn't bother stripping the hangers off the shirts or the jeans, frayed at both ankles, or even the green velvet dress with tags still attached, just dropped the bundle in the roller suitcase. Smoothing the clothes down flat, I made a safe home for the art pad and tugged on the zipper. A tag from the dress caught in the metal teeth, blocking my path until I swore and ripped it free. Who cared that the dress had come from an expensive mall store and not the Goodwill?

"We're wasting time," Collin said, dragging Danny toward the closet we shared. "At least Dad gave us more time than the night we came to Atlanta."

"But I wanted to start fifth grade at the same school," Danny said. "What will Tommy say?" His face twisted, somewhere between gloom and acceptance. "He'll never know, will he?"

Drawing the roller up, I climbed to my feet and aimed for the door. "We've been through this a million times. Once we go, we're gone."

"It's not fair," Collin said, glaring at me. "Normal people don't live like this. You know that, don't you Jes?"

As much as I wanted to scream at them for ratting me out over the pictures my friends posted online, part of me wanted to stretch an arm around each of the twins and assure them this move would be different. I hated that part of me; what I needed most was a heart of stone. What about the friends I'd never see again or the stray cat that climbed through the window most nights? Instead of screaming, I grabbed my bags and pillow and headed for the door.

The air outside was dark and about as tight as an oven might feel. I lifted the only proof of my existence and threw the bags into the back of the van. Maybe Dad would commend me for being first this time.

I turned and the trailer loomed before me, each light disappearing as if Mom had blown out a series of candles. Fifteen for the birthday party I never had this year. The odds of a sixteenth seemed even less. Mom and Dad pulled their roller bags through the door and called the twins.

Smiling, I climbed into the van. Time to forget Atlanta and everyone I would never see again. The tinted windows brought another layer of darkness into the van, if that were even possible. Everyone piled in, yet no one said a word.

Dad cranked the van and drove until only a few eighteen-wheelers danced around us through the six lanes, each fading to a square of red dots along the highway ahead. I propped my pillow against the window as one of the twins snored from the backseat. Mom poured coffee from a thermos, an aroma that left me torn between our many late nights on the road and perfect mornings afterward.

He managed a small laugh. “Atlanta wasn’t a total waste. The doctors at the hospital were great and the kids finished nearly a whole year at one school.”

I’d heard it all before. Every city had a good and bad side, though the fear that brought us to Atlanta had not faded from my mind. Next would come the speech about how he’d find another job that better suited his skill set, he was thankful Mom worked all those extra hours at the Waffle House, and of course their kids were healthy. Lucky us, but he never said what he was really thinking.

Someone had found out about me.

* * * * *

The van was deathly still when I opened my eyes and the only light was a burning halo beyond the windshield. As my eyes adjusted to the light, I recognized the outline of Aunt Charlie's house. "How long did we drive?"

"Hush," Mom said, "don't wake the boys."

Sweat formed a river down the side of my face, soaking into the pillow. We'd stopped at the home of Mom's only sister Charlene. I straightened, peering at the cookie-cutter houses now visible from either side of the van, each aglow with their own little dot of light. Mom and Aunt Charlie sometimes talked on the phone, but almost three years had passed since we pulled into this driveway for a visit.

"About two hours," Dad whispered.

"Why did we stop so soon?" I wrinkled my nose. Had the boys taken off their shoes?

Mom turned and patted my hand. "We're in Credence."

Any other hick town with a name I'd never heard of and I'd be snoozing again, but not Credence. Not the town where Mom grew up. "We haven't stopped in Credence in three years and that was only for Christmas."

"There's a job here," Dad said. "Mom can finally go back to teaching."

I thought of Mom waiting tables, of how she'd talk about teaching while counting a stack of bills from the night before. Her eyes always lit up when she remembered working with kids, as a math teacher and then a social worker. That was back in the years before my adoption. I often wondered how much she missed her old life.

"It's been a long time," Mom said, her voice a mixture of exhaustion and weary hope.

"We'll be living with Aunt Charlie?" I asked.

"No, honey," Mom said, "the house next door is empty, has been since May. It was perfect timing since we needed… a new home."

Yeah, our typical perfect timing. "How long will we be staying?"

Dad groaned. "Hopefully longer than in Atlanta."

I sucked in a breath, feeling the old guilt pressing closer. It was my fault we always had to move.

"You'll have your own room this time," Mom said. "You won't have to share with the boys. This is a real house, not a two-bedroom trailer like our last place."

"Everyone I knew in Atlanta lived in a trailer." I glanced at the houses to my left and right, wondering which one might be ours.

Mom laughed. "There's nothing wrong with living in a trailer. We've lived in several, even that pop-up Dad pulled behind the old Ford. I'm just saying give this house a chance. More room, more possibilities."

"I've got two bags," I said. "The last thing I need is more room."

"We'll get you more stuff," Dad said. "We'll stay with Lorraine's sister for a few days while we get some furniture. School here starts tomorrow, but maybe by the weekend you'll have a new bed."

I thought about how careful I'd been to hide the truth about my past. I never Googled my real name at the library or said a word about what happened in New York. Staring at Aunt Charlie's house, I wondered who'd scared Dad into packing us up this time.

* * * * *

Aunt Charlie had managed to order everything from the stepping-stones, which led us through a virtually flat lawn, to her museum of a living room. Everything had to be clean and in the perfect place—even Aunt Charlie's signature hugs had their own perfect rhythm. First, she sealed me within her arms. Then she tightened her grip as if I might flee. Finally, she giggled and let out a sigh. This she repeated until I pulled back and inched closer to Mom.

"You do remember Bailey and Pade?" she asked after Dad cleared his throat.

Did she think I'd forgotten her kids? "Yes," I said, remembering the few times I'd visited and hung out with Bailey. She was my age and Pade was a year older. Bailey and I had become instant friends. I wondered, maybe even hoped, it might be the same though we hadn't seen each other for years. "I remember coming here for Christmas."

"Charlene," Mom said, her voice rising. "It's only been three years. Jes doesn't have a memory problem anymore."

Great, it was starting already. I couldn't remember anything before Dad found me at four, standing in the middle of a dark highway. Mom and Dad always acted like I was a fragile piece of glass, about to crack and break at any moment. If only they'd treat me like a normal person.

"Unless," I said, "you ask me about something that happened before the night I met Mom." Instead of letting Mom comfort me, I pulled away as she tried to put an arm around me. "Don't we have this discussion every time we visit? And you guys worry about me not remembering."

Red crept into Aunt Charlie's face. "I'm sorry."

It was my fault and they all knew it. The moves, the secrecy—it was all about a time I couldn't remember. Maybe I really was crazy.

Dad cleared his throat again. "Where are the kids?"

"Pade's playing some kind of video game and Bailey is probably on the phone."

"The sun is barely up." Dad glanced at his watch.

Aunt Charlie grinned. "Come on, Justin, think like all you have to worry about in the world is what's for dinner and what trouble you can find for Friday night. It's not early, it's late. Go on upstairs, Jes. Bailey's room is second door to the… oh, sorry. I'm sure you remember the way."

Mom managed to shift the conversation away from me as I climbed the steps and took a right. I tiptoed past the first doorway but stopped when I heard voices. Easing closer, I slid the door open.

Pade leaned back in a desk chair, eyes closed. Bailey laid across the bed with a phone in her hand.

"You never take sides," Pade said. "Why now?"

"It's not fair how Tosh and Lisa treat people." Bailey didn't bother looking up. "If Sarah Beth's good with that, don't expect me to just hang out and play nice."

"Yeah, my sister finally takes a stand and it's against my girlfriend. Way to stab me in the back."

Bailey tossed her hair, a thick mass of midnight black falling halfway down her back. "Angel and Rachelle are my best friends."

"Tosh promised not to mess with Angel or Rachelle."

"When you're around. What do you think happens when you're not?"

Pade sighed. "Part of staying popular is keeping good with everyone."

"Angel and Rachelle don't care about being popular. Why should I? You're the one who does the football thing. Class president, honor society—you can have them all."

"Angel and Rachelle don't care because they could never be popular."

Bailey lowered the phone. "I thought you liked my friends."

"I do, but they're weird, come on admit it. You wouldn't think—" Pade's eyes opened and landed on me.

Intense dark eyes took in the length of my body, eyes the same shade of midnight that curled around his ears in a childish way, much too short for my tastes. Stopping on my face, his eyes took on a look of irritation. 'How dare you sneak up on us,' he seemed to say.

"Hey." Bailey jumped from the bed. "How long have you been standing there?"

Pade pushed the chair back in a guarded motion. "Glad you're back, short shit."

"Why?" I asked.

He laughed, not taking his eyes off me. "I called you that before, remember?"

"There's nothing wrong with my memory." I steadied my tone. "Why are you glad to see me?"

Pade stopped laughing and looked to Bailey, then back to me. "You're serious." His eyes narrowed. "What happened to the Jes Delaney who had a sense of humor?"

Bailey stepped to my side. "Leave her alone. She doesn't understand your jokes yet. Jes needs time to get to know everyone here."

He shook his head. "I know what you're thinking. You're not bringing her to the party. It wouldn't be a good idea."

"It's the best idea," Bailey said. "Angel and Rachelle, Terrance, Skip—they'll go easy on her. Better for Jes to meet them before someone like Tosh or Lisa. Hey, I bet Mom would let you drive the car."

Pade shook his head again. "I'm not babysitting. It's Angel's party and I promised her that me and Terrance would bring the drinks."

Drinks? I smiled while imagining Dad rant. "When do we leave?"

* * * * *

Pade stared ahead as the orange Mazda bounced, intent on tracing two cuts of dirt that seemed to guide us around the deepest pits. Pine trees lined both sides of the road, stretching in infinite rows like the corn fields had in Nebraska. Nearing the last turn, the trees opened to a 'Y' with rows of trailers in either direction, some deserted. Almost all brandished a fence with 'beware of dog' posted on the gate. Half included rusty cars on cement blocks, in stark contrast to the occasional medley of azaleas and brightly painted garden gnomes. One had black trash bags over every window, reminding me of a haunted house.

After every major bump, Pade's eyes found mine in the mirror and I looked away. Bailey stared out her window, maybe beyond the trailers, quiet for the first time that day. The music blared, with a screeching guitar and pounding drums, as the silence became more than I could bear. Did Pade listen to heavy metal like this all of the time?

As if Pade heard my thoughts, he pressed buttons until sounds of country music filled the car.

"We're almost there," Bailey said. "Don't let these trailers scare you."

I laughed, though she probably couldn't hear. "We lived in a trailer park in Atlanta."

"Oh." Eyes still fixed outside, she allowed the second half of the song to pass in silence, making me feel like the worst friend ever. Then she turned around and smiled. "Bet you didn't have an ex-military bus driver, a voodoo shack, or a pot farm—see that long driveway? Angel says no one goes there after dark."

"It will be fun," she said. "You'll really like Angel—she always tells the craziest stories. Your life will seem boring after an hour of hearing about hers."

"Not likely." I turned to my window. Couldn't the day go any faster?

The trees thinned behind the trailers, leaving a vast opening just beyond the turn. Sunshine and wispy clouds filled the opening as faraway trees became apparent. We climbed the last little hill at the turn, rising until I had my first view of sparkling waves.

Pade slammed on the brakes and spun to face me.

"What the hell," Bailey screamed.

"Angel lives on the river," he said. "Just moved here a week ago."

"So?" I asked.

He silenced the radio with one twist. "Mom says you're afraid of water."

"Pade!" Bailey slapped his arm. "Now you're really being mean."

"I want to know," he said, not taking his eyes off me. "Tell me that you're shaking and can't find the words. Show me you want to turn back."

"I. Am. Not. Afraid," I said. "How's that for shaking?"

"Keep driving," Bailey said. "It isn't her fault."

I rolled my window down, almost welcoming the haze of dust and the smell of the river ahead, along with the need to gag. Everything was my fault. "What did I do?"

"Damn it," Pade said, hammering his palms against the steering wheel.

Grasping for the handle, I pulled until the door clicked, but stopped. Anyone else and I would have gladly stalked right back up that road of endless pits and found my own way home. It wouldn't be the first time, or the last, but this was family. Credence had to be different. I shuddered, for one day they'd know the truth—if Mom and Dad didn't whisk me away in the middle of the night first.

Bailey faced me again. "We didn't know how you'd react to the water."

"Remember the pool in our backyard?" Pade asked. "Mom had it covered a month ago, because you were afraid of water."

I rubbed my eyes. "I'm sorry." But a month… that meant Dad had actually planned this move… which meant we might be staying.

"Pade's angry because we always had pool parties. But it's okay," Bailey said. "Mom said you were scared of water and we don't want to give you a reason to leave."

"Speak for yourself," Pade said, but his words had softened.

Somehow, I managed to roll the window back up without breaking into a full-blown fit of tears. "My parents say I was petrified, but I don't remember anything from before my adoption. If they know, they're not saying. We've never had a pool and we've definitely never lived near water. My dad would be on the way with the van floored right now if he knew about this place."

Bailey smiled. "Good thing we haven't told Mom. She still thinks Angel lives at the apartment."

I laughed despite the feeling someone had punched my stomach. "It all sounds crazy, doesn't it?"

"Well, Sis," Pade said and eased onto the gas, "sounds like she'll fit right in with your crew."

CHAPTER TWO

The Dare

Bailey introduced me to everyone at Angel's party, and then shoved me into a bathroom that barely held a sink and shower, much less a washer and dryer. She pulled an eyeliner pencil from her purse and applied a black stripe under each eye, on top of an equally dark line. The floor crunched under my feet, but I didn't need to look for the litter box I'd smelled from the hall. A creamy-white cat rubbed against my legs and I stooped to pick it up.

"Angel's been threatening to make everyone play spin the bottle," Bailey said. "How lame is that? I'm having flashbacks to fifth grade."

I shrugged. "It's Angel's party."

"And I'd cry if her parents hadn't left the liquor cabinet unlocked. We're trying vodka this time." Bailey laughed. "Angel said that bottle has the most and last time her parents almost caught on to the fact a third of the rum evaporated."

"Evaporated?" Rachelle poked her head around the

door. "Maybe she should take Skip's stupid advice and fill the bottle back up with water."

"This is too much drama when everyone's only gonna get one sip." Bailey shook her head. "Angel's lucky you keep her from listening to Skip."

"It's not easy." Rachelle glanced down the hall, where Angel and Skip laughed. "Angel doesn't seem to have a brain when he's around."

Bailey closed her purse, content with only the eyeliner. "Did you hear why Skip got the ticket? No one gets a ticket for driving too slow, and of course his dad took the keys."

"If my dad was the principal, I'd lose the keys too." Rachelle laughed. "Oh yeah, Angel's ready for us."

At the entrance to the kitchen, Angel rounded the counter and grabbed her phone off the charger. "Everyone who's playing spin the cell phone—in the living room. Except for you Pade. You're making me a drink with the o.j. you brought."

Pade laughed. "Spin the cell phone? You've got a whole liquor cabinet to choose from."

I found a seat on the only section of wood floor not covered by a rug.

"Sure you want to do this?" Rachelle asked.

I stared at the floor. "Like I've got a choice."

She moved closer. "You don't always have to try so hard to fit in, not around here. Was it bad at the other schools?"

Her words brought a smile to my face. "Not bad, really. We just never stayed anywhere long enough to worry about not fitting in. Starting school in Credence, well, I guess it's like coming home." I met her eyes, feeling sure about one thing at least. "If fitting in is a package deal, then I say bring it on."

She blinked, perhaps wanting to say more, but pulled back as Bailey squeezed between us.

Angel strolled in, foam cup in hand, followed by Pade. "Since it's my party, I get to pick, and the new girl goes first."

"What?" I glanced from Pade to Skip to Terrance, as all three stared back. I held my breath as I spun the phone. The case swooshed, easing to a stop in front of Pade.

With everyone laughing, Bailey slipped an arm around my neck. "One kiss won't hurt."

I pulled away. "Am I the only person who thinks this is crazy? Why do I get the feeling you're up to something?"

"Up to what?" Looking around the circle, she shrugged. "This wasn't my idea. Maybe Pade wants to kiss you."

Of course he didn't want to kiss me, and now he couldn't not kiss me. If only the phone had stopped in front of Skip or Terrance. Still, one option might keep my name out of gossip. "You know me kissing Pade would be yucky weird since we're related."

Angel squealed. "Nice try. Too bad everyone in this room knows you're adopted. Bailey was right—this is lame, but I've got a better idea." She rubbed her hands together and jumped to her feet. "Instead of just kissing, why don't you go somewhere alone?"

"Hey," Bailey said. "We won't be able to see them."

"What about Sarah Beth?" I asked.

"This is just a game," Terrance said. "Sarah Beth has been to these parties. If the phone had stopped on her, she might have kissed you herself."

Angel turned so fast she nearly fell. "Everyone follow me." She led us through the kitchen, green and white linoleum dotting our path from beneath a layer of clothes and more cat litter. At the pantry door, she stopped. "Five minutes in the pantry. You can even decide to make out with the light or without."

"Fine." I pushed open the door before anyone could notice my cheeks.

"Really?" Bailey asked with wide eyes. "No arguing?"

Pade followed and grabbed the string above. "Light on or off?" He grinned, pushing the door closed behind us.

I lowered between a vacuum and a shelf of cans, finding nothing but a stack of old *Seventeen* magazines to sit on. "Seriously?"

"Are you counting the minutes already?" He sighed and sat down opposite me, legs crossed, within an arm's length. The safety of nearly a foot in height difference disappeared. "We should at least act like something's going on in here."

"I guess we could *say* we kissed." Maybe turning off the light wasn't such a bad idea. "How would they know if nothing happens?"

We sat, unmoving, while silence tied a knot at the base of my tongue. I waited for him to make a joke, laugh, or somehow act like the same Pade I'd seen ripping through foil paper under a Christmas tree. Though meeting this guy had once been fun, kissing him might make me hurl. Knowing him could be even worse.

"You never wanted to kiss me before," I said. Did he notice the way my fists clenched?

"I've never been alone with you in a pantry before."

His smile faded as a question grew in his eyes. Time slowed to nonexistent as he crossed the gulf, with my heart on pace to beat loose from the safety of its cage. Each thud sent new warmth through my blood as I tried to catch my breath.

One kiss, I told myself. Other guys had kissed me. Well, maybe one other guy at my last Homecoming dance and one before we moved to Atlanta, but neither had made me feel as if something great was about to end. Or begin. I couldn't decide.

Inches from my face, Pade paused and inhaled. We were frozen in time and I trembled, fearful he'd never close the distance, never end the torture building inside. Without warning, he brought his lips to mine, first in a feather touch, and then holding as if an eternity could pass before we'd gasp for air.

Clapping brought us back to the party, to Angel's house, and I remembered who sat across from me. I pulled back, red gleaming in my cheeks, and not only from embarrassment. I was ready to hit somebody.

"Did you get it?" Bailey asked.

Skip lowered his phone. "Not a good shot. Can we try again?"

I scrambled to my feet. "Please tell me that won't be on the Internet tonight. You don't understand—my dad will have a stroke."

Pade grabbed my arm, guiding me to a back corner of the living room. His voice shook as he leaned down. "My sister can't say no when Angel gets these wild ideas."

"Well," I said, "this is some welcome, but why kiss me? We could've lied and said we kissed. Who would've found out?"

"I wanted…" His eyes locked with mine. "How it would feel, I had to know."

My cheeks flamed again. "Are you out to get me now because of the pool? Or is it something else?"

Pade looked away. "You've got it wrong. I don't hate you."

"Then why let them embarrass me?"

"It was just a game, just a kiss," he said, shaking his head. "It wasn't supposed to mean anything."

"It didn't." I ran for the back door, not sure where I was going, not caring who was in my way. Out onto the red wooden porch and down the steps I ran, a panorama of water spreading before me.

Bailey yelled, her steps closing on mine. "Where are you going?"

Hot air filled my lungs as I rushed toward the water. "I can't believe you."

"For letting Skip record you? A year from now, we'll be making jokes about the look on your face."

"He's got a girlfriend."

She laughed as I reached the bank. "Pade's always got a girlfriend. Sarah Beth is like the rest—boring."

I dropped to my knees, stretching for the water. "You're an expert on girlfriends?"

She grabbed my arm, pulling me back. "You can't get in the water. Uncle Justin really would have a stroke."

Pushing her away, I reached again for the water, this time dragging the tips of my fingers through the river's edge. The sky didn't fall. The world didn't come to a screeching halt. Looking around, nothing had changed with the boats speeding by. My insides still pulsed and life before I met Justin and Lorraine Delaney remained a blank canvas. Laughter floated down from the house. "I thought it would be colder."

"Jessica Ray," a voice thundered behind us.

I jumped and lost my balance, nearly toppling into the water. Dad rushed forward, pulling me to the bank as if a single drop might mean my end.

"You should have told me," he said. "You shouldn't be here."

"You followed us?" I bit my lip to control the anger, but Bailey had receded to the shade of a nearby tree. What had she said about an apartment? "Angel can't help her parents moved to a trailer park."

"We've lived in more trailers than I can count on my left hand. I can't believe you hid the fact they live on a river. You know how I feel about you being near water. You've freaked out before and scared us."

Would it matter that Bailey and Pade had set me up? "It's not like I remember."

"You used to cry out in the night. You wouldn't put a toe through the bathroom door without Lorraine's hand attached to yours." His eyes blazed as he pulled me close, his voice dropping to a whisper. "Something happened to you that night in New York, something that made you fear water. Don't you ever worry that going near water might bring back a past you don't want to remember?"

I looked at the water behind me, gleaming in the sun—a river the size of an Atlanta highway. A boat parted the mass of glitter and another shot by, pulling a tube with two girls flat on their stomachs. A jet ski rode the waves left in their wake and shot an endless stream of white drops into the air. I longed to jump off one of the many wooden docks, clothes and all, if only to prove him wrong about my fears.

"Your mom should have come with you. We thought you were old enough, that you would understand how to stay safe."

"I promise I didn't know about the water."

"Like how you promised not to post pictures of you and your friends online when we were in Atlanta? It's a good thing I made sure you put on sunscreen before you left this morning. Have you quit doing that too?"

The man was anal about everything. Maybe he had every right to be mad, but when would he tell me why he worried about the water more than I did?

* * * * *

At dinner that night, my family sat around the huge table in Aunt Charlie's kitchen. Bailey took the chair across from me as I glanced around. Everything in the room looked like it cost a fortune. Not only did the polished wood table extend longer than our last kitchen, the counters overflowed with gadgets Mom admired for most of the night. She'd never mentioned wanting a red mixer before. Mom cooking our first meal together in Credence while her sister went into work at the hospital felt weird.

"People can't stop getting sick long enough for us to eat," Mom said with a laugh. "What a shame."

Maybe the weird feeling had something to do with how Pade had refused to come home, insisting on staying the night with Terrance.

Dad didn't mention Angel's place or the fact her backyard included a dock, and Bailey knew better than to remind him. He stared at his plate, dragging the meatloaf and green beans from one side to the other.

Mom talked about the afternoon, how she and the boys bought new clothes for school, and all of her plans for the first day of class. If only I'd been there, she had enough money to buy me a new outfit for every day of the week. "Maybe we'll go Saturday," she said, but Dad simply nodded. Her latest attempt at meatloaf wasn't much better than some of the worst cafeterias I'd known, but he'd never tell her.

"Are we ready for tomorrow?" he asked, but didn't look my way.

The boys spoke and Dad watched their tug of war with interest. Unlike me, he understood their 'twin talk.' Danny would start a sentence and Collin would finish. Or Collin would start and Danny would finish.

Born almost a year after I met Mom and Dad, Danny and Collin were the younger brothers my real parents never gave me. They made fun of my clothes and were smart enough to crack every one of my passwords. Danny and Collin were responsible for Dad knowing about the pictures online. No rules broken, no violation of any state or local laws. Just friends hanging out at the bowling alley, but he acted as if they caught me popping pills or worse. No one could find out I came from New York. For the first time, I didn't feel grateful for how they hid me. No, protected me, as Dad always said.

A silent table jolted me to Dad's stare. "Where were you just now?" he asked.

"I was, I…" My voice trailed off as I tried to think of words that wouldn't make me sound like a total freak. I couldn't help I still *felt* like one. "I was thinking about tomorrow."

Dad sighed. "Why are you so anxious for school to start?"

I shrugged. "I'm not anxious. This year will be the same as last, only I'll be in tenth grade."

"Same as last you say?" Dad raised an eyebrow. "How long will it take you to add up enough tardies for a write-up? You'll find your typical share of trouble this year, no doubt."

"Uncle Justin," Bailey said, "what kind of trouble did you find in high school?"

"I found my fair share," he said. "Enjoy it while you can; you're only fifteen once."

'Live in the moment' was one of Dad's favorite sayings. I guess almost dying cleared him of worrying. Unlike me, tossing at night, sleepless as I worried about every mistake I'd made throughout the day. Not to mention the fact I could never forget I was adopted.

Bailey laughed. "I bet the entire school begged to hang out with you. You probably even got to be class president."

"Yeah…" started Danny.

"You'd make a great one," finished Collin. He glanced at Mom. "What do you think?"

Mom lowered her glass of sweet tea. "Your father is a talented speaker. Before Atlanta, he gave inspirational speeches whenever he traveled for his job with the weight-loss company."

Danny looked at me. "Inspir what?"

"Inspirational means he makes people feel good and shows them how to be creative."

Dad gave a rare wink, his smile widening. "I guess you could have considered me a popular student where I went to school."

Great, sounded the cold irony in my head. Another thing I couldn't have inherited from him.

"By the way," Dad said, "you're looking at the newest rep for Health Made Simple."

Collin scraped his fork across his plate. "Does that mean we can be good speakers too one day, just like you?"

"Son, the two of you can be anything you want."

"What about Jes?" Collin asked.

No one took a breath until Danny broke the silence. "She can't be like Dad, silly, she's adopted. Tommy says his dad told him adoption means we're not related, not actually."

Collin looked to Dad. "Does that mean Jes is not really our sister?"

Dad's face tensed. "Of course Jes is your sister. The fact she's adopted means she has different biological parents than you. It also means she's here because we love her and want her to be part of our family." The finality of Dad's tone kept the twins from asking what biological meant, leaving four eyes to search mine.

Mom's smile relieved the sinking in my stomach. "What Dad's saying is that he and I aren't Jessica's father and mother by birth, but we love her like she's our own. You do love her too, don't you?"

"Yeah," the twins answered.

The silence that took over dinner branded me a true outsider. All the years we'd been together, playing this game called family, and the truth was clear. The meatloaf became a mass of rubber bands between my teeth, and I spit the wad into my napkin. When I pushed the plate away and glanced up, a ghost flickered in Dad's eyes.

He carried his plate to the sink and turned on the

water, full-force. "I believe Jes will surprise us all one day, with talents of her own." Hands forward, he braced himself against the counter and closed his eyes. Steam rose while the sink filled. Dad stood, unmoving, as if preparing to step out of the curtains and onto a stage. When water slipped over the ledge of granite and rained around his feet, he jumped and grasped for the handle.

Mom snatched a towel from the fridge. "I've got it." Her voice was high, strained as she laughed. "I needed to mop this floor."

With a nod, Dad turned for the porch. He allowed the door to slam behind him, which he normally yelled at us about.

Under the table, my socks gleamed as if still warm from the dryer. I watched her jagged strokes, the way she gripped the towel, before rising. "Can I help?"

She glanced at the twins, who were scraping the last bit of ketchup from their plates, then squeezed my hand. "Don't worry about your father. He gets in these moods sometimes, but he was right."

Bailey finished her tea and slammed her glass onto the table. "Let's go upstairs."

I nodded as Dad's words repeated in my head. If only he'd been my real father, I might have inherited some of his confidence.

* * * * *

Despite the night's heat and Bailey's nonstop hums and half-finished sentences, I clung to the comforter, carefully tucked in one side of her bed. I touched my lips, which still tingled from Pade's kiss.

"Are you okay?" Bailey whispered. "Am I keeping

you up?"

I wondered if she talked in her sleep every night. Did she even know? Well, I wasn't the person to drop that bomb. "I'm fine, just can't sleep."

Bailey sighed. "We can't have people thinking you spent all night studying before the first day of school. I'm sorry your house isn't ready yet. I could sleep on the couch."

"I've got a lot on my mind."

"You can tell me," she said.

No, I couldn't. "Do you ever miss your father?"

Bailey leaned back on the pillow and stared at the ceiling. "You mean the snake who sends us presents on birthdays and at Christmas? I guess Mom would probably miss his check if it didn't come in the mail every month."

I sighed as a silence fell between us, the kind that signaled a bad storm approaching. Maybe asking about her father had been a horrible idea. About the time I decided she'd fallen back asleep, Bailey gave a muffled cry.

"I haven't talked to him in over a year. No visits, only one call for Pade; what else can I say? Do I miss him? Yeah, but he's the one who's staying away." She sniffled. "Pade doesn't want to see our father ever again." Her voice became a whisper. "I overheard him tell Mom he wasn't going to Colorado because I didn't get invited."

Though my head screamed for me to stop, seldom did the opportunity to talk about my real family present itself. I might not remember them, but the articles online about my real parents made sure I'd never forget. "You've got your mom and at least you know *who* your dad is."

"I definitely wouldn't call him dad." As the meaning of my words sank in, Bailey rolled over to face me. "Sorry, I forgot you're adopted."

"How can you forget? Mom and Dad never let anyone forget."

"Aunt Rainey and Uncle Justin love you, anyone can see that. You can't tell me you don't believe…"

I stared above, knowing I should stop, but at the same time desperate for someone to hear me, maybe even attempt to understand. Why should it matter now when it didn't a year, a month, or even a week before? "I know they love me—I'm just not their daughter. If I was really their daughter, if they even thought of me as their daughter, they'd stop reminding everyone I'm adopted."

"I don't see how they remind anyone."

"They always tell people I'm adopted. It's like 'hello world, this kid's not ours.'"

"What should they do, lie?"

"Yeah."

"Have you ever told them?"

"They should be able to figure it out. You know what, it doesn't matter."

The outline of her smile was a razor blade to my heart. "Do you ever think about your real mom and dad?"

"I try so hard not to. My real mother and father…" I swallowed back tears threatening to drown the words. "They didn't want me. I'd never call them mom and dad."

"How can you say that?"

A noise sounded from the hall and Bailey lowered her voice. "How do you know they didn't want you? Did they tell you?"

"I can't remember… before. Dad told me. He hated to say their names, but he did finally tell me."

"Mom said Aunt Rainey found you when she lived in Canton—Ohio, right?"

"Right." What a joke. She knew just like everyone else in Credence would soon hear. Mom had been working in Ohio right before my adoption and even her own sister seemed to believe the lie. Well, not a lie as Dad would say. 'Merely an embellishment to protect your identity' was his justification on more than one occasion.

She tapped a finger to her chin. "I can't believe Uncle Justin actually said your real parents didn't want you."

"He didn't say it like that, but Dad does give some details when I ask."

"At least he talks to you. There's so much I could never tell my father. Oh yeah, maybe if he were here…" She sighed. "As for Mom, there's lots of drama I could never tell her."

The humor in Bailey's voice reached through the moonlight and carried me back from the edgy pain of self-pity. "He met Mom right after she found me." Even though Dad found me, not Mom, our story stayed the same no matter who asked. "They got married and poof—*happily ever after* for us all. They've always loved me and taken care of me, it's just that…"

"You want to know where *they* are."

"I'd like to know why they didn't come for me, if they've ever bothered to look for me."

"Do you think about your real parents all the time?"

I rolled over, still feeling a sting from her smile of

pity in disguise. "You know what scares me the most? I can't remember my real mother's face. I can't remember being held by my real father or the sound of his voice. Eleven years have gone since we left… Canton."

"Are you thinking about going back one day?"

"Would yes be selfish?" I asked. "Or just bad?"

"My mom is always saying people are never happy with what they have…"

Yeah, I'd heard it before. "Until they don't have it anymore. I don't see how this applies to me since I can't remember my real parents."

Footsteps drifted down the hall and we both went silent.

"Girls," Mom said, as she opened the door. "Was that you I heard?"

Even with my eyes closed, I knew Mom watched in silence. She probably hoped for movement, though neither of us flinched. Eventually her steps faded back into the night.

CHAPTER THREE

Chase

"Jessica Ray," Dad called from the stairs. "It's six-fifteen and Mom will be leaving in thirty minutes."

Was it morning already? I took a deep breath of the strange smell around me—carpet cleaner or maybe a gallon of Febreze. Mom had always been a freak about eating off the floor in the kitchen, but Aunt Charlie was like that about every room in her house. I climbed from the bed, praying our new house might be ready before the weekend.

When I walked into the kitchen, Bailey was at the bar, finishing a glass of orange juice. She frowned at my tangled hair and wrinkled T-shirt. "You better hurry and get dressed."

Mom handed me a plate. "Not before we get some food in you."

Aunt Charlie trudged through the door, her eyes fixed on the coffee pot. "I'm glad I made it home in time." Cup in hand, she hugged Bailey and put an arm around my neck. "You girls enjoy your first day. If only I was fifteen again."

"Sure," Dad said from behind a newspaper. "Then I'd feel sorry for all the boys at Credence High."

As Aunt Charlie laughed, Mom shook her head. "Charlie was quite a heartbreaker in school. She stole a couple of boyfriends from me once upon a time."

"Thanks, Charlie," Dad said. "I owe you one."

Aunt Charlie shrugged. "Most often life works out in ways we never envision. Look at me now, a woman of leisure. I'm free to spend the rest of the day cleaning my filthy house."

Dad lowered the paper. "I'm sure the only house on this block cleaner than yours is empty next door. How you can rule the world of obsessive and still work as a nurse is a topic I'd never take on for a lecture." He stood to kiss Mom on the cheek and stopped by my side for a hug. "Don't forget your sunscreen."

I rolled my eyes. "Do I ever?"

He smiled. "Skin cancer is nothing to play around with. Watch out for the sun today."

"Dad, we're in Alabama. Ignoring the sun is like you telling me to put on sunscreen every morning. It's weird."

"Wear the sunscreen and we'll have nothing to worry about."

"We've already lived in half the states. Why not try somewhere like Washington, where it rains all the time?"

"The sun glares at us, even on a cloudy day." He glanced at Mom and Aunt Charlie, both laughing as they talked, and lowered his voice. "Lorraine's only family lives in Credence. Let's make sure we stay as long as possible."

I considered asking if he'd planned this move, but simply nodded and forced the scrambled eggs down my throat. Aunt Charlie still rambled about 'those idiots' at the hospital when I reached the stairs. After changing shirts four times, jeans three times, and shoes twice, basically everything I had, and plastering on my daily ration of white sludge, I finally felt good about the girl in the mirror. At least good enough to climb into the van.

Danny stretched across the backseat, crowding Collin. "Can't we go any faster?"

I settled into the middle, next to Bailey. "We're not moving yet, stupid."

Collin gasped. "Mom, Jes used the s-word."

Mom's tone was even as she climbed into the driver's seat. "One with more than four letters, I hope." She cranked the van and turned up the radio. Elvis again.

"Are we in 1970 or what?" Bailey pulled out her eyeliner. "This music has to be at least that old. I bet your mom wasn't even born then."

I laughed. "As if that would make a difference."

With only twenty minutes before first bell, Bailey spotted Angel and Rachelle by the band room and I almost ran to keep up. Only Angel played, but several 'non-banders' hung out there in the morning. Outside two doors painted with black notes on a white ribbon, and around a corner, was a place she called The Spot. From our vantage point, higher than most of the courtyard, we could watch almost everyone along the crisscross of sidewalks.

Angel stood as we approached. "Jes, you really tore out of my house quick yesterday. How was that kiss?"

"What kiss?" asked a voice from behind us, and I

turned in time to see the girl's eyes roll. "Who are you and who on earth would want to kiss you?"

My first instinct was to laugh at the checkered tie around her neck, but Bailey spun around, glaring. "Tosh, this isn't your spot to be."

Tosh smiled and moved close enough to block Bailey's path. "If I wanted it to be, I could build a house and live here."

I'd known people like this at every other school and Bailey was not fighting for me on the first day of class. "I'm Jes Delaney." I extended a hand. "Bailey's cousin from Atlanta."

Tosh stared at my hand while shifting closer to loom over Bailey.

"It's not your business," Bailey said, "but Pade kissed her at Angel's party."

"Kissed your cousin?" Tosh snickered. "Isn't that creepy or illegal?"

"Jes is adopted. But that's not the point."

Tosh glued her hands to her hips and puckered out her bottom lip. As her eyes narrowed, tiny freckles were lost in the crease of her nose, freckles that exactly matched the Raggedy Ann hair jutting from both sides of her face in pigtails. "He must have felt sorry for her."

Bailey opened her mouth but stopped as I grabbed her arm. She hadn't noticed Pade and Terrance weaving through the crowded sidewalk in our direction.

Pade smiled, which immediately drew Tosh to his side. "You're looking nice today."

She lifted a foot, bracing it against the wall in an effort to tie her shoe, and the pleated skirt rose higher. "I'm glad you noticed."

Terrance cocked his head in amazement and turned

to Angel, barely covering a laugh. "I heard you and Bailey got stuck with the new English teacher."

Angel frowned. "Mrs. Pearson. She's taking Mr. Hancock's place since he moved over the summer."

Pade turned to Angel as if Tosh had disappeared. "Mr. Hancock never cared if I missed class as long as it was school related. Glad he didn't quit last year, since I can make just about anything school related."

There was that smile again. Did Pade have to be charming to every girl at Credence High?

Tosh lowered her foot and moved closer to Pade. "I heard she'll make everyone in her classes write five term papers."

When Terrance spotted more of the football team and motioned to Pade, Tosh leaned down to whisper in my ear. "Don't think for one second he's got any interest in scrubby tenth-graders. You're the lowest of the low."

"Tosh," Pade said, and she brightened. "Want to walk with us down to the drink machines? I'll buy you a coke."

She tossed her hair and winked at me before following Pade onto the sidewalk. "Maybe next time, Delaney."

Anger flared in Bailey's voice. "I hate that bitch. She thinks she's got the whole school taking second place to sexy. My brother can't possibly like her."

"Of course he likes her," Angel said. "All guys like her. Only Tosh could get away with wearing a skirt and tie."

Several guys stopped along the sidewalk to observe her confident walk, smiling as Tosh passed. Life seemed so unfair and yet so typical. This girl lived for any opportunity to make fun of the 'outs' like me, while the 'ins' loved her, guys especially. I wished for a way to hurt her, to make her feel the same fear and know the anger gnawing like a hamster deep in my heart.

Bailey waved a hand in front of my face. "Hey, don't look so evil."

"Evil implies I have the power to make Tosh trip in front of everyone waiting for class."

She frowned and pulled a lime green page from her backpack. "Don't make that face. Hurting people doesn't suit you."

"Time to find a schedule," I said as a bell rang out over the courtyard. "You know, make this real."

While Bailey walked to class, I ran to the office. Inside the tiny room, I squeezed through the crowd and found a space to stand. From one foot to the other I shifted, doing a kind of dance in line, but no position felt comfortable. The clock ticked and then ticked a little more, seeming to almost stop a few times. I covered my face, imagining eyes staring, all the faces in my first class, if I made it to first class.

"Jessica Delaney," I said as I finally reached the counter. "This is my first day and I need a schedule."

The woman tapped her keyboard without looking up. A man in a gray suit leaned across the counter. "Delaney? You must be Rainey's daughter."

I stared at him while trying to figure out why his dimpled face seemed familiar.

"You've got the same pretty brown eyes and hair." He grinned. "Lorraine and I attended this very school, more years ago than I like to admit."

"We're not finished," said a guy to his side.

The man straightened. "We're about as finished as

one of those meetings I've got to…" He turned back to me. "I'm Dr. Greene, by the way."

I laughed, realizing his face was simply an older version of Skip. "Nice to meet you."

Dr. Greene pulled a page from the printer. "Your first class is Mrs. Pearson. This should be interesting." He handed me the paper. "Chase here can help you find the way."

When I looked closer at Chase, a strange feeling washed over me. Behind thick glasses sat two of the bluest eyes I'd ever seen, rivaled only by the ones looking back from my mirror at night. I'd worn brown contacts for years, the same shade as Mom's eyes. I fought a grin as I realized he'd have no idea my eyes were blue.

Dr. Greene shuffled into a nearby office, leaving Chase to argue as the door slammed in his face.

"Move along, dear," said the woman behind the counter, still without looking up.

"Where's your first class?" I asked as Chase shook his fist at the door.

"Just follow me," he said, pushing through the crowd. "Try to keep up."

I was out of breath by the time we crossed the courtyard and passed three long brick buildings with empty halls. "Is there a second bell around here?" Avoiding tardies this year might be impossible.

"First class number equals building," he said as we stepped through the doors of building five. "The office and cafeteria was building one."

"Mrs. Pearson's new this year and I heard she'll be tough."

"Sounds like this year *will* be interesting." As he

laughed, his blue eyes took on a shine, forcing me to scrap the weird feeling and label him a nice guy.

We entered the class, barely in time to hear my name.

"Jessica Delaney?"

"Here." I headed for a seat in the back. Chase followed and eased into the empty seat next to mine.

A clipboard holding the list of names lowered as our teacher looked at me. "I assume you will be in that seat on time tomorrow, Miss Delaney."

"Yes ma'am."

"Good. Skip Greene?"

When the embarrassment of being late finally passed, I glanced around the room. Posters covered all four walls, one with only black and white, while the other three glowed with a rainbow of costumes spread across the stage of a theater. Bailey and Angel sat straight ahead, side-by-side on the front row. Ahead to the left, Skip stared out of the window, maybe imagining himself on the other side. The rest of the names were new until 'Chase Pearson.'

"You are here, of course."

Mrs. Pearson stood before her desk, not bothering to look up as she marked his name off the list. Every inch of her long-sleeved suit hung perfectly smoothed, down to the skirt that landed at her knees. In grape-colored heels that exactly matched her suit, she seemed to loom over the class.

Her hair, a mixture of honey and gold much darker than Chase's white-blond, was pulled back to a bun behind her head. Thick glasses covered her eyes, but I imagined they were a blue as deep as the guy sitting next to me. Remembering my comment about her being tough, 'he must think I'm such an idiot' flowed through my head at lightning speed. Bailey turned and mouthed "he's cute."

"Bailey Sanders."

Bailey swung around. "Here."

"Miss Sanders, while in my classroom you will face forward and be respectful. As long as you continue to do both, we will get along. Do you understand?"

"Yes ma'am." Bailey's head bobbed, though her tone spelled a gigantic no.

Mrs. Pearson finished the remaining names and passed out a syllabus, not once smiling. After every point came chalk on the board and a chance for Bailey to whisper to Angel. Every time I looked at Chase, his hand moved as he wrote across pages in a black binder. I groaned, sure of two things: No way would Bailey 'get along' with our new teacher, and someone had finally found a way to make me hate English.

* * * * *

At lunch, I followed Bailey into the cafeteria as she looked for Angel and Rachelle. Nearly dragging me to the end of the long table where they sat, Bailey pulled my arm until I landed in the seat next to her.

"Ooh, cute guy alert." They followed Bailey's gaze while I glanced over the line and made a mental note to bring my lunch the next day. "Check out the cutie I'm calling at the next table." She slapped the table in front of me. "Oh, I forgot, you've already met."

Chase sat, surrounded by empty seats, with a sandwich in one hand and a book in the other.

"Oh my god," Angel said. "Is he really going to sit

by himself and read during lunch?"

Rachelle laughed. "You're the one needing the glasses, Bailey. You've found yourself a real bookworm."

Why did I feel the urge to defend Chase? "Why don't you both stop? He's a nice guy."

"Who belongs in a library." Angel rolled her eyes. "Maybe he'll read Bailey a bedtime story."

Bailey drummed her fingers on the table. "You guys are just jealous since I called Chase first."

"You go right ahead," Rachelle said, "but you may have some competition. I saw Jes walking rather close to Chase on the way to first block."

"I know." Bailey looked at me. "You've got to give me the scoop on him. How did you get him to sit next to you?"

"Since we were both late, seats were kind of limited. I didn't ask him to sit next to me."

Angel exploded in laughter. "Yeah, right you didn't."

I turned to Rachelle. "You really think I have a thing for Chase?"

"Don't you?" she asked.

"Dr. Greene asked him to show me the way to first class. I didn't realize it was because he was going there too."

"First block," Rachelle said, grinning. "We say blocks here, not classes. And I can see how that might suck."

I leaned closer to Bailey. "Speaking of things that suck, you do realize Mrs. Pearson is his mother?"

Her eyes doubled in size. "You're telling me that mean woman in first block is related to my cutie? The Wicked Witch of English?"

As her voice thundered in my ears, I glanced around to see if half of the cafeteria had taken notice. Satisfied no one was watching us, I grinned. "If there's a tornado, I know where I won't be standing."

Bailey laughed and pointed to the line. I glanced at the clock. Exactly fifteen minutes left to get our meals and finish.

"If only Chase would lose the glasses," Bailey said as we reached the end. "Rachelle and Angel could see how cute he is. Why don't you fill him in on the advantages of contacts?"

"Hey," I said, gripping her arm. "You can't tell anyone."

"That your eyes are really blue? Seems like a dumb secret."

Turning my back to the line, I pulled Bailey closer. "Yeah, I'm sure it is dumb to someone who has lived in the same town with the same friends since kindergarten. I wear contacts because I have to, and why not make them brown like Mom's eyes?"

"Maybe dumb was a dumb word to use," Bailey said as we made it through the doorway and grabbed trays.

"Chase might not speak to me after today." I reached for a plate, wondering if anyone would tease me for buying three pieces of pizza. "He barely spoke to me this morning."

"But he watched you during English."

I almost tripped as I spun around. Why did Bailey's words send my thoughts into panic mode?

"While Mrs. Pearson wrote on the board, I checked him out. You were too busy looking through the new English book, but he definitely watched you."

As we reached the table, I laughed at Bailey, but

déjà vu weirdness lingered from my first meeting with Chase. "'Likes me' watched or 'stalker' watched?"

"I don't know," she said. "Maybe you should ask him."

From my view, Chase seemed like a harmless loner who didn't care who caught him reading a book during lunch.

Her smile turned devious. "Should I tell Pade to watch out for his new competition?"

I smiled, dreading the knowledge Pade would hear about Chase somehow. "I think we better find out more about Chase."

* * * * *

After fourth block, I fumbled with the combination of the locker Bailey and I would share, hopefully all year. While on my knees and trying to force open a latch along the dreaded bottom row, my palm slipped, hugging a sharp edge. Pain fired up my arm, fighting a current of red racing to fill the wound.

"It's her," Tosh said. "Lisa, check out the new girl."

Lisa laughed. "That's Jes Delaney?"

"Or shall we call her De-lame-y?" Tosh's nasty laugh followed.

I stared at the floor, forcing the pool of blood out of sight as they stopped behind me.

Tosh leaned against the lockers, eyes boring into me. "What are you doing on your knees, De-lame-y?"

"The Lamester sure is quiet today," Lisa said. "Come on Jes, tell us about that kiss."

Tosh slammed her foot into the next locker. "Damn it, Jes, look at me. You *will* answer my question."

Her voice rose. "Shithead… why ya… on ya… knees?"

Shame scorched my cheeks as I peeked around to spot people staring. Although class had ended more than twenty minutes before, no one seemed in a rush to leave Credence High. Hot tears formed in the corners of my eyes, intensified by the memory of Dad's words to 'never fight, no matter what.'

If I looked up, Tosh's hands would grab my hair, revealing my inner struggle to keep the tears from falling. After choking on the smell of strawberry gum, I imagined her hands on me at any second. What I didn't picture was a tidal wave of cold liquid down my arms, through the lengths of my hair, and soaking into my shirt and jeans.

"What the hell are you doing?" Tosh howled and I glanced at the skinny blonde who stood open-mouthed. Lisa's cheerleader skirt shook as much as the empty cup in her hand.

"Sorry, Tosh," Lisa said. "I didn't mean to spill it. I… I swear the cup just flipped in my hand."

A throat cleared from the end of the lockers. "Lisa Johnson and Tosh Henley, what have I told you about drinks inside the building?" Dr. Greene frowned. "Clean up this mess."

"Yes, sir." Lisa ran to the nearest bathroom and emerged with a handful of paper towels.

Dr. Greene regarded the scene in silence, the disapproving kind that usually carried detention or worse. I felt his eyes stop on me, maybe in an attempt to figure out my role in this, maybe urging me to open wide and scream denial. When he disappeared down the hall, Tosh bolted to a set of double doors in the opposite direction.

Lisa spun. "Where are you going?"

Tosh shoved open the doors. "Clean up your own mess."

The crinkled paper fell around me as Lisa dropped to the floor. Expecting her to follow Tosh, I sat back in amazement as Lisa stretched across the floor, soaking up the sugary puddle. I grabbed some of the towels, blotting the sticky mess from my face and arms, then swabbed the tiles around my knees.

With most of the floor dry, Lisa gathered the towels and looked up, finally meeting my eyes. Loose hair forked from the braid down her neck, with a few strands coiling around her face. "Why did you help me? You didn't have to, I…" She pushed back the hair and closed her hands over both ears, eyes now skyward. "I mean I'm sorry. Thanks for helping."

"You're welcome."

Her hands lowered and her shoulders seemed to relax. Her fingers no longer shook, but her eyes fixed on me again. "I don't understand why you're being nice to me."

"Free country," I said.

Lisa stood and walked toward the doors Tosh had used. I forced my eyes to the locker door, wishing I had the nerve to start a normal conversation before she left. My hand still throbbed as I reached for the locker, but my whole body froze when one of the hall doors opened again and I caught a glimpse of white-blond hair. It was the new guy. Chase.

I followed him, stumbling through the door in a mad dash to discover what humiliation Chase might have witnessed. Down the walkway and around a brick wall, emptiness spanned my first snapshot of the courtyard. Bushes with tiny leaves lined the concrete trail, alongside wooden benches, but nothing large enough to cover Chase.

Laughter welled in my throat because of the same weird feeling from earlier. I forced my feet ahead, not sure if I wanted to know how Chase had disappeared.

Circling back to the front office, I entered by the library and almost crashed into Pade.

"I'll see you later," said the girl next to him. She flashed a weak smile as she passed me and shoved open the door. She rounded an outside corner before Pade said anything.

"Hey," he said, but didn't move.

I hesitated before meeting his stare. "Hey."

"How was your first day?"

"Fine, except for the shower." I expected either twenty questions or an encouraging joke. "I think Mom's waiting."

Pade halted my escape with a spark as his arm grazed mine. "I intended to break up with Sarah Beth, but now her parents are getting divorced. Jes, she needs me."

"Sarah Beth's a nice girl. I can see why you like her."

His smile returned, but with a careful twist. "She likes almost everyone, maybe even you if you'll let her." His eyes dropped, along with the cool confidence. "Sarah Beth has no idea you're the one she should fear."

I swallowed the pain in my throat. "Don't go there."

"I won't if you tell me the kiss didn't mean anything."

"Technically we're family, so how could it?"

Pade laughed as his eyes recovered. "You do remember we're not blood related? It's not as if the thought never crossed my mind, I just didn't expect kissing you to feel so… different."

"If people think we're dating, they'll be all grossed out. You could never pick me up for a date—my parents would freak."

"So that's your answer? We stay just friends?"

"Staying friends would require us being friends first."

"What about the kiss? Look in my eyes and say it didn't mean anything."

For only a second, I considered cutting my heart out and exposing years of hope and fear packed inside—as if we were speeding through a Cinderella movie. Then I remembered this was the guy who not only embarrassed me with that kiss, but probably hated me over a stupid pool. "It didn't mean anything." I turned and walked to where Mom had the van running, not once looking back.

CHAPTER FOUR

Phone Disaster

On Friday morning, I stared at my plate. The eggs were cold and the hash browns, well, Mom had made better. Maybe a thin layer would make my plate look halfway eaten—my only problem was the silent twins. Every dab of plate versus fork echoed through the kitchen. Dad scanned the paper, drinking his coffee by the drop, still refusing to give in over the water fight. Mom had a section of the paper, filling in blocks of a crossword puzzle.

"How was your first week of tenth grade?" he asked.

Dad's words made me jump. "One more day and I'll say fine."

He smiled. "No problems?"

I matched his smile. "No problems."

"No write-ups for being tardy yet? How are your teachers?"

"Fine, Dad. Everything's cool."

He nodded and raised his cup, but paused before taking a sip. "What are your plans for tonight?"

I swallowed and took a deep breath. "Aunt Charlie said she'll drop me and Bailey off at the Fun Connection."

"The Fun Connection? Charlene said she'd take you there? Tonight?"

"Yes, Dad, tonight. Remember when you said you'd quit being a creepy-stalker parent and let me go out with friends? No hiding in the crowd with the twins while I skate?"

"When have we ever hid?" He looked at Mom and dread swirled in my stomach.

"Now, Justin, we did tell her that."

"I don't remember saying anything of the sort." He turned back to me. "You're only fifteen."

"Angel and Rachelle said they've been dropped off for three years."

"But you're not Angel or Rachelle. You're…"

"Different? A freak? Most normal tenth-graders have their learners' license by now."

Dad choked on his coffee and leaned back, arms crossed. "I think the words normal, tenth-grader, and license are mutually exclusive."

I shook my head. "I don't even know what that means."

He glanced at Mom and then back at me, frowning. "Maybe you can drive when you're a senior, like Pade will. He worked all summer and saved, and after next summer, he'll be able to afford a car. No one can use a license without a car."

"I'm not fighting about *that* again. I just want to go out for one night."

He smiled. "One night and you'll be happy for the rest of the year?"

"Dad!"

"The Fun Connection is thirty miles away. That's too far to drop you off, come back home, and then make a one-eighty to pick you up."

"Aunt Charlie is dropping us off. All you have to do is show up at ten."

Dad's face was firm, until I noticed the corners of his mouth twitch. Mom laughed first, but he did follow.

"We talked to Charlie last night. She's in agreement with us," Mom said, eyes pointed at Dad. "You and Bailey are now old enough to stay out until ten."

"Nine-thirty," Dad said.

"We want to go too," the twins said.

My skin turned cold as I scrambled for a twin-worthy excuse, but Dad's tone silenced their complaining. "You can't go out after dark without us until you're fifteen. Since your mom and I aren't going, neither are the two of you."

With the boys on mute, my heart soared, ready for half a dozen 'oh my god' sessions with Bailey and an end to another long day of school. I stood in a rush, but Dad motioned for me to sit back down.

"Jessica Ray," he said. "Except for certain recent events including that party at the river you failed to mention and the pictures online, you've acted both responsible and respectable, thus proving we can trust you. As long as these exceptions are not repeated, your freedom will continue. Do you understand what I'm telling you?"

"Don't mess up," I said.

"Smart girl. I believe we have an understanding?"

"No exceptions."

"Since you'll already be gone when I get home, we'll discuss the rules now."

I nodded, not about to open my mouth and possibly change his mind.

"When Charlene drops you off, you are to enter the doors and not leave again until Lorraine picks you up at ten. You and Bailey are to stay together at all times." He reached in his bag and pulled out a box, which he slid across the table. "We got you a cell phone. It's activated—just make sure it stays charged and call us if you have any problems. Can you do all of that?"

"Yes, sir."

"Jes," Dad said as I scaled the steps to Bailey's room in pairs. "Have a good time."

"Thanks, Dad."

* * * * *

When the first bell rang, I was already at my desk. Mrs. Pearson assigned an essay and picked a few unfortunate souls to read one of Shakespeare's plays. Again, Chase lowered into the seat next to me, silent as every day before. Even when I dropped my pen and he reached down, Chase managed yet another day of invisibility in his mother's class.

After hours of comedy that brought only tortured silence, our teacher finally passed out vocabulary tests. She was counting pages to pass down the aisle when her hand paused midair, swooping like a hawk to Bailey's wrist.

"Miss Sanders, are you texting?" She scooped up Bailey's phone before my friend could stammer an excuse.

Mrs. Pearson turned off the phone, dropping it into her desk drawer with a slam that sent waves of uncertainty coursing through me. Bailey couldn't get in trouble, not today.

"As I said on our first day, school rules dictate phone usage is not permitted in any classroom. If another phone is found in any state but off, it will also be confiscated for the duration of the semester."

Bailey opened her mouth, but the look on Mrs. Pearson's face was a red light even she couldn't ignore. "We will finish this discussion after class."

When the bell rang, I stood outside, counting the seconds until I felt like exploding. Ultimately, I gave up and ran to second block, confident Bailey would monopolize every bit of thirty minutes to detail the chewing-out session at lunch.

I stepped into chemistry only tragic seconds after the late bell. As Mr. Larson called the class to order with one of his trademark whistles, I scrambled into the nearest seat, praying he didn't notice and mark me tardy.

"Does everyone know what today is?"

"Lab day," Ronald Pitts said, from the front row.

Mr. Larson grinned and pointed at Ronald. "That's right. On Fridays, we get out of this boring classroom and do some cool stuff." Whoops and hollers surrounded him. "Now, I need everyone to take a seat in the lab. Two people per table, please. Find yourselves a partner you can work with all semester."

Most people rose at once, but I hesitated. Every school was the same sad story, as choosing partners always seemed to translate into one more popularity contest. I had no friends in Mr. Larson's class, no one sympathetic enough to end my suffering. Even the newest guy in school would surely hear a 'yes' before me.

At an empty table, I lowered onto a stool, broken along the edge with no back. Several students gathered in the center of the room, discussing who would get who. I pulled the drawing pad from my backpack and opened to a page creased at the corner, ready for my escape.

"That's pretty good."

I looked up in surprise as blue eyes admired my latest sketch. "Thanks."

Chase reached for the pad and claimed the seat adjoining mine. As he flipped the pages like a cartoon in slow motion, his eyes grew wider. "These are better than good. They're great."

Everyone in lab negotiated a seat, but still no movement from Chase. Mr. Larson paused at our table with an array of manuals. "Color?"

"Green," we said, at the same time.

Chase grinned. "Looks like we'll get along just fine."

I reached for the folder. "How did you know I'd say green?"

"I didn't," Chase said as Mr. Larson walked away. "Green is my favorite color."

He must be kidding. "Mine too."

"Sounds like we have something in common."

The need to discover more about this mysterious guy was increasing, and not only for Bailey's sake. "How was the vocab test this morning?" *Idiot*, I thought, wanting to kick myself for reminding Chase of the scene in his mom's class.

He shrugged. "When your mom's an English teacher, not doing well is kind of a waste."

"What do you mean?"

"If I ever failed her test, she'd stay in teacher mode after school. Some girls that first day were saying how 'cool it would be to have a mom who's the teacher.' I say they're crazy. If I make the smallest grammar mistake, she's all over me, and she hates contractions. Why do you think I was talking to Dr. Greene on the first day? The stupid computer placed me in *her* class and I was trying to convince him to have my schedule changed."

I listened, fascinated by the way his hands moved, by the animation in his voice.

"You have no idea how it feels." He took a heaving breath. "I bet you think I'm weird."

"I'm not the best judge of weirdness."

Chase shook his head and laughed. "You're the worst liar."

"It's just that you can't be any weirder than me. And I do know how it feels to have a mom who's a teacher."

The laughter stopped. "How can you know that?"

"Because my mom's a teacher here too. She's Mrs. Delaney and math is what she's teaching, though I'm glad pre-cal isn't on my schedule this year."

His eyes raked over me. "Her room is next to my fourth class. You have the same brown eyes and hair."

"She never minds helping with my homework. You might have her class next year."

"We move around a lot. I'm sure I'll be at a different school next year."

"Moving's a pain," I said, but he'd opened the binder and started writing again.

* * * * *

"Can you believe that woman?" Bailey asked. After complaining for two-thirds of lunch, she showed no sign of stopping. "Hey, are you listening to me?"

"Yeah," I said, "but I'm also trying to eat."

"You don't sound happy. What's wrong?"

She blinked and I prepared for her next move, while hoping she'd drop the subject. How could I explain the depression I felt after Chase ignored me for the rest of lab? I couldn't talk about him, not even with Bailey. I gripped the fork until red lines sank into my skin. "What are you going to do about Mrs. Pearson?"

"Don't you mean what are *we* going to do?"

"We?" An image appeared of Dad screaming at me twice in the same week.

"We're gonna fix this before my mom finds out. If she hears about me texting in class and Mrs. Pearson taking my phone, she'll say no going out tonight. You know if I can't go, you can't go either."

"How do you know Mrs. Pearson hasn't already called Aunt Charlie?"

"Because I had Pade call her during first lunch. If Mom had changed her mind about letting me go, she would've said."

"You told Pade?"

"Pade and I always cover for each other. Besides, he wants you to come."

I dropped the fork. "Pade's going to the Fun Connection?"

She smiled. "Football games don't start 'til next week."

"What about Sarah Beth?"

"Forget Sarah Beth—she won't even be there tonight. Her parents are going away for this 'save your marriage' retreat and they're dumping her with the grandparents."

"But she and Pade are still dating, right?"

"Don't even act like you feel sorry for that girl. She's not as nice as people say." Bailey raised a hand, brushing away our argument. "Pade's *my* brother and I've known him since before you were born."

"Like the difference between November twenty-fifth and January second makes you an expert on everything." I shook my head and sighed. "You were saying about Mrs. Pearson?"

"I've got an idea."

* * * * *

Fifteen minutes after the last bell, Bailey and I slipped through the side door of building five on careful toes. Eerily silent, the hall stretched before us with open doors to either side. After passing three empty rooms and an abandoned janitor's cart, we stood in the doorway of our first block. I hesitated, taking a step back, but Bailey pushed me inside. She put a finger to her lips.

"Do you wanna get us in trouble?" she hissed.

I shook my head. "Just making sure no one was coming."

"Her meeting should give us enough time, but we've got to hurry."

As we reached the desk, looming like forbidden treasure at the front of the room, Bailey snatched open each drawer. She dug through the papers with record speed. "Here's next week's vocab test."

"Just find the phone." I no longer hid the urgency

in my voice or the desperation to escape Mrs. Pearson's room.

"I've got it." Bailey held up the phone, her voice filled with satisfaction. "She'll never know what happened."

I reached down to close the bottom drawer. "Let's go."

Bailey pulled a black binder from the drawer before I could slide it shut. "This looks like the one Chase was writing in yesterday. Aren't you a little curious?"

"I think you've got the phone and we should go."

"Oh Jes, you're no fun." She laughed, opening the front cover and flipping through several pages of notebook paper. Chemistry notes. Instructions on how to search for an I.P. address. Maps of Delaware and Alabama. About halfway through, she paused and glanced up. Names filled the left side of the page from top to bottom, the names of every girl in first block. Notes followed to the right and some names were marked through, including mine. "Are you seeing this?"

I swallowed hard. "I'm seeing."

Steps sounded outside the doorway and we sank behind the desk. Bailey still clutched the binder.

"You should not be here," Mrs. Pearson said as the door slammed. A man answered, but I couldn't understand his words. I lowered an ear to the floor and glimpsed the gold shoes our teacher wore during first block. The man's shoes were twice the size of hers, black, and curved at the toes.

"What should we do?" Bailey whispered.

"You could be jeopardizing our mission by coming here," Mrs. Pearson said.

Sympathy for the man bubbled inside of me, his

foot twitching in preparation of a run for the door. His voice shrank from hers and, despite a few English words, quickly changed gears with a language that made no sense. The gold shoes shifted forward and her voice rose, also spewing words I'd never heard.

My cheek flattened against the cold tile as I struggled to catch a view of him. The man was dressed in the same dark green as the other janitors I'd seen.

Mrs. Pearson pointed two fingers at the door. The handle turned and the door creaked open, bringing a rush of air against my face. I gasped when I realized no one stood on the other side.

The man bowed and turned, his shoes silent across the floor. When he reached the hall, the sound of a cart echoed, metal on concrete, rolling away.

Our teacher faced the desk and I froze, but instead of approaching, she spun and followed the janitor's path. Her shoes clicked down the hall as if her heels were marching inside my ears.

When the sound faded completely, I released a breath. Bailey shoved the binder in the drawer and we ran all the way back to the hall door we'd used earlier. Free in the sunshine, Bailey halted, staring down at her hands.

"My phone," she said in agony.

Again, I saw the door open with no hands touching it. Then the notes next to my name: *draws great, brown eyes, brown hair, no confidence.*

"Jes, you're gonna call me an idiot. I was in such a hurry, I threw my phone back in the drawer with that binder. We've got to—"

"I'm done with sneaking into *her* room. Let's get out of here."

Bailey crossed her arms. "What about tonight?"

"If Mrs. Pearson hasn't called your mom yet, maybe she won't. You can apologize on Monday and she'll probably give your phone back."

"I've tried already."

"Well, try again."

"There's something weird about that woman."

Really, she just figured that out? I grabbed my backpack from the bushes and started walking.

Bailey followed, in a fog. "Did you hear what Mrs. Pearson was saying? I can't stand how formal she talks. Sometimes her words don't even sound like English."

"She was talking to a man, a janitor I think."

"Don't you mean chewing out a man? I don't care what language she spoke. I'd be taking upset to another level."

"Did you see them leave?"

"I couldn't see anything from under the desk, but I did hear the door when they left. Did you read what that creepy notebook said? Talks more than Lauren. Who is Lauren and how could he write that about me?"

My fear had begun to subside, replaced by anger since the conversation was once again all about Bailey. "I don't know why Chase would be writing anything about us." Or why my name was marked out.

"Maybe Chase is a pervert or creep or something. His mom probably found the binder and took it." She brightened. "Or maybe he's trying to find a girlfriend."

Mrs. Pearson's words played again in my head. *'You could be jeopardizing our mission.'*

"You're not listening," Bailey said.

"I was just thinking about what Mrs. Pearson said."

"What did my mom say?"

I froze at the sound of Chase's voice. How had he walked up without us hearing him? Before I could ask where he came from, Chase stopped in front of me.

Bailey stepped between us. "That she won't give back my phone."

His eyes narrowed and filled with darkness as he stared at me. Then, just as quickly, the darkness faded and he smiled for Bailey. "My mom is stuck on the rules. She doesn't like to be disrespected."

Bailey's voice sweetened. "What do you think I should do?"

His smile widened. "You might apologize and be real nice about it."

Even worse, Bailey raised her eyebrows and mirrored his smile. "That sounds like a good idea."

I thought of the day she 'called' him in the cafeteria. How could she be so sure about a guy without even speaking to him? He was cute, but an image of me flirting with Chase forced a round of giggles. I covered my mouth in an attempt to stop the laughter exploding next. Chase and Bailey gave each other the 'this girl's crazy' look, which only made me laugh more. Heat flooded my cheeks as tears filled the corners of my eyes. I struggled to a nearby bench and dropped down, swatting the tears.

Bailey lowered by my side, leaving Chase at a safe distance. "What's so funny?" She put an arm around my neck. "We're like sisters now. You can tell me anything."

Sisters. A wave of fear passed over me. What would happen when we had to leave again?

Chase smiled. "I'm sorry about my mom."

Bailey looked up at him. "I was only worried about the phone because we're going to the Fun Connection tonight. If my mom finds out your mom took it, she'll have a fit. And we'll both be stuck at home."

"Fun Connection? Is that in Credence?"

"The Fun Connection is across the river," Bailey said. "About thirty minutes from here."

Chase looked from me to Bailey. "I get it. You don't need to worry about my mom tonight." Turning, he walked away without another word.

Bailey stood. "You don't think he thought you and me…"

"No, let's go. Mom's got to be waiting."

"I hope he was right about his mom."

When we climbed into the van, air rushed from the vents and cooled the fire in my cheeks. Already my fears were fading. Bailey would never be lost to me, and I only imagined a door opening itself. Door handles couldn't really twist without someone on the other side. And Mrs. Pearson's words—that was probably French or Italian or something other than the three months of Spanish I'd taken in the town outside of Phoenix.

I placed a hand flat with the tinted glass and watched as people outside rode atop lawn mowers, filled every stall at the car wash, and followed wiener dogs down the midtown sidewalk. *Maybe the night will turn out good after all.* Just as the thought escaped, a noise filled the van, above the easy sounds of Mom's typical sixties' rock. Bailey jerked to attention and rambled through her backpack, until the noise had words, and a tune.

Mom glanced in the mirror. "That's probably Charlie."

Bailey wedged the phone between her shoulder and her ear as she linked her hands in a silent prayer of thanks.

CHAPTER FIVE

The Fun Connection

As the sun went down, Aunt Charlie dropped us off in front of dark glass lining the main entrance to the Fun Connection. Pade followed, until he noticed Terrance and Skip and almost ran in their direction.

I'd barely completed a sentence around Pade since telling him the kiss meant nothing. The thirty-minute ride had consisted of Bailey recapping the week next to me in the backseat. Aunt Charlie cut in once, just to ask if Bailey had every class with Chase. Each time Pade's dark hair stirred in front of me, I remembered the softness of his lips touching mine. Excitement burned inside of me, though an image of his face after my words stole the thrill.

"Do you realize we're finally parent-free?" Bailey asked.

Two elbows and a pair of skates grazed the side of my head. I moved closer to Bailey. The ceiling opened as we entered the main atrium, with six rows of glass that held back the stars. Yellow wallpaper shined like the sun, descending from the roof to the floor. My shoes squeaked along the tile, but no one seemed to notice the awful sound. Most people flowed from double doors to our right, dumping bags of popcorn as they passed. In front of us stretched the skating rink and to the left a putt-putt golf course. Up a winding staircase, each step aglow, rose an entire level called Gaming Galore.

"How 'bout pizza?" I shouted, above music that shook my feet and merged with at least a dozen conversations.

"Don't you ever think about fun before food?"

"Just a quick slice," I begged.

Bailey chewed on her Slurpee straw and checked a text as I shoveled in two slices of pepperoni pizza covered by a cheese explosion. "Angel and Rachelle are getting their skates already." She tossed her phone onto the table. "How do you think he did it?"

I stared at the phone, giving up on savoring the sticky warmth against the roof of my mouth. "What?"

"You know what," she said. "Chase put *this* phone in *my* backpack and I never saw him do it. Did you?"

"I didn't see him near your bag."

"It had to be him. He even said 'don't worry about my mom.' I can't believe Chase did that for me."

"He could be grounded for weeks if she finds out."

"Isn't he great?" She stared beyond me, through the glass that separated us from the skating rink, until her smile died. "Do you think he heard me call him a creep?"

"Have you changed your mind?"

"Maybe." Bailey's voice sounded at first uncertain, but changed as she studied my face. "He must be an okay guy. I mean, come on, do you think he would have gotten my phone back if—" She covered her mouth as her face streaked with red.

"He didn't like you?"

Hope flashed in her eyes. "You think he likes me?"

Jeez, I'd never act like a fan-crazed groupie over a guy in public. "He was flirting with you."

"When?"

"You know, after you flirted with him."

"I did not…" She smiled again as my eyebrows shot up. "Okay, maybe I did."

"You did and you were shameless."

"The 'shameless' flirting did get my phone back. Maybe he felt sorry for us."

"Maybe he felt sorry for you. He didn't even speak to me except to ask about his mom."

"But Chase… well, I guess he didn't. I'm sorry."

"Don't be—you called him and you can keep him."

"You really don't like him?"

I shoved in the last bite of pizza. "Chase is cute." Did she really think I'd go after Chase when she was that determined?

"I bet every girl in English class would love to date Chase and you've got to be different. Pade will be so happy," she said, with a hearty laugh.

I rolled my eyes. "I'm glad we finally decided Chase isn't some creep or pervert."

"Chase is great and definitely not a creep. Do you think he might be here tonight? We could ask him about the phone."

"I don't know. His mom seems strict."

Bailey grabbed her phone. "If anyone is creepy, it's that woman."

"Do you think she'll get creepier when she realizes your phone disappeared from her desk?"

"Let's not think about it now," she said. "Let's get you some skates."

I sat on an empty bench and tightened the laces of my rented skates, with music hammering against the smooth wood beneath my legs. Bailey sat next to me as she put on the pair of inline skates she'd brought, an expensive gift from the father who never called. The skates had orange and white flames with blue laces, marked by a name known mainly to those with parents who could afford designer skates. Only Pade's would gain more respect, black like a star-filled sky, with laces that glowed on the floor.

Because of the amount of people, finding a comfortable groove became a struggle to weave in and out of the crowd. Since Bailey could out-skate me any day, I found myself alone after only a couple of rounds.

Rachelle fell in beside me, her words sketching a guy she'd just met. "…and he's sixteen with a Mustang. What do you think?"

"Sounds cool." It was a safe answer at least.

Her lips parted and curved at the edges, revealing a smile Bailey seemed to envy. A hundred tight braids fell around Rachelle's face, fake I knew, but beautiful against her dark skin. "He's pretty cool—even said he'd take me to the movies. My mom and dad might let me go next month, after I turn sixteen. I told Angel, but she wasn't impressed."

Laughing, I nearly tripped and reached for the wall. "You know how Angel is."

Rachelle laughed. "I'm no stranger to her wannabe fame, but she is my best friend. She could've listened and been happy for me."

"Sometimes people don't think, even when they're our best friends," I said, as if I'd ever stayed somewhere long enough to have a real best friend.

"Hey," Angel said, appearing at Rachelle's other side. "Limbo is next." Before Rachelle could open her mouth, Angel launched into a story about a guy with a Corvette.

I slowed as the next opening came into sight. "I think I'll find Bailey."

Angel rolled her eyes. "She's over by the lockers, talking to Skip."

Bailey's arms stretched across the back of a bench between two rows of lockers, her fingers only inches from Skip's ball cap. He laughed and I almost turned away, but she looked up and waved. "You've got to hear what Skip said about Tosh."

"What about me?" Tosh asked, as she and Lisa rounded the lockers. "If you can tell the Lamester, you can tell me." Her voice filled with spite as she stopped. "I can't believe your parents let you out tonight. Now we'll all die of boredom." She drew out 'die' and her laugh tinkled like a porch lined by windchimes might, each in a different key. With a smile, Tosh reached for my arm.

I stepped back and looked around, each set of eyes burning into me.

Bailey yawned and stretched her arms further. "Did I say Tosh? I meant Mia."

The lines on Tosh's face tightened as she moved closer to the bench, but Bailey didn't move. "What about that Philippine bitch?"

Skip frowned. "How did Mia get on your hate list?"

Tosh opened her mouth as Lisa leaned forward, whispering in her ear. The stern look faded, replaced by a smile and the tinkle of laughter. Tosh swirled as Pade and Terrance came around the lockers.

Pade looked from Tosh to Bailey, and his sister shrugged. Then his eyes stopped on me. "Why is everybody so quiet?"

"Pade," Tosh said, moving to his side, "the limbo contest is about to start. Want to check it out?"

Bailey leaned forward, one fist balled at her side, feet firm on the ground below the bench.

"Sure." Pade gave Bailey a quick shake of his head when Tosh turned.

"It's too bad De Lamester can't skate better." Tosh started for the floor. "Looks like she'll miss out again." Pade followed with Lisa and Terrance shadowing his exit, neither meeting my eyes as they passed.

Skip opened the bottle of coke in his hand, guzzling half of the contents in one swig. "I'd like to hear Tosh say that about Mia in front of Terrance."

Bailey's eyes narrowed. "Tosh would never talk bad about Mia in front of Terrance. They've only been dating for two years now, and that's a lifetime at Credence High." She shook her head. "I can't believe Pade left with Tosh. My brother shouldn't even speak to her after what she said to Jes."

Skip shrugged. "Tosh is cool and she's an eleventh grader. What guy wouldn't want to hang out with her?"

Bailey stood and glared down at Skip. "I'll pretend you didn't say that."

"I'm just saying most people don't know the real Tosh. And I didn't say I liked what she said about Mia *or* Jes."

"Tosh is the enemy and you need to remember that. I wouldn't talk to you if you associated with that stuck-up bitch, even if you are the principal's son, and even when you show up at the house with Pade."

"Tosh doesn't hang with tenth-graders."

Bailey grabbed my arm, urging me to a nearby locker. "He missed the point." She gave Skip an evil look and he shrugged again, leisurely as if his bench might be the most comfortable spot in the whole building.

After stowing our skates, we headed for the stairs to floor two. I silently counted each step on our climb to the gaming level, desperate to think about anything other than Pade. When Bailey left to get tokens, I crossed to the far wall and banged my head against the glass panel. The sound echoed in my ears, but no way could anyone below hear. Two of the skating refs held a bar as people took turns dancing underneath. Pade stood next to Tosh in line, her excitement growing with each downward inch of the bar.

Deciding how to feel about Pade escalated to war inside my head. On one hand, I felt the distinct urge to make a loop around the floor at his side, several in fact. On the other, I felt the urge to smash every die-cast car lining the shelves in his room. If only he could see the real Tosh, the way she was with me at least, and then don the armor and shining sword. I was furious at him for walking away with her and not even looking at me. I was furious at myself for wanting to believe in him.

"Guys are real idiots," Bailey said.

"It's okay."

"Even if you forget the fact he's my brother and you're my friend, he still should have told Tosh off."

Sighing, I took a last look at Pade and turned. "Let's just play skee-ball."

With each round, I swung harder as my anger rose to new levels. Bailey topped my score in each game and managed to get an entire round ahead. I aimed at the hundred-slot and fired up the ramp. My eyes widened as the ball flew in, along with the next nine.

"Wow, that's ten in a row. I've never seen anyone hit that many hundreds before."

With my anger dowsed by the thrill of winning, we played the virtual snowboarding game. My mood improved and even soared across the snow. Even though I'd never liked cold weather, my fingers ached to remember grabbing a ball of the white, wet slush. I closed my eyes, willing myself to remember making a snow angel or laughter from a snowball fight, but I only saw the headlights of an old Ford and heard the screeching of brakes. Snow wedged between my toes, biting at the tips of each nail.

Bailey gave my arm a squeeze. "You beat me at this game too. Are you ready to go back to the floor?"

I forced a smile and nodded, pushing away the memory. At least one of our nights couid improve.

We entered through a door near the skate rental counter. Since Pade and Tosh were nowhere in sight, I relaxed. "Maybe they left."

"Maybe, but I bet Pade isn't far."

As I found a rhythm on the floor, pulsing music brought new courage to venture from the wall. Even better, Pade returned to the floor alone. He passed close enough to rustle my hair in his wake, but I couldn't meet his eyes. He sped around for the third time, just as a boy about the twins' age fell in front of me. With a forward plunge, my nose nearly crushed against the stone, but strong arms pulled me back.

"Are you okay?"

Unable to believe Pade gripped my hand in his, I squeezed tighter, cringing with the thought he'd realize my secret prayer. We passed the closest opening. I exhaled and looked for the next, fearing Pade would guide me to safety. Instead, he pulled me to the center of the floor, into a groove wide enough for two. Another round and my feet fell into sync with the left then right flow of his.

Only the last notes of the song and seeing Tosh along the outside wall spoiled my mood. Pade's thoughts were evident in the way he led me to a bench on the other side of the room. After asking if I was okay again, he backed away and weaved through the crowd in Tosh's direction.

I lowered to the bench. Bailey giggled and dropped down beside me, her face glowing with victory.

"Tell me how it felt."

"Great until he saw Tosh."

Her smile faded. "I'd kind of hoped she left for the night, but my brother did skate with you."

"He kept me from falling over that kid."

"He was holding your hand. He gave you the look."

As much as I longed to believe what Bailey thought she saw, I realized that no one, *no one*, would believe Pade Sanders had an interest in me. The center of every joke at school on Monday morning would be Jes Delaney. "Look who he's with now."

"We've got to do something about her," she said.

"You're not making me feel better."

"Sorry."

"You should go back to skating," I said, when the next song began.

"I'm not leaving you on this bench alone."

Okay, plan B. "I'm going to the bathroom, see you in a few." When I reached the bathroom door, I glanced back with a smile. Bailey was circling the floor.

After locking the stall, I pulled out my new phone and scrolled through a text from Mom. When had she learned to text? My fingers froze when voices echoed through the empty room. I pulled myself up to stand on the toilet.

Tosh laughed, probably admiring herself in the mirror. "Can you believe that girl? She must actually think Pade likes her."

"That's crazy," Lisa said. "Obviously, Pade likes you. He's been hanging with you all night."

"You know it."

"Jessica is so pathetic."

"Yeah, it's too bad Pade had to feel sorry for her. We could've skated that song together. Did you see how he had to slow down?"

Lisa laughed and I wondered if she enjoyed herself as much as Tosh.

"Pade is so cute when he's being nice…" Tosh said.

"…to people who don't deserve it," Lisa finished.

I gripped my phone, hoping it wouldn't go off. The ringer needed to be on silent, but I didn't trust my shaking fingers.

"I'll make sure he's not thinking about her," Tosh said.

"What are you going to do?" Lisa asked.

"You'll see." Their voices faded as the door squeaked shut.

Bailey was halfway around the rink when I reached the floor. She'd leaned over the wall to talk with Angel. I skated into a haze of people, amidst strobes of lights and my favorite dance song. If only Pade… no, I must focus.

"There she is," Skip shouted from my left.

Despite an effort to look away, my eyes met Pade's for one heart stopping second. *Get to Bailey. Almost there.* I tore my eyes to the right as something caught my foot, sending me stumbling ahead. Leaning forward, I extended my arms, desperate to regain my balance. Both feet slipped out from under me. My hands hit the concrete first, followed by my back. For a moment, everything stopped.

The stone heaved a chilling breath through the fabric against my skin. My throat knotted around a sobbing mess no fifteen-year-old deserved, though tears were useless at this point.

Arms outstretched, I could feel my left hand, but not the other. Pink and green stars danced across the ceiling, jarring with bass chords of music like a thunderstorm. My favorite song, but all I could picture were the people who left me in New York. I closed my eyes and their faces glared in black-and-white, not as my parents, but as crinkled newspaper clippings.

Somewhere a switch flipped and row after row of fluorescents hummed to life, glowing beyond my eyelids. At the same time, the music died in a massive screech. The darkness in my heart dissolved with the voices around me. I opened my eyes to see Pade shoving through the crowd.

He dropped to his knees beside me, taking my good hand in his. "Are you okay?"

Instead of his eyes, I focused on the skeleton face

that glowed from the front of his T-shirt. The sunken eyes tugged at the corners of my mouth, reminding me of, well, something like hope.

His fingers tightened around mine. "Tell me where it hurts."

Pade's cologne teased my nose, threatening to unearth a longing no one could know about. A fog surrounded us as I raised my eyes to his. Voices pressed closer, threatening to steal his dark eyes, but I banished all thoughts of who he really was to me. I tried to push up with my free hand but crashed down hard on my elbow.

"Hey," he said, in a flurry, and reached for my damaged hand.

I jerked back. "It's fine."

A ref dropped to my other side. "Let me see. Try to move your fingers. Good." She turned to Pade. "The wrist isn't broken, but she needs to have it checked out. Are you…"

"Yes," Pade said, with authority. "I'll call her mom."

"Get back everyone." The ref helped me to my feet.

"Don't call, please." I reached for Pade, but he was already cutting our path to a set of benches.

Lights switched off above and the music returned, which brought clapping from every angle. Since the ref had my good arm, I stared down and not at the faces.

"Just relax," she said, nudging me ahead. "Let your boyfriend handle this."

As she smiled, my heart sank. The girl was older, not really a woman, but definitely older than the sixteen years Pade could claim. Her eyes sparkled and I realized two things: she liked Pade and she was happy for me. I wanted to tell her Pade wasn't my boyfriend. The words were in my mouth, at the tip of my tongue, but I failed to spit them out. Explaining would be weird after the way he'd held my hand.

Bailey sat down next to me when the ref skated off. "Does it hurt? This war between you and Tosh has gone way past funny."

"They'll be here in ten minutes," Pade said, lowering the phone.

Bailey stiffened. "They? I thought Aunt Rainey was picking us up."

"Aunt Rainey and Uncle Justin took the twins shopping at the new mall. They'll be out front in ten minutes."

My stomach twisted. "I told you they couldn't leave me alone, not even for one night. I bet they're watching from the gaming level. They're stalking me, I swear."

Bailey put an arm around my shoulders. "They're not stalking you Jes, they're just… uptight."

"Slightly neurotic makes more sense."

Pade yanked the laces on my skates, nearly pulling me from the bench. "Sorry," he mumbled and reached for my hand. "People care about you. Why is that so hard to understand?"

"Yeah right," I said, moving my hand away.

He sighed and slid off my skates. Without looking back, he zipped around a row of lockers to get my shoes.

Bailey stood and turned for the lockers, her voice rising while the distance between us grew. "Sometimes I think you'd rather push everyone away. And you don't tell me the important stuff about Jes Delaney, like why you're so worried about what they might do."

After Bailey moved out of sight, skids sounded in

front of me and Tosh leaned down with a smile. "Well, Delaney, I give that fall an eight point five. You even had people on the floor above staring, but a broken neck might have gotten you a ten. You should be more careful. Next time—"

"There won't be a next time," Pade blasted from behind.

Tosh spun, her face pale. "I didn't mean—"

"To trip Jes? You hooked her foot right before she made the second turn."

Anger grew behind Tosh's eyes, flaming as a house would, burning in the night. "You don't know what you saw."

"You've gone too far this time."

Tosh clenched her fists, though Pade's glare never wavered. Her smile returned as she drifted back to the floor. "See you on Monday."

Pade slid the grungy running shoes onto my feet, a pair once white and blue with striped laces. Although Bailey had already given up on convincing me to trash the best fitting shoes ever, I cringed as I stared at the perfect shoes on Pade's feet.

"That's Aunt Rainey texting," Pade said, looking at his phone. "Let's go."

"Where's your ride?" I asked as our eyes met. "Aren't you spending the night with Terrance?"

"Not tonight," he said softly.

Outside the wall of glass, the silver van gleamed under the lights. At the sliding door, Danny and Collin inched closer to the pavement, no doubt wishing to ditch our parents as only ten-year-olds could get away with. Someone laughed behind us and Pade pushed ahead, refusing to let me turn around.

The air slapped me, feeling more as a scalding bath would than the heat Atlanta had wielded without mercy. Bailey was recounting the night already, pausing only to hit my elbow and mutter "sorry" under her breath. Clutching my wrist closer, I tried to shut out the constant movement of her lips. At the sidewalk's edge, my parents rushed forward and I shuddered imagining the guilt trip Dad had in mind.

"Let me see your hand." Dad poked and prodded, while gauging the look on my face.

I thought of the concrete, cold under my body, and the pain took a backseat in my mind. They could never care that much. I wasn't really their child; our blood was not the same. In the end, I'd be alone, just as when we met. I'd—

Dad pressed harder and I winced. "That's what I thought. Okay Lorraine, next stop is the hospital."

"Really, Dad?" I bit my lip. "You should know how much I hate that place."

"Humor me," he said, turning to Pade. "Are you staying or going?"

"Going," Pade said, without hesitation.

Inside the van, Mom turned on a light and caught my hand. "Where did you get this cut?"

I glanced at the half-healed wound. "My hand slipped at the locker. On the latch, first day of class."

Her eyes took on a look of torture. "Why didn't you tell me before?" She caressed my hand, sending guilt through every vein.

"It's no big deal." I pulled back. "Did you guys really drive over here after Aunt Charlie dropped us off?"

Dad cleared his throat. "We took the boys

shopping."

"I thought we agreed I'm old enough to go out after dark."

"Sorry, honey," Mom said. "After dinner, the boys wanted ice cream. No reason to wait until late before driving over."

Dad cut in front of a lowered Nissan with blue lights, ignoring a hand that shot from the driver's window and waved a lone finger. A horn blared when the van changed lanes, and then another when we rounded a corner and merged between a Cadillac and a dump truck.

"Kick it," Danny screamed.

"Faster," Collin said, laughing.

"I'm not dying," I said, but a quick peek in the mirror showed the strain in Dad's eyes.

Air filled the van, tasting heavy and metallic. I shivered and angled the nearest vent away, consumed by a strange new thirst for the heat outside the glass. "I can't help you guys usually pick these redneck towns with no McDonalds."

"Hey," Bailey said, "easy on the home town. I thought you liked living in Credence."

Dad slammed the brakes, though the next red light was two blocks ahead. "Other than our months in Atlanta, the only 'city' we lived in was Canton, and we're never going back there."

I rolled my eyes and twisted to look at Pade, but he was staring through the layers of tint.

* * * * *

After spending three hours at the hospital, despite the

fact Aunt Charlie worked there and 'hurried' us through, I got a brace for my sprained wrist and finally got to go home and sleep. In the early morning hours, I dreamed, something I couldn't remember doing since before we went to Atlanta.

A woman spoke, in a voice filled with pain, and then a man. I couldn't understand their words, but I felt a closeness to them in the deepest part of my soul. They were my real parents. And they were fighting again.

At first, not understanding seemed a result of their lowered voices. From my hiding spot in near darkness, I willed my legs to move closer, before my brain registered a total lack of control over the dream. Fear set my heart in motion.

The angry voices approached, only the sound melted into sadness. Though I still didn't understand their words, nearness to the sound soothed my fear. They stood merely feet away, almost close enough to touch…

His voice disappeared from the room first, causing my heart to land somewhere near my feet. "Daddy," I wanted to scream to the room, to the world, and make him turn around. She cried out in anguish, words meant for her ears alone, as if caution mattered to the empty room. Steps fell against the stone, first heavy thuds and then fading to gentle clicks, merging with tears I could only imagine.

CHAPTER SIX

Secrets Online

I awoke the next morning astonished. After eleven years, I finally had a tiny glimpse into the life that was once mine. The smell of the room, lavender I think, and the sound of her voice resonated within me, yet at the same time tortured my thoughts. I'd vowed to hate them forever. My father's voice was filled with pain and fear. My mother had cried, and the clicking of her heels as she ran from the room sent a chill through me.

The weekend involved more shopping than I'd ever known including stores that only sold new clothes. We bought furniture for the entire house and even a red mixer for Mom. With every stop, Aunt Charlie produced a credit card that was accepted no matter how many times she swiped. She teased Dad about 'finally being useful', but he only smiled. I wondered how much Aunt Charlie really made as a nurse and if my parents could pay her back before I graduated.

On Sunday night, I opened the striped bag and

placed my collection of drawings in a drawer below my new desk. Sinking into the chair, I hugged the bag, wondering if I should empty it completely. Credence was different, but if our stop here wasn't the last… No, it was 'fate' as Mom always said. Fate was why Dad found me, out of a million-plus people who could have been driving down that highway. Fate meant we'd finally come home.

One by one, I pulled out the contents of the bag and removed the paper towels that protected the treasures of my life. I sat each on the cherry-wood dresser. At least the sales guy had promised it was cherry-wood, as if I'd know the difference. The stone box Mom gave me at the cave in Tennessee. The brass pirate ship from a yard sale I helped with near Chicago. The snow globe Dad gave me that first week at the foster home. My old glasses.

I dumped my new clothes on a bed that didn't have sheets yet. Within the heap were jeans with designer labels, shirts I'd only dreamed of, and dresses that almost made me cry, especially the black one that stopped above my knees. In the smallest bag was a bracelet Mom handed me in the van. She said it was real gold, but I wouldn't have cared if the bracelet was a piece of string with bottle caps like we made after the first move. Maybe I'd wear it on the wrist not covered with a brace. I pulled out the old green dress and stared at the label for the last time.

In six years, I'd never worn it, and probably couldn't anymore. But that was okay. All of the new things were me now.

On Monday, Mrs. Pearson rushed into class less than a minute before the bell, followed by Chase. His eyes fixed to the brace. "What happened?"

"I was skating at the Fun Connection—tripped on the concrete."

Chase opened his backpack, though his eyes never left the brace. "Anything broken?"

I focused on the black binder in his hand. "Doctor said it was only a sprain."

The binder slipped from his hand and Chase grabbed air, only able to watch as his pages spilled across the aisle between us. "Thanks," he mumbled, as I reached for detailed formulas I refused to learn for chemistry. He opened his mouth again, but Mrs. Pearson called for class to start. I shifted my attention to our teacher, preparing for any mention of Bailey's phone.

"Good morning, I have your first vocabulary test graded." Smiling, her voice became a cheerful opposite of the usual strictly business attitude. "I am pleased at how well the entire class performed." She lifted a stack of papers from her desk. "Someone even received a perfect score."

"Chase."

I glanced around for the owner of the voice. Several girls in front of us giggled, but Chase refused to raise his eyes.

Mrs. Pearson crossed her arms. "Chase has to work harder than most to impress me. He does not make good grades simply because he is my son. Actually, Jessica made the one-hundred."

She passed out the tests and it was my turn to feel like the only one not wearing green on St. Patrick's Day. *Never ace a test in her class again*, I told myself. More giggles. *Ugh!*

Mrs. Pearson dropped the paper on my desk and

flashed another smile. "Congratulations." Her smile faded as her gaze settled on my wrist. She hovered for a moment before passing out the remaining tests.

When she reached the board, her voice had lost all trace of a smile. "You can review any missed words before the next test. I may have neglected to mention these tests will be cumulative." Groans sounded around the room. "There will be a new test each week, but I will include frequently missed words."

She held up a sheet of paper. "I will circulate a list of selected works for book reports. These reports will be due on the third Friday of each month and I expect four pages, typed and double-spaced. Twelve-point font is preferable in Times New Roman."

Four pages didn't sound like the assignment from hell. Term papers would be worse, but our teacher hadn't mentioned the 'T' word.

"Oh," Mrs. Pearson said, as she faced the board, "I do expect you to actually *read* the books you choose."

*****

Every morning Chase brought a renewed excitement to finish first block and race to second. Although week one was edgy for us both, the next four made edgy seem like no more than a false start. His jokes wiped away Tosh's evil words for nearly half the day, as did his thirst to see each new page in my drawing pad.

Instead of hanging at The Spot until first bell, I embraced the habit of being on time. Before the end of our usual gossip exchange, my path to Mrs. Pearson's room began. Our teacher never had to scold me for being late after the first week. After the second, I felt convinced she'd never mention the phone.

Chemistry became interesting for the first time. Chase seemed born to teach and spared no effort in shining light on all of Mr. Larson's chemistry experiments. I marveled at how he enjoyed my least favorite class, his attitude a summer day when compared to our wintery first block. Only when called upon did Chase speak, and Mrs. Pearson rarely called his name.

It took Bailey those four weeks in entirety to ask Chase about the phone. After listening to her daily dose of speculation, I finally convinced her to approach him. The only problem? It took even less time for me to wish I hadn't.

"You'll never guess where I'm going Friday," she said on a Tuesday afternoon, late in September.

I laid across my bed in silence, knowing she didn't have the willpower to make me wait.

Light from the window splayed across her face. "On a date to the movies."

"Oh?" I asked and rolled away. "Well, have fun."

Bailey grabbed for my shoulder, giggling. "Guess with who."

"Skip Greene."

She threw a pillow at my head.

"Ronald Pitts."

"Ronald, come on. That was so ninth grade." Her laughter made me grin. "Besides, I've raised my standards. I only date the cutest guy in school now, the dreamy Chase Pearson."

The grin faded as I rolled back, alarms flashing in my head. "How did you get him to ask you out?"

"I kept pestering him about the phone. Chase said he slipped it in my backpack when we were on the bench. He asked if there was any way I'd believe him." She smiled wider. "That's when I said only if he'll go to the Fun Connection on Friday night."

I was impressed and somewhat jealous. Of Chase? No, that couldn't be. "You really asked him?"

"You know I go after what I want."

"How are you going to sell this to your mom? Dad banned me from dating until my sixteenth birthday, as if three more months will matter."

Her eyes gleamed. "The question is how are you going to sell this to *your* mom and dad?"

"What do *I* have to do with you and Chase?"

"Think double date."

"Oh, no."

"I've got it all planned out. You and I will be going to the Fun Connection on Friday night."

"I just got the brace off my wrist. Mom and Dad will freak if I ask to go back there."

"Yeah, if you ask to go skating. Tell them we want to see a movie."

"Just you and me?"

"Mom will drop us off and we'll meet Chase inside the theater. It'll work great, trust me."

Only one part of her plan kept me from relaxing. "I thought you said 'double date.' Who am I supposed to be meeting?"

"You won't be meeting anyone." Her laugh cut short my sigh of relief. "Pade will be riding with us."

I jumped off the bed. "You're lying. Friday night is football."

"Are you sure?"

"Yes." I slapped a hand to my forehead. "Credence is off this week."

"Just be glad you don't have to hide *him* from your parents."

* * * * *

On Thursday, I slipped into the library after school and signed in for a computer. Since Bailey left early for a dentist appointment, I had time to get online, though I'd watched the clock in every class as I wrestled with the possibility.

Credence was different. Risking our new home was wrong. I knew I shouldn't even think about typing my real name, but I hadn't looked in more than a year. I sank into a padded chair and read the 'Research Only' sign posted above each of the six stations. Fortunately, no one sat at the other five.

I opened the browser and typed 'Jessica Naples' and 'New York' in the search box. More than ten thousand hits appeared, but I knew the address would be on the first page. As the link hesitated to load, I slid the mouse over the close button in case a quick exit became the only thing keeping us from having to move again. Using the keyboard, I scrolled down as the page finished loading.

A picture took form in the center of the screen. Strings of hair and smudges of dirt hid most of the girl's features, but I knew the shape of her face by heart. Snapped less than a month before meeting the only man I remembered calling dad, the picture was a mesh of black and white creases. I touched the shiny surface, squinting at the bear in her arms. The fact I couldn't remember the bear's color didn't seem quite so bad this time.

I scrolled back to the headline of the article, 'Mother Pleads for Safe Return of Daughter.' Paragraphs followed describing her tearful pleas, and I read them like all the times before. *Liar*, I charged at the unseen face, as if hurting her would erase the mark upon my soul. Each time the words appeared, I hoped to learn more about the life just beyond memory.

Something hit the floor and I turned from the screen. As before, every chair but mine offered freedom to surf. Sounds of laughter drifted through windows amid sunshine and stale gossip from students waiting for rides. After three days of rain, I imagined warmth on my face instead of a cold electric glow.

"What are you doing?"

I jumped, but one click of the mouse left only standard library wallpaper to greet me.

Chase stared. "Did I scare you?"

"Maybe a little." I wondered how much he saw before the page closed. "I was just doing some research for my…" jeez what could I say, "book report."

"Really?" He dropped into the chair next to me. "You must by trying hard to impress my mom. You don't need to bother. I can tell you she's already impressed." Chase turned to his screen and logged on.

I laughed, imagining jealously. "I'm not trying."

"Mom can be tough, but you're good at English. It drives her crazy knowing I'd rather be in any science class than hers."

"I've always been good with letters, but seriously, I won't make another perfect score in her class. I haven't since that first test."

His eyes stayed on the screen. "If she finds out you're missing questions on purpose, she'll make you wish term papers were never invented."

"Why should she care?"

"She cares about all of her students, probably too much. Mom is always talking about making a difference. Helping people means more to her than anything and being a teacher was always her dream."

With all my issues, a teacher on a mission would be like adding twelve lines to a haiku. "How do I make her leave me alone?"

"I don't know if you can." Chase's screen loaded pictures of a blond girl who deserved a life-sized trophy in any beauty pageant.

"Who is that?"

"Lauren's a friend from my last school."

Lauren, who Bailey had wondered about almost daily since seeing Chase's binder. "You talk to her from the library?"

"Mom won't let me contact anyone there."

I connected with the familiar sadness in his voice. "I've moved a lot too. There were several times I had to leave friends behind." When Chase remained silent, finding something else to say seemed harder than the worst chemistry test. "Where'd you go to school last?"

"New York City."

As in *my* New York City? Looking away, the sadness beneath his words made me want to squeeze his hand. "You're from New York? I can tell you've got some kind of accent."

"We lived there less than a year. We tell everyone we're from California."

"Why Credence?"

"Why not?"

I thought of how Dad gave the same evasive

answers and smiled, before remembering the day Bailey and I snuck into Mrs. Pearson's class. "Is it just the two of you?"

He nodded. "My dad died in an accident when I was five. Mom falls over her own words to make me proud of the man, but I can't remember him."

We'd left New York by my fifth birthday. "A car wreck?"

"Something like that."

"No brothers or sisters?"

"I had a sister." He sighed. "How about you? You said your mom's a teacher here. What about your dad?"

"He's a consultant for Health Made Simple."

"Never heard of it," Chase said.

"Dad gives motivational speeches. You know, he sells all that live your life better stuff."

"So, you're saying he helps people, like my mom."

I shrugged. "I've got two younger brothers, Danny and Collin. They live to drive me *insane*, but they can be cool sometimes. As if I'd ever tell them."

He closed Lauren's page. "I wish my mom would finish her meeting."

"Me too. Crap, I forgot about the conference." I logged off the computer and grabbed my backpack, nearly falling as I scrambled out of the chair.

Chase jerked to attention. "What's wrong?"

"Mom's gonna kill me. I'm supposed to get my brothers from the fifth-grade building."

"I'll walk with you," he said.

"Not necessary." I spun, meeting Chase's eyes. His face was inches from mine, with the computer behind showing only a library logo, and his backpack draped neatly over each shoulder. "How did you…?"

"You can ask on the way."

Chase stared ahead as we crossed the pavement that divided the high school and elementary school. I wanted to ask about what happened in the library but couldn't find the right words. Tired of trying to solve the mystery of Chase, I dropped my bag and danced into the sunlight. Since all the buses were taking students home, pavement stretched ahead for the length of the five elementary buildings. I spun on the tips of my toes, arms spread wide.

He watched from the covered sidewalk. "You seemed to brighten when you stepped into the light."

"After days of rain, sunshine makes me feel better than any Saturday."

"You're going to think I'm weird again."

I stopped spinning, although the pavement felt like a steep drop beneath my feet. "Weirder than you logging out of the computer before I could've clicked escape?"

"I hate the sun."

Laughing, I raised my arms to the sky. "What do you mean, you hate the sun?"

"I burn really easy."

The look on his face ended my laughter. "Don't feel bad, just get some good sunscreen. My parents are bent on skin protection—they practically make me bathe with the sticky white goo every morning. Dad gets sunscreen that's like SPF one thousand."

After a laugh from Chase, I lowered my voice. "My dad had cancer."

His face fell.

"It happened about a year before we moved to Credence. He had dark circles under his eyes and went to a specialist in Atlanta I'd never heard of. It was a whole school day and beyond at the hospital just to see him. No lie—I actually did homework on a table next to the bed while nurses drew his blood."

"What kind of cancer?"

"Most people would guess lung cancer or a brain tumor, but the disease killing him was skin cancer."

"Is he okay now?"

"He's in remission. Dad had treatments I couldn't pronounce, even radiation."

Chase's eyes grew. "Radiation?"

The terror in his voice sent me stumbling back. "It saved his life."

Chase recovered and stepped off the sidewalk. "If too much sunlight causes skin cancer, how can you like the sun?"

As we stood in the heated afternoon, I looked down at his palms, which faced skyward. They were pale and smooth like mine, but larger. His fingers shook slightly at first, but the longer we stayed in the sun, the more each trembled.

"The warmth makes me feel good, even if it's only for a minute." I returned to the sidewalk with his feet close behind mine.

He sighed. "I feel like I could tell you anything."

"If you can tell me anything, explain how you got Bailey's phone back in her bag." When Chase smiled, I reached out and squeezed his arm. "You can tell me anything and I'll believe you. Unless you say you're from another planet or something crazy like that."

His smile faded for a moment, and then returned. "And if I tell you something crazy like that?" Chase searched my eyes, his face close enough to make being kissed a fear.

"Jes," Danny shouted from the main entrance.

Chase stared as the boys approached, but I couldn't read the expression on his face. They only let him get out a short 'hello' before taking off down the sidewalk.

"Beat you there," Collin said.

Although I was prepared to run after them, Chase stumbled in his effort to follow. "They're twins?"

"What's wrong with that?" I asked when the boys finally stopped.

"Nothing," he muttered. "I'm just… surprised."

Collin looked up at Chase. "It's cool to have a twin."

"I'm sure it is." Chase turned to me. "What about you? Do you have a twin?"

Yeah, okay. I fought an urge to laugh at the impossibility of Chase's question. If only he knew where I'd come from, we'd be laughing together.

Danny jumped in front of us. "Jes can't 'cause she's—"

I caught the back of Danny's shirt. "Shut up!"

Chase glanced from me to Danny, eyebrows drawn together, but I wasn't about to fill him in on the drama surrounding my life. Collin changed the subject—fortunately, both got bored with any conversation about me unless they knew a way to make trouble. They mentioned a new computer game Danny wanted. Chase fell into their 'gaming talk' and owned the twins' attention until we reached the van.

"Who's your new friend?" Mom asked as the door slid open.

"Chase," they answered, perfectly in time.

Mom extended her hand as the boys climbed in. "Nice to meet you, Chase."

Chase shook Mom's hand, smiling as if he'd just received a PhD in charm. "Yes ma'am. Nice to meet you."

"Where are you from?"

"California, born and raised." Chase checked his watch. "Sorry, I've got to go. My mom's waiting." He waved at the boys. "It was cool to meet a set of twins."

Danny and Collin whined as Chase bolted. Mom shut the sliding door, watching me curiously. "You haven't mentioned a new friend."

"Mom, don't go there."

"Chase does have pretty blue eyes, just like someone I know."

I shook my head. "Chase and I are nothing alike. He's my lab partner and probably the only reason I'll pass chemistry."

"Okay, okay. So, Chase is from California?"

"Yeah."

"We've never lived in California. Maybe you can learn something from Chase."

"Maybe." Like how to lie better than you taught me.

* * * * *

Chase was from California.

Chase thought it was cool to have a twin.

Chase knew how to reach level nine of *The Dragon's Keeper*.

He was all Danny and Collin talked about that night at dinner. As I swallowed my last bite of taco, the boys found yet another opportunity to talk about Chase. I groaned and Mom smiled. Dad listened until the table was clear and the boys climbed the stairs for their hour of TV. After helping Mom with the dishes, I slipped into the living room where Dad was watching the news.

"Dad?"

He looked up, giving me his uncomfortably full attention.

"I was wondering if we could talk."

"Uh-oh," Mom said, from the doorway. "This sounds serious."

"I've been thinking about when we were in New York."

Dad frowned. "New York?"

"I've got some more questions."

He switched off the TV and waved me over to the couch. Mom took the seat to my other side. "You know we've always tried to answer your questions as honestly as possible. Have you remembered something new?" It was always Dad's first question when I mentioned the past.

"I remember when you and Mom adopted me, but before that…"

Mom put an arm around my neck and pressed her head to the top of mine. "Honey, there's nothing wrong with not remembering. You were so young then." She pulled me closer. "Perhaps some things are best left in the past."

I turned to Dad. "What was it like in New York?"

"Life was much faster than in Credence."

"Did you always live there before we met?"

His brow creased. "Come on, Jes. Have you forgotten I'm from Colorado? Bailey's dad and I attended college together. How do you think I met Lorraine?"

They met in New York. Or did they? It was so long

ago. My head was foggy as I looked to Mom and then back to Dad. "What about your family? Mom always talks about hers."

Dad cupped my cheek with his hand. "You are my family."

I brushed his hand away. "You know what I mean."

"My parents passed away years ago. What else would you like to know?"

I took a breath. "Why didn't my real parents want me?"

Dad's face tightened and his arms surrounded me. "If only you *could* remember." He sighed, as if giving up a fight. "They disappeared before the hearing. That's why Lorraine and I signed those papers and kept you for good. I still have a friend in New York, with the police. No one has found any trace of the Naples since the night I found you. That means no paper trail, no money trail—nothing for the police to follow."

"I get it. They don't want to be found. But why can't I talk to anyone else? At least I could tell Bailey the truth."

"Remember what we talked about before? About the reporters who swarmed the foster home and how I moved us from New York when your adoption became final?"

Dad had made it painfully clear that no one in Credence would ever hear my former last name. No one could learn my pathetic story. Which was fine, I could deal. I might cry myself to sleep at night, but I'd never reopen a wound for the people who loved me.

He sensed me holding back and pulled away. "No matter what happens, we won't let you go. We'll do whatever it takes to keep you safe." His words felt like a shield from torture Tosh had yet to discover.

* * * * *

The dream came again that night. I heard my parents argue and then sad voices. The powerless feeling overtook me as thoughts of my mother's last words seized my heart. When I awoke, my tear-stained face clung to the pillowcase.

CHAPTER SEVEN

Date Night

"I told you my plan would work," Bailey said on Friday evening. She smiled in my bathroom mirror as we got ready for the movies. "If anyone catches us, we just *happened* to be watching the same movie."

I groaned as the curling iron grazed my ear. "Are you sure Pade thinks this is a date?"

From her purse, Bailey pulled a compact and a tube of crimson lipstick. "You should've talked to him instead of hiding all week. Trust me, guys hate that."

"I still can't believe Sarah Beth broke up with him."

"Not every girl in school would choose Pade, especially when he's willing to set them up with a senior on the football team. If he was so in love with her, why would he do that?" Bailey laughed and smeared on a dark layer of eye shadow. "Imagine you and me on our first real dates together. You'll be with Pade and I'll be next to Chase. On different rows, of course."

"Of course." She really had thought of everything.

That is, everything except for harassment times two.

"So," Danny said from the cracked door. "Jes is going on a date with Pade."

Collin pushed him aside. "And Bailey's going on a date with Chase."

I spun, throwing open the door, but the twins were halfway down the hall before I stepped outside. Laughter sailed as they flew down the stairs.

Bailey scowled in the mirror. "Those boys get on my last nerve."

I shut the door tight. "At least you don't have to live with them."

"Do you think they'll rat us out?" she asked.

"Danny and Collin? Rat us out?"

"Right. Let's leave before they have the chance."

Bailey gathered her makeup and headed for the stairs. I followed close behind, preparing to sneak out of the back door. Danny and Collin had finally pushed me to the breaking point. If they told Mom and Dad and ruined our plans, we'd have serious issues.

Dad sat on the edge of the couch, spreading papers across the coffee table. Mom reclined to his right and flipped through a cookbook. Announcers on the news channel mouthed headlines without sound.

She noticed us first. "I want you both to be careful. Don't leave the doors of the Fun Connection until Charlie pulls up to the curb."

Bailey ran for the door, nearly tripping on the carpet. "See you in the car."

Dad was concentrating on his papers, but looked up in time to stop me. "What movie are you going to see?"

"*The Summer Show*," I said.

"What's that rated?" he asked.

"PG-13."

He lowered the papers and leaned back, his face sagging as if he'd run a marathon. "Are you sure?"

"Next week will be October. I'll be sixteen soon."

Dad smiled. "Jessica Ray, I'm well aware of that."

I reached down to recover a page as it slid off the table. Unfortunately, I failed to notice the twins standing in the doorway.

"Jes is going on a date," Collin said with a smirk.

"Date?" Dad eyed the twins. "How do you know that?"

"We know everything," Danny said.

Mom chuckled. "You've got a long way to learn half of everything."

Dad grinned at me. "Just who is this mystery boy?"

Danny and Collin stopped in front of me. "Pade."

Dad's grin disappeared. "Pade?"

"Jes and Pade sittin' in a tree..." Collin said, pointing to Danny.

"K-I-S-S-I-N-G," Danny shouted.

"First comes love, second comes marriage..."

"Then comes Jes with a baby carriage."

I glared at the twins. "I think I learned that one in second grade." My eyes shifted to Dad, as he exchanged a glance with Mom. "Bailey and I were talking in the bathroom and the boys overheard us. A girl at school likes Pade. Not me."

Dad leaned forward, both hands meeting in an 'A' below his nose. "Boys, go upstairs. I think you've caused your sister enough grief for tonight."

Danny and Collin laughed, bolting out another verse as they mounted the stairs.

Mom closed her book. "A girl at school likes Pade?

Other than the one who broke up with him?"

Tosh flashed in my head. "That's what I've heard."

"How do you feel about that?" Dad asked.

Like pulling Tosh's hair out. "How should I feel? He's Bailey's brother."

"And he's going with you tonight?"

"He's going to the Fun Connection. Once he gets there, he'll probably go skating."

"Skating?" Dad's voice filled with concern. "Please don't tell me you plan to go skating again. I can't go through another night like the last time."

"I can honestly say Bailey and I are going to watch a movie. No skating. Promise."

His face relaxed. "And that stuff about Pade?"

"I'm sure Pade will be hanging out with Terrance or whoever else he's meeting." I looked at Mom. "You know I could never like *Pade*." My eyes rolled for an extra edge of drama. "Right?"

Mom smiled, but the smile didn't reach her voice. "What have you got against Pade? My nephew seems like a nice young man, and charming. Do you know something about him we don't?"

Why couldn't they just let it go? First, my parents worried I might like Pade. Then they wanted to know why I didn't. Was I the only sane one in our conversation? "Pade is a great guy, really."

"Then what's the problem?" Mom asked. "He seems quite popular at school."

"Popular is not my thing."

"Oh," Mom said. "I thought you might feel weird since Pade is sort of related to you."

"*Lorraine*!" Dad held up his hands.

Her face colored. "I'm just saying…"

"She's already confused enough." He turned to me. "Maybe you've doubted me at times, but I can promise you're not related to Pade. There is *nothing* similar about the blood in your veins."

"What's so bad about me forgetting I'm adopted, just for once?"

"Oh, honey." Mom stood, putting her arms around me. "It feels wonderful knowing you'd want to forget, that you'd even think of us as your real family."

Not wanting to argue the point she missed and filled with sickness over the thought of a warm family moment, I looked back at Dad. "Can I kill those boys now or do I have to wait 'til they're older?"

Dad's smile returned, but his voice mirrored the sadness in Mom's. "Give them a few more years, Jes. They'll grow out of their obnoxious stage. Maybe you'll even beat them to it."

"Beat them? Come on, Dad. I'm not obnoxious."

He laughed with me. "I'm sure all teenagers have their moments."

I grabbed my phone from the bar and headed for the door. "Did you guys really think I had a thing for Pade? That would be weird." Silence filled the room, far from the laughter of only a moment ago. Surely, I convinced them.

As the door sealed my escape, I fought a surge of dread, unable to shake the sight of Dad with lines at every corner of his face. For months before his cancer diagnosis, Dad came home with an exhaustion ten hours in bed couldn't fix. The prospect of his cancer returning had the potential to rain a flood of anxiety over the entire evening. No, I'd push the fear away by concentrating on my first date. At least I could control that part of my life.

Bailey chatted nonstop until we pulled into the parking lot of the Fun Connection.

"Enjoy the movie, girls." Aunt Charlie watched Pade rise from the front. "Son, be careful skating."

Even though I knew Pade should be going to the movies, I touched the edge of crazy while waiting to see if his plans included skating. He certainly looked ready with his skates in hand. Maybe Bailey had our date all wrong.

Chase stood inside the main row of doors, eyes coasting a room full of noises and people rushing by. After spotting us, he seemed almost relieved, at least until Pade eyed him and nodded.

"Hey man, what's up?" Pade's voice was relaxed, but his eyes stayed on Chase.

"Not much." Chase shrugged, though his voice was cautious, like he'd been asked to believe a lie.

Bailey pulled Chase's arm, oblivious to the signals passing between them. An entire conversation, some kind of challenge, and maybe even a grudge had formed in six short words.

I considered possibilities as Pade rented a locker to stow his skates. "Jessica Ray," I said, under my breath. "Focus on your date." Giddy warmth overtook thoughts of Chase as Pade held out his hand and smiled.

Bailey and Chase stopped midway up the aisle for screen eight. Pade gestured up and I nodded, continuing to the top. I settled within a whisper of Pade, munching on the popcorn between us. He talked about a new action movie, maybe hinting at another date, while I wondered what to do next. Take his hand? Wait for Pade to make the first move?

When I checked my phone, a whole hour of the movie had passed without Pade reaching for my hand. Below us, the shadow of Bailey's head bent, merging with Chase's shoulder. Jealousy of her success rippled through me.

Pade leaned close, his breath a tickle of heat against my ear. "What are you looking at?"

"Nothing," I said.

"Bailey and Chase seem like they're really into each other."

"Yeah." I closed my eyes and slid lower in my seat, not wanting to talk about Bailey or Chase.

Pade sighed and leaned back, once again focused totally on the movie.

Reaching for my drink, I took a huge gulp, which was so not needed in my situation. As I replaced the cup, my fingers grazed Pade's and I froze, electricity catching me by surprise. I needed to breathe. I needed to pee. Then his fingers slipped through mine.

The most depressing part of that movie turned out to be the end. After sitting through all of the credits and nearly dragging Pade alongside empty rows of seats, he finally released my hand at the door. We found Bailey and Chase outside, but my first stop was the bathroom.

Bailey checked into the stall next to mine. "Oh, my god, that was awesome!"

"Yeah," I said, sighing in relief. "The movie was cool."

"Please don't tell me you actually watched that movie." Bailey gagged. "Didn't you have better things to think about?"

For two hours, I'd banished thoughts of Dad's illness. The feeling poured over my heart again, tearing me between laughing and crying.

"Are you going to answer me?" she asked.

"I didn't watch the *whole* movie. Pade did hold my hand."

"Of course, I had faith in my brother." She checked her makeup in the mirror and almost ran to Chase's side.

At the locker holding Pade's unused skates, my hand touched his and Pade pulled away. "We should talk more."

Color faded from the world around me. "About what?"

"You, me." The space between us widened. "If we're going to be more than friends, we should at least talk about stuff. If you could ask me anything, what would it be?"

I shrugged, able to think of only one question, but gutless to say the words. "What do you want to do after graduation?"

He raised an eyebrow. "I can see we've got to work on the opening up part."

"You said anything."

"Yeah, but I meant…" He sighed and yanked his skates from the locker. "I want to be something big with math like an accountant or engineer."

"No pro football?"

"What are the chances of that happening?" Pade slammed the locker door, muttering under his breath. Without warning, he turned and smiled. "Did you like the movie?"

I envied the confidence in his voice. "Yeah. I'm glad—"

"Pade!" Tosh crossed the floor and stole a spot between us. "I didn't know you were here." She gave me a look of pointed daggers, but smiled at him with the sweetness of a candy store. "Come and skate with me."

For a scary moment, I thought Pade might follow Tosh. Instead, he pulled out his phone. "Sorry, my mom's picking us up in a few."

"Fine." She shrugged as if the world could end before she cared. "See you on Monday."

As Tosh walked away, weaving her tight jeans close to a group of guys who'd stopped talking to stare, I pictured her face against the floor, hair in knots between each of my fingers, with my foot pressing down on the back of her neck—

"Don't let her get to you," Pade said.

"I'm cool," I said.

"What were you saying before she walked up?"

"Nothing."

He sat next to me on the way home, leaving a gap between us. I welcomed the distance for the first time. While Bailey created an entire script to satisfy Aunt Charlie's questions, I fought an urge to admit the movie was everything except one I'd see again. After pulling into the driveway next to the van, we climbed out of the car and Bailey followed Aunt Charlie inside. Pade remained lost to the night until curiosity snowballed into enough nerve for me to turn.

In the shadow of the van, Pade leaned down and pressed his lips to mine. An edge of sweat and sweet cologne filled my nostrils, and I burned the scent into memory. Darkness mixed with moonlight in the cool air around us, making me want to scream above the pulsing in my head. Maybe Pade planned to kiss me deeper, but I didn't move, fearful of opening my eyes to discover the whole date was no more than a dream.

When Pade stepped back, he spoke with a huskiness somewhere between wonder and torture. "Goodnight, Jes." He crossed the path to his house without another word, but I still felt on top of the world.

* * * * *

Since I missed breakfast the next morning, my stomach growled before I could climb from the bed. While Bailey ran home to shower and change, I found Mom in the kitchen making lunch for the boys.

Butter sizzled on the flat iron as she opened the bread. "I bet you're starving."

"You're making grilled cheese sandwiches?" I asked.

"Do you want ham or just cheese?"

"Ham, definitely."

Dad walked in, with circles hanging under his eyes. He opened his arms and I fell into his embrace.

"Are you okay?" I asked, a cold hand clutching my heart.

He released me, confusion on his face. "Of course. Why?"

"You look tired."

"Oh, that," Dad said. "Mrs. Greene stopped in and watched the boys while your mom and I went out."

"Since when do you guys go out without us?"

"Didn't you wonder why Charlie dropped you off *and* picked you up? Lorraine and I went to the movies."

I gasped.

"Thought we'd see *The Summer Show*. You know, find out what all the fuss is about. Jessica Ray, is there anything you want to tell me?"

"Dad, I…" My eyes zoomed to Mom.

She laughed. "Quit giving her that look."

Dad opened his mouth but laughed before he could form another word. "I can't believe you messed that up. She was about to rat herself out."

Mom handed me a plate with two sandwiches. "Parents shouldn't know everything."

"Maybe not," Dad said, still grinning as he lowered to the table. I watched as his face began to glow again and I let out a long sigh. Maybe I'd made a mistake.

"Alright, boys, I was thinking we could all go out tonight. How does the fair sound?"

While Danny and Collin made a victory lap around the table, Dad looked at me. "How about it, Jes? Is fifteen almost sixteen too old to hang out with your parents?"

I shook my head. It was going to be an awesome day.

* * * * *

Everyone piled into the van as a silly high set the mood for our trip to the fair. Aunt Charlie sat on the floor between the boys, all the way fighting with Dad over top honor with the best joke, keeping the rest of us scrambling for tissues. Bailey and I sat in the backseat, with Pade wedged between us. He held my hand when no one was looking and pretended to be teasing me when they were.

Since we arrived in the parking lot four hours before dark, I prepared myself for the sunscreen lecture. Mom and Aunt Charlie climbed out with the twins, plastering a generous white film across their cheeks. Dad remained in the driver's seat long enough to cake on his.

He handed me the tube. "One day you'll thank me for making you wear this."

I applied the thick substance. "Yeah, whatever."

"The sun can be harsh, so don't make fun of skin protection."

I forced a frown. "Does that mean when I'm thirty I'll look like I'm twenty?"

He laughed. "Next time I'll go for the vanity angle first."

Bailey stood at the end of a long row of cars. I ran to catch up, wiping my sticky hands on my jeans. "What should we do first?"

She pointed to a double Ferris wheel. "Rides."

Mom looped her arm in Aunt Charlie's. "That sounds great."

"Yeah," Aunt Charlie said. "Just like when Daddy used to take us."

Dad left with Danny and Collin, looking amazed as they argued over where to start. Danny and Collin never argued.

Mom and Aunt Charlie bought a ticket for everything Bailey and I rode. The Himalaya was my favorite, with music beating as we screamed on a grounded rollercoaster. My second favorite was the Gravitron, although I couldn't feel my legs when the ride stopped spinning. Only three rides went upside down, but I refused to get in line for those.

Excitement crammed the air around us as the sun dropped behind the trees. Flashing lights came on, seamless rows of neon purple and green outlining the rides. Dad returned with Danny and Collin, both pouting over all the rides they couldn't get on until they were taller.

"Sorry boys," he said. "Your mom was always short for her age too." He put an arm around my shoulders and squeezed. "There are advantages to being the oldest."

"Nothing useful."

"Don't bet on that." He handed me a twenty. "Why don't you and Bailey try some games?"

"What should we play?" I yelled as voices fought with music along the outer section.

"No one's lining up to collect those dusty toys." Bailey paused at a booth boasting the largest stuffed animals. She grabbed the tail of a monkey hanging from the tent above our heads. "Look at this."

I stared across row after row of old coke bottles and the frenzy of rings flying from every corner of the booth, each trying to ring the neck of a bottle. "You'll never win that."

"No, I spent my money already. But you could."

"I don't think so." Then I spotted Bailey's true motive. A guy with tattoos worked our side of the booth.

He smiled as if Bailey and I hovered on the brink of college. "Five dollars buys you twenty rings."

"Go on," Bailey shouted in my ear.

Deciding on a tiger above his head, I laid the twenty down.

Bailey reached in the box he handed over. "What are you waiting for?"

"I'm watching how people aim." I lifted a ring, molded from thick red plastic, and tossed it across the booth. The edge bounced off the rim of a bottle and fell out of sight.

"You'll never win that way. Hey, can you show my

friend how to play?"

"Sure." Tattoo guy tossed a ring, landing it on the neck of a bottle, probably for the hundredth time that day. "That's how you win."

I was down to my last two when Pade walked up.

"Having fun?" he asked.

"Maybe if I could land a ring on one of these bottles."

Pade lifted a ring, turning it in his hand. "I don't see how it can fit."

Tattoo guy cleared his throat. "All games are completely winnable, that's our rule."

Bailey stepped closer. "He's right Pade—Jes and I saw him ring one. There's no reason why *you* can't win."

I tossed the ring in my hand and watched, helpless as it disappeared into the abyss between two rows of bottles.

"Last one," said tattoo guy, as he leaned against the counter.

Pade cut his eyes to me. "What are you trying to win?"

I pointed to the tiger and Pade nodded. His face tightened as he stared across the sea of green glass. He lifted his hand and aimed, tossing my last ring with a gentle flip. To my amazement, the ring landed perfectly around the neck of a bottle.

Squealing, I gave Pade a high five. Bailey hugged her brother and bounced as if we all stood on a trampoline.

Tattoo guy grinned. "Great shot, man. What'll it be?"

"Tiger," Pade said, calm at the center of our excitement.

"Alright, ladies' choice."

The tiger, overstuffed orange and black stripes in my arms, dragged the ground around my feet. As I grabbed the tail, Pade's eyes met mine. Under his gaze, my heart pounded, each pulse accelerating as the games disappeared. Every funnel cake and laughing face and old metal bell blurred around me. I longed to rewind time and amend the day I said our kiss meant nothing, clearing the way for me to drop the tiger and throw my arms around Pade's neck.

Bailey's voice pierced the fog. "I'm going to catch up with Rachelle."

Pade put an arm through mine. "You're welcome."

Minutes passed as we walked the rows of games, maybe hours, before Pade spoke again. "Homecoming is four Fridays away. What will you be doing that night?"

My breath caught. "Hopefully, same as you."

"You mean before or after I throw the winning play and get every coach in the Southeast on a plane to Credence, begging me to sign for their school?"

I pushed him away. "Obviously, I'll be dancing while you're passed out in the locker room."

He laughed and recaptured my arm. "Can't you let a guy dream?"

"I thought Bailey said your dad's already planned for a college in Colorado."

The sparkle in his voice withered and died with the happy lines of his face. "Next year I'll be eighteen. He'll be done choosing my life for me, and if he's not, I'll make sure he understands what 'legal' means."

The amber glass of a beer bottle rolled beneath my feet. I stumbled with a goofy 'ouch', nearly falling.

Pade grabbed my shoulders. "Are you okay?"

Before I could answer, he shoved me into the shadow between two tents. His lips brushed mine, softly at first, but urgent with the next touch. The smell of canvas surrounded us, reminding me of a camping trip before Atlanta. Warmth flowed all the way to my stomach, like when I gave in at a party once and drank a shot of flaming red liquid.

"Go with me to the dance," he said.

I searched for his eyes. "You can't take me to Homecoming, not *really* take me."

"I can take whoever I want."

"No," I said, biting my lip. "You can't pick me up."

"I've got a license. Mom will let me borrow the car."

"That's not what I mean. You can't tell your mom who you're taking. You can't meet me at the bottom of the stairs and shake Dad's hand. We can't arrive together; people will make puking noises behind our backs."

"Don't you think you're taking this 'related' thing a little far? Besides, this is Homecoming, not Prom. We'll just meet up after the game and hang out on the dance floor."

"Hang out?"

Pade took my hand, pulling me back to the fair. "We'll figure something out."

We spent the next hour checking out the fair, side-by-side, with no mention of the dance. He looped his arm in mine again, but this time kept a safe distance. Only when Mom and Dad walked up from behind did Pade release my arm. Their loud voices tipped us off.

Dad never said if he saw us together.

* * * * *

That night, I had my strangest dream yet.

The stone floor chilled my toes as I followed my father's voice. I tripped on the edge of my nightgown and almost fell. With a trembling hand, I jerked the edge of the nightgown up from the floor. For a terrifying instant, he was lost to me. My feet bolted toward his anxious sound, the only sound. No longer worried he might send me back alone, I needed the security of his arms around me. Maybe I could stop him, make him turn around. Whatever his reasons for leaving, my heart didn't doubt his love. If only he would slow down.

Around the last corner of the hall, a narrow door rose to my right. I stood on my toes and stretched both arms to reach a square handle. Because of my change in height, the dream began to feel contradictory—happening both in the present and in the past. Both real and unreal. Even more unreal came when the door opened.

Before me was a spaceship, complete with flashing lights and swirling engine noises. The outside, shaped like a racecar, glowed under the lights, but the mass of metal could have overflowed a garage. Seams from a door drew my attention to a stairway that spiraled to the floor. Between my feet and the stairway stretched a lighted path of metal, some kind of bridge, and to each side dark water, pooling below the platform in battered waves. The same waves of wind caught my hair and threatened to force me back.

I tripped on the edge of my nightgown as the ceiling split. Darkness hovered outside, glittered with stars, causing my head to feel as if it floated ten feet above my body. A voice called from behind, above the fully charged engine. I closed my eyes and pictured myself at the top of the stairway.

When I opened my eyes, silent darkness surrounded me. In shadows of moonlight, my room in Credence looked exactly as it had before the dream.

Aunt Charlie liked to say, 'Dreams are just a twisted reflection of recent experiences. Dreams are how people work through issues during sleep.'

Had I somehow mixed the lights and noises from the fair into my dreams of the past? Were my dreams really of the past? If all of this actually happened, where had I come from?

CHAPTER EIGHT

The Game

Bailey and I hung out for most of Sunday, riding our bikes in the woods beyond our row of houses. A simple drop from silent black road to bumpy gravel led us to trails that branched from either side of the one-lane road. By following her imaginary map far enough, she promised we'd cross several shallow creeks and emerge at power lines leading to the river.

The woods thickened as we entered the area she called Ghost Town. Deep pits of muddy water lined the road. Down a hill and along a creek lay foundations, representing a once thriving town. Bailey talked of how she and Pade would walk the water's edge, pretending the heart of that old town had somehow found life support.

Swirling waves gurgled before the water came into sight. We weaved through the trees, walking a tight rope around fingers of poison ivy, until we reached the bank. I removed my shoes and socks, wasting no time in joining the weathered stones. Leaves fell around us, blanketing the water with a splash of color. The air smelled of dirt and rain, and calm, despite the rushing water.

"You know our parents would freak if they found us here." Bailey laughed at her own bold statement. "If Uncle Justin ever saw you in that water…"

Dad would be furious. He'd tell me how scared I should be, when my heart overflowed with enough happiness to squash any fear. I grabbed a handful of water and washed the dirt and sweat from my face. The water chilled my toes and at times nearly took me for a ride along the rocks. If only I could drift away, be someone else, or maybe have another life.

"Yeah, I know," was all I said, but I stood in the ankle-deep liquid beauty until we absolutely had to leave.

When the afternoon washed into a purple and orange sky, we wheeled our bikes back across the blacktop. Bailey crossed the yard and I parked behind the house, slipping through the back door. I tiptoed through the kitchen, to where Mom and Dad were talking in the dim living room.

"I think it's time to tell her," Mom said.

I flattened against the wall beside the living room entrance, preparing for a detour from the usual 'kids only' version of the truth. My stomach fluttered with the certainty they were talking about me.

"You may be right," Dad said. "I just want her to enjoy being young. You know it's a luxury my parents didn't allow."

Mom sighed. "Knowing her past, I sometimes wonder if I have the right to say she should hear more of the truth, especially when I know she'll hurt."

"Lorraine, you have every right. In Jessica's eyes, you're her mother and I'm her father."

"She can't remember her real parents and I feel horrible. Not knowing what became of them has to plague her mind, even though she hardly tells us."

"We can't erase what was done for her protection," Dad said. "She loves us both and that will never change, but let's focus on now and not then."

Mom sighed again, frustration spilling from her voice. "She'll be sixteen soon."

"I know." Dad's words were a leaking tire.

"You should be the one to tell her."

"When she's ready."

"And when will that be?" she asked. "In case you haven't noticed, Jes is growing up fast."

"She held it together so well last year, but I'm afraid she won't face the truth without pain in some form."

Oh god, he was sick again. He'd waited so long to tell me before.

Silence filled the room until Mom spoke. "We can only hope for the best."

"I must take my battle to others and maybe then a cure can be found. It may take a year or more, but the future is worth everything. No matter what happens to me, you must see her through this."

"You know how much she means to me."

I drew myself from the wall, ready to cry my eyes out. Dad was sick again, I knew for sure. How long had he hidden the truth this time?

"I'll talk to her tonight, before I leave. But I'll only tell her what she needs to know for now."

Shaking, I managed to climb the stairs and sneak by the boys' room. Nearly an hour passed as my pillow soaked up a steady stream of tears. I pulled the comforter over my head when Mom opened the door.

She stumbled to a halt. "Jes, I didn't hear you come in. How long have you been back?"

I tried to hide the shaking in my voice. "Just a little while."

"Honey, are you okay?"

"I'm fine."

"Are you sure?" Mom sighed. "Dinner's in twenty minutes."

When darkness settled beyond the window, I crawled out of bed and snuck from my doorway to the bathroom. I splashed water on my face to hide how I'd been crying, but it brought no relief from the sick feeling inside.

At the kitchen door, I heard Danny's voice. "She was there and Bailey—"

Collin jumped in. "They were at a creek."

"Let me get this straight—the two of you saw Jes and Bailey at a creek." Dad looked at me. "Jessica, go to the living room. We need to have a talk." His eyes burned as they moved over me and cut back to the twins. "You two are never to go there again, do you hear me?"

"But, Dad—" Collin said.

"You were both told not to leave the pavement on your bikes. That's two weeks with no bikes."

The boys whined as Dad followed my slow progress to the living room. He motioned to the couch but didn't claim the seat next to me. Instead, he chose to stand in front of the fireplace, with his back to me. The clock ticked endlessly as my thoughts of what to say were in chaos.

Dad rubbed his eyes and turned. "Jessica Ray, I'm very disappointed in you."

I cut my eyes to the floor. "I know."

"I've expressly told you *not* to go near water, and look what happened. Your brothers followed you down there."

My head drifted lower.

"Anything could have happened down there. Your mom and I can't always protect you, especially if you sneak off."

The tears returned. "I'm sorry."

"Sorry doesn't get it. If you ever..." His voice choked. "I don't know what I'd do without you."

I straightened. What would I do without *him*? When was he going to tell me?

Dad's eyes narrowed. "What do you have to say for yourself?"

As I shook my head, he clenched one hand and shoved the other through his hair. "You're grounded."

"Grounded?" An entire grade had passed since the last time Dad made that threat.

"It's time you start taking responsibility for your actions."

Responsibility? Was he for real? *He'd* been lying to me. I rose and stomped back to the kitchen.

"Jessica," he shouted. "I'm not finished."

Mom sat in silence, her eyes following me as if I might dash for the porch door at any moment.

"Jes is in trouble," Danny said, laughing with Collin.

"So are you," Mom said, as I calculated my escape. Hunger faded while I debated between the stairs and the door.

Collin jumped up. "Jes can't speak—she's

grounded."

"What the hell ever," I blasted, quoting one of Tosh's favorite lines.

Mom stood, blood draining from her face. "Jessica!"

I turned as Dad grabbed my arm with one hand.

With the other, he hit me.

The searing of his hand on my cheek sent heat rushing across my face. In all my years, neither Mom nor Dad had ever hit me. My eyes met Dad's with all the fierceness I could gather from my heart, from my soul. I inhaled, ready to stand my ground if he hit me again.

Dad's hand rose. "Jessica Ray."

Courage welled from a hidden source. "Go ahead, hit me again."

"You will respect your parents."

"You're not my real parents. I wish I'd never met you."

An eternal minute passed before Dad's sad words. "Be careful what you wish for."

"Justin!" Mom's broken voice rang in my ears. The sound carved a path to my heart and made me want to cry all over again. I looked at the boys, who watched with quiet worry. Then I escaped the room, along with two sentences I'd give a year's allowance to take back.

Dad didn't follow.

* * * * *

The clock on my nightstand glowed nine-thirty when someone tapped on the door. Elbows resting on the comforter, I pushed the book I'd opened under my pillow. "Come in."

"Hey," Dad said, crossing the room. He lowered to the edge of my bed. "Are you okay?"

I watched his shadow on the wall, etched by the dim lamp. "You didn't hit me that hard."

"I'm sorry."

Something in his voice brought tears to my eyes. "Me too."

He faced the window. "I've never seen your eyes filled with such determination, as if your heart had been clad by iron. What happened?"

"I got mad."

Dad laughed as his eyes returned to my face. "Mad? You were furious. You reminded me of…"

"Of who?"

When Dad spoke again, his voice was a whisper. "Your mother."

I rolled my eyes. "Mom never gets mad."

"You don't know her like I know her."

"Dad, I'm sorry. I shouldn't have talked like that."

"No, you shouldn't be disrespectful." He rested a hand over mine. "I'm leaving tonight."

My breathing stopped. "You're going to work?"

"I have to go to Tokyo."

"Tokyo is on the other side of the planet. How long will you be gone?"

He sighed. "At least four weeks, maybe six."

I sat straight up, shoving back the comforter. "A month? You're leaving us for a whole month?"

"I'll be back before you know it."

A fresh round of tears burned in my eyes, a river this time, anything to make him stay. "Please, Dad," I said, as if time had not separated me from the fears of a five-year-old. "Don't go. Not now."

"Why not now?"

"You've never been gone for a whole month." I rested my head on his chest. "Please."

Dad hugged me tight. "One day you'll understand the importance of my work. I promise."

How could I ever understand him leaving me?

* * * * *

Dad was already on a plane before breakfast the next morning. After choking down cereal, I wasted almost forty-five minutes with my clothes. When I climbed into the van, Danny and Collin amazed me with a hug.

"We're sorry," they whispered.

Bailey leaned over the seat. "Are we having a moment?"

Their faces brightened as I smiled. "We're good."

Mom shifted the van into drive. "Okay, you guys, don't forget about PTA tonight."

PTA? That meant the absolute first time Dad wouldn't be there to nag about meeting all my teachers, the first time I'd miss complaining about him embarrassing me. I closed my eyes, bracing for a long day.

First block came, but no Chase. Mrs. Pearson directed class as usual, not once casting her eyes on his empty desk. I flipped through the pages of my English book, desperate for a story to read, anything to shut out her voice. When the bell rang, I stared at the door and the surge of people pushing through to escape. Instead of following, I approached her desk.

"Mrs. Pearson?" I asked.

Her eyes rose. "Yes?"

I took a step back. "I just…"

"Speak, Miss Delaney, I do not have time to waste."

"I wanted to ask about Chase."

"Chase?"

"I wanted to know if he's sick or something…"

When she spoke again, her voice had softened. "My son was not feeling well today. He is resting at home."

"Will you please tell him I hope he feels better?"

"I will."

My heart sank, but I managed a smile. "Thank you." Without looking back, I headed for second block.

Bailey reached for my arm as I left the building, pulling me from the flow of traffic. "Did you ask about Chase?"

"Mrs. Pearson said he was feeling bad and stayed home."

Bailey's voice echoed my depression. "That sucks."

Second block crawled along, much the same as first. No Chase. I pulled out my art book and started a new drawing. The rest of the day was dedicated to a picture of my favorite spot on the creek.

Since PTA began at six, Mom took us out for dinner. Aunt Charlie had plans to meet us at the restaurant, but a last-minute emergency kept her at the hospital. Our table made for a huge contrast to the clatter of plates and laughter from the next booth as even the boys struggled for happy thoughts.

Back at school, I waited outside the doors of building one, on a bench next to Bailey. "Did you hear how long Dad might be gone?"

She nodded and bit her thumbnail. "I talked to my father last night. He might come home for Christmas."

I leaned back until my shoulder blades reached the

brick. "What did your mom say?"

"Mom has always loved him—I just can't figure out why." She shoved her phone in her purse, nearly ripping the zipper. "He only stayed around long enough for me and Pade to be born."

I thought of Pade. "There must have been *something* great about him."

"Mom is so devoted. I can't understand why she doesn't divorce him and go on with her life. He'll never give up his job in Colorado; not for her, not for Pade, and definitely not for me."

"But isn't he from Colorado? Dad says—"

"What, how nice the weather is in Colorado? It doesn't matter. He should live where the family chooses. It's three against one."

"Do you think we should go inside?"

"Let's wait 'til the meeting is over."

"Too bad Dad isn't here," I whispered.

"You're doing better than me. At least you have one parent at open house. I guess Mrs. Greene will keep the boys until your mom talks with our teachers and Pade's."

"Good thing she's teaching him pre-cal. That leaves only three if he and Terrance bother to show up."

Bailey laughed. "Terrance has a car. Where would you be, right now, if your best friend had a car?"

"Not at PTA, that's for sure."

When Mom appeared to lead us around, Bailey hung back. "Do you really have to talk with all of them? Don't you work with these people every day?"

"I've seen Mrs. Pearson, but I haven't had the chance to talk with her. Besides, talking to other teachers during school hours is not the same. Tonight, I need to be a parent, not just a teacher. Do you know what I mean?"

"Sure," Bailey said, but shrugged when Mom turned away.

Mom took a sweeping look around Mrs. Pearson's room. She admired the classic playbills that I barely thought of anymore, along with scenes from some of Mrs. Pearson's favorite plays, including those she bragged about attending.

"Wow," Mom said, "she loves Shakespeare."

Just as Mrs. Pearson finished with Angel's mom, Bailey's pocket buzzed her latest ringtone. Mom frowned and Bailey headed for the door, leaving Mrs. Pearson to stare at the phone.

The two women shook hands as Mrs. Pearson introduced herself. "You have a smart daughter, Mrs. Delaney."

Mom smiled. "Her father and I are proud."

Mrs. Pearson's next question seemed only natural. "Where is your husband?"

"He's out of the country, traveling for his job."

"How unfortunate."

"Also unfortunate is my sister being detained at the hospital tonight."

Mrs. Pearson filtered the words with an emotionless face. "Yes, I was looking forward to meeting Mrs. Sanders."

"Oh?"

Mom's curiosity was an open invitation for Mrs. Pearson to tell all, but instead she turned to me. "I talked with my son this evening and can gladly say he will return tomorrow."

I remembered the folder tucked under my arm. "I

took some notes in chemistry for Chase. He probably hated to miss it."

She reached for the folder while Mom went to find Bailey. "He does love science." To my surprise, she opened the folder and glanced over the pages. When her fingers paused, she pulled my penciled masterpiece from beneath the stack. "This is…" She raised her eyes. "Wonderful. You drew this?"

"Since Chase looks at my drawings every day, I thought it might make him feel better."

Her smile warmed. "Thank you."

Mrs. Pearson closed the folder and tossed it on her desk. Her face settled into a fake smile and her words were all business again. I escaped into the hall as Bailey made the long walk to stand before her favorite teacher.

Rachelle stared from a doorway across the hall. "Your eyes remind me of a puppy someone dumped on the road next to our house. A cocker spaniel I think, but Dad wouldn't let me keep her. Said the curly hair was too long already."

"Is he here tonight?"

"Yeah. Too bad yours couldn't make it."

I tried to smile. "I'm getting kind of used to being disappointed. Life story, you know. If only my real parents—"

Her nostrils flared. "What? Cared about you? Bothered to stick around?"

"I can't stand to think about how they didn't want me." I glanced at the woman in the room behind Rachelle. "You look so much like your mom. You're so lucky."

She smiled, but her eyes were glossy, bitter almost. "Latasha's not my real mom."

"What?"

"You heard me. Latasha is not my real mother. She didn't give birth to me."

I gasped, for the hall had narrowed around us. "I don't understand."

"My real mom is Latasha's sister. She's a crackhead in D.C."

"Why are you telling me this?"

"So you'll know I understand." She stepped forward as I retreated against a locker. "So you'll know you can't fool me with the *'I'm adopted and can't stand it'* B.S."

"But my parents love me. I love them."

Her laughter was a low, throaty sound. "Then start showing it." Rachelle backed up, smiling again, and this time her eyes danced. "Trust me, life could be worse. You could've been stuck with those people who didn't want you."

* * * * *

The whole family attended Pade's next two football games, except for Dad, and the second was the only game scheduled on a Thursday. That night the glow of the stadium threatened the darkness above as fall gusts blew through my hair. Everything had begun to spin out of control except for my relationship with Pade. Bailey and I paced before the chain-link fence and cheered while Pade threw the ball as if Credence fought for the state finals. In a way, his accomplishments felt like part of me.

We passed Tosh and Lisa with a group of juniors on our way to the concession stand. Bailey and I ignored the taunts and kept walking. I bought a hotdog and drink from the counter, and smiled at my friend, knowing nothing could spoil the night.

As the clock counted down, impatient people spilled onto the field in a massive flow. Cheerleaders clapped and screamed. Band members danced, Angel included with her clarinet in hand. Even though I never led a single drive, I enjoyed the skyscraping high.

While we waited for the team to emerge from the locker room, Bailey talked with Rachelle on the fifty-yard line. I stole glances at the doors that separated me from Pade. When Rachelle spotted Angel, still in uniform, Bailey leaned over. "You know he's not going any faster just 'cause you're watching."

"I know."

She put an arm around my neck. "Are you finally going to admit that you like my brother?"

"I like your brother." The words were out before I could think of consequences.

She hugged me closer. "Just think, one day we could be real sisters."

"That still doesn't mean he likes me."

"He does, Jes, he really does." Although I shook my head, her smile never wavered. "Trust me. Hey, is that Chase? We've got to check it out."

I eyed the doors, this time collecting every inch of nerve. "You go ahead. I think I'll find Pade."

With a deep breath, I started toward the locker room. Slow steps built the confidence needed to tell Pade I was ready for that step beyond 'just friends.' A stream of players passed on their way out, but no one seemed to notice me in the shadows. At the entrance, I hesitated before grabbing the door. How embarrassing would it be to get sick on the floor of the guys' locker room?

Inside, lockers formed a barricade of silence. The staleness of sweaty socks filled the air, but underneath floated the smell of his cologne, though maybe I simply imagined the warmth as I remembered our last kiss. Only one sound penetrated the wall, gentle waves hitting highs and lows like music seeping from a speaker. I rounded the lockers before realizing the sound was laughter. The tinkling grated my nerves, but I froze after hearing a male voice.

They stood disturbingly close despite a thousand empty tiles surrounding the showers. Pade had cleaned up and changed, his hair tousled and still wet. The loosened straps of Tosh's lacy tank hung from her shoulders.

"Why do you have to be so mean to everyone?" he asked.

Her words were honey. "I'm not mean to *everyone*."

"You know what I'm saying."

Tosh leaned back against the wall. "Maybe you should help me understand."

"Please, Tosh, I'm trying to be nice about it."

"I've heard you and your sister are close. I can't help she hangs out with a bunch of scrubby tenth-graders."

His face was only inches from hers. "You can help it. Just leave them alone. They've got nothing on you, Tosh. I don't understand why you feel threatened."

"I don't feel threatened. Your sister is okay, but her friend's got a crush on you." She raised her eyes. "I don't like competition."

"Jes isn't your competition. She's family, like my sister." Pade didn't break contact with her bold eyes. "I thought you were old enough to understand."

Tosh licked her lips, glossy under the fluorescents, and placed her hands against the tiled wall. Pade leaned in slowly and touched his lips to hers. As if watching an amazingly horrible movie, I stood breathless while he pressed her to the wall and the kiss turned to fire. She stretched her arms around his neck and the kiss deepened, leaving me with barely enough strength to turn and walk away.

I never looked back, only dragged my feet to the field. Since a fit worse than tears threatened to expose my suffering to the world, surely Bailey wouldn't be fooled. I approached her near one set of goal posts, but her eyes remained on Chase. Mom and Aunt Charlie reached us through the crowd, about the time Pade walked up. Tosh was nowhere in sight, but I couldn't meet his eyes.

"Pade," said Aunt Charlie, "I thought you were going to eat with the team."

"I don't feel well," he mumbled.

I wondered how to survive the ride and begged my tears to wait, tears I'd sworn to never let him see. We climbed into the van, the boys taking second row with Bailey insisting I squeeze between her and Pade. I fixed my eyes on the lights of cars speeding by and held every inch of skin away from the chance to brush his. The closeness of the backseat and Bailey's constant chatter nearly suffocated me.

Bailey asked her mom to spend the night as planned, but I held a hand over my mouth. After announcing I also felt sick, she turned away, though not fast enough for me to miss the pain in her eyes.

Aunt Charlie shook her head. "I hope you and Pade

haven't caught the same bug."

With every other light in the house off, I stood before the bathroom mirror, filled by awe over how my entire life could spiral out of control this fast. I pictured Pade, holding my worst enemy, kissing her with a force he'd probably never felt when kissing me. After all, I was 'family' to him.

My stomach wrenched and I grasped for the sink. Collapsing on my knees, I puked twice, a film of bile burning the roof of my mouth. Above, I gripped the counter's edge, drawing myself up. My hand slid across the marble, knocking my brush to the floor. I lifted the brush, staring at the bristles that prickled against my skin, but in a flash used the handle to shove every item from the counter. The towels, creased and rolled on the wire shelves, were plush in my hands as I hurled each at the wall in a fury. I spun to the mirror. Two brown pools stared back. I ripped out both contacts and fired them across the room, not caring where my fake vision landed.

The mirror was a blur and I moved closer, watching my real eyes, deep blue like the calmest ocean. The air was silent, grieving around me, until the flood of tears erupted. With a final curse of the world, I dropped to the floor again, this time hugging my knees close. My head rested on numb arms as sobs shook my entire body.

Even dreams stayed away that night, allowing hours to grasp the most painfully great truth of my life: I loved Pade Sanders.

CHAPTER NINE

The Wreck

Soft light glowed on my window the next morning, which had been left half-open. Birds chirped outside the screen. My skin tingled as I gripped the comforter, pulling it over my face. Coffee and bacon filled the air, for the morning was perfectly normal.

Until I opened the holder for my contacts.

I ran into the bathroom and dropped to the floor, feeling across the tiles. My fingers grazed one contact and I released a breath, holding the tiny bubble in my fist. A single brown eye would ensure I didn't starve, as long as its blue counterpart failed to meet either of Mom's.

After clearing my plate in record time, I gave the bathroom floor another shot. My knees were shaking when a honk split the air. I bolted around the room in dismay, hating the low probability of ever finding the other contact. Back in my bedroom, I sifted through the top drawer until my fingers found the small case. The lid creaked open to reveal a set of glasses, unworn for more than three years.

I raced down the stairs as Mom waited next to the van, arms crossed. A quick charge should have propelled me inside, but her firm grip stopped me from climbing. The twins leaned forward and whispered as Bailey's voice crackled behind them. To my surprise, Pade also sat in the backseat.

Mom's voice trembled. "Where are your contacts?"

"I lost one last night," I said.

"That was your last set? Oh dear, and your father isn't here. He usually gets them for you."

"I've got my old glasses. I can see fine and they still fit my face."

She sighed, ushering me into the van. "My mess magnet."

During a ten-minute ride that seemed to restart twice as many times, Pade refused to let Bailey complete a full sentence. Unlike the day before, I had his full attention. Also unlike the day before, I contemplated a restraining order. Pade continued to ramble about the game while each play infuriated me more.

He followed us to The Spot and I entrenched myself in a Bailey-Angel debate over what to wear for the Homecoming dance, ready to block out yet another recount of the night before. Tosh appeared on the sidewalk, but Pade hovered by my side until the first bell rang.

"Look at Delamester," Tosh said. "She's wearing blue contacts now."

Tosh laughed, but Pade quickly changed the subject. In a perfect world, I would have simply smacked her and asked, 'Who the hell wears contacts with glasses?'

When I lifted my backpack, Pade touched my arm. "I like the blue eyes, Jes." He gave a smile with the power to melt my heart only twenty-four hours before.

I mumbled thanks and sped off, reaching first block with a minute to spare. Mrs. Pearson followed her usual path to the front as Chase's stiff body maneuvered into the seat next to mine.

He stared at the desk.

My stomach tightened. "What's wrong? Chase, talk to me."

"You wouldn't understand."

"Your morning can't be as bad as mine."

"You have no idea." The squeal of chalk on the board drowned out a groan as he looked up, his face shifting from disgust to surprise in the space of the last bell. "Your… eyes."

"Usually I wear contacts, but I've lost my last pair."

"But your eyes are blue."

I pressed the metal frames higher, rubbing the sore spot on my nose. "My eyes are blue, but I wear contacts that make them look brown."

"Why would you want people to think you have brown eyes?" he asked.

"My mom and dad and brothers all have brown eyes."

"And yours are blue. Like mine."

"Chase," Mrs. Pearson said. That's when I noticed the room had filled with silence. "Stop talking in my class."

He leaned across the aisle. "Tell me why."

Mrs. Pearson slammed down her planner and circled the desk, heading in our direction, but the clicking stopped when I looked up. Her gaze flowed from me to Chase, then back to me. "Class, open your literature books and read *Twelfth Night*. Silently." I tried to think of something, anything to say if called upon, as she turned and ran from the room. Everyone glanced around, but no one said a word.

I met Chase halfway, voice lowered to a whisper. "I'm adopted."

* * * * *

A trip to the bathroom kept Chase from asking more questions and made me late for second block. I opened the door to Mr. Larson's class and approached my desk under the cover of silence. As I eased my backpack to the floor, Ronald Pitts raised his hand.

"Yes, Ronald?" Mr. Larson asked.

"Jessica's late for the fourth time."

My hands gripped the desk in a motion that could have strangled Ronald as laughter erupted from every direction. With my eyes focused on the board, I prayed Mr. Larson hadn't marked down all four tardies.

He glanced at his roll book. "I guess Ronald's right. We'll deal with this after lab."

When everyone rose to enter the lab, my eyes found Ronald's. He grinned and whispered to a couple of girls, both giggling as I passed.

Anger burned inside me as the lab began. Chase collected supplies for our experiment without a word, including his typical insistence for my help. After preparing all the beakers, Chase asked the question I'd refused to elaborate on in first block. "You're really adopted?"

"I'm really adopted."

He lifted beakers and poured fluids at random, making green and orange bubbles. "Why didn't you tell me before?"

"My past isn't something I usually talk about. Besides, it's not some big secret. You would've found out." I evened my tone, not wanting to sound bitter about Chase knowing the truth. "I can't believe you haven't heard already."

"Trust me, I'd remember hearing you were adopted."

"I'm surprised Bailey hasn't told you."

He pulled a small bag from his pocket and poured a white powder into one beaker, before sloshing the beaker in a circle. "I've tried asking about you, but she only wants to talk about herself."

I smiled. "You'll get used to it."

"How long have you known?"

"About being adopted? I've always known."

His eyebrows shot up and liquid in the beaker rippled, splashing several drops onto the black surface. "Always?"

Green smoke rose from the liquid. Without thinking, I reached for the bubbling ooze, which appeared to be burning a hole into the table.

Chase swatted my hand. "I wouldn't touch that."

"This isn't TV. I didn't find out about being adopted last month. My parents have always seen the truth about my adoption as need-to-know for *everyone*, which is probably why no one bothered to tell you."

"That's cool. I mean, it's cool you've got parents who are honest with you."

I wanted to agree but couldn't reverse the titanic flip of my stomach.

"What about your real parents?" he asked.

"I don't talk about them."

"Are they dead?"

"They gave me up."

"Jes," Mr. Larson said as he approached the table. "I'm sorry," he whispered and pushed a folded yellow slip under my lab manual.

My throat was dry. "It's okay." My first write-up in Credence.

"Mrs. Pearson asked that you stop by her class when second block is over." He glanced at our table and his watch. "If you guys are finished, you can go ahead and leave. That way we can make sure you aren't late for third block."

"I guess Chase will have to clean up this mess," I said.

Mr. Larson glanced at the table again. "What mess?"

I gasped. All five beakers formed a neat line, at the center of the table, same as before the experiment. The liquids were gone, as if Chase never filled the tubes with green and orange bubbles. I pressed my fingers to the black surface, a long sheet of wax without a single hole. Chase had retired to his stool, hunched over the black binder, writing again. He didn't move when I touched his shoulder. Grabbing my backpack, I ran to first block.

* * * * *

Students nearly trampled me as the bell rang, but Mrs. Pearson was already moving a chair next to her desk and waving me over. "Miss Delaney, I have your vocabulary test graded."

My heart skipped a beat as she pulled a clip from a

stack of papers, the one with my name resting on top. The staple was missing, which made spreading the pages in front of me easy.

"Is there something you would like to say?" she asked.

"It looks like I made an A."

"If not for misspelling two words, you would have made a one-hundred." She leaned back in her chair and inspected my face. Slowly, she arranged five more tests in front of me. "I reviewed your old tests and discovered you missed words you previously spelled correctly." Her voice lowered. "I think you planned to miss those words." The silence continued and she sighed. "You had the ability to make a perfect score and purposely answered incorrectly?"

"Yes ma'am."

She winced. "Jessica, I am very disappointed in you." Her use of my first name brought a sick sense of closeness compared to the impersonal Miss Delaney. "What do you have to say for yourself?"

My eyes focused on lines marking the floor. I intended to answer, eventually, but she gripped my most recent test and marked out the grade, drawing a huge '0' with a slash through the middle.

"You're giving me a zero? I've never made a zero in my entire life. I only missed two answers. I earned an 'A'."

"You have not *earned* anything. You wasted your chance to excel. You cheated and cheaters in my class get zeroes. Jessica, you will learn not all people are blessed with such gifts. Drifting through life while carelessly wasting what you have been given is not fair to yourself or those around you."

Bitterness charged my words. "Life is not fair." Dad had used that line many times.

Our eyes locked and I wondered how long our 'battle of wills' could last. Just when I felt sure I'd be the first to look away, Mrs. Pearson removed her glasses and rubbed her eyes. "That may be true. Ironically, you are the only one who can even the odds."

* * * * *

I shouldn't have stopped on the way to lunch, but I really had to go. Tosh was washing her hands as I slipped through the bathroom door. No way would I make it to another building. A quick effort shifted the stall's lock into place.

Tosh's cruel laugh echoed in the empty room. "Lame, lame, always lame."

The silence that followed brought no end to my fears. When the outer door closed, I breathed relief into the surrounding air and dashed from the stall. Because every soap dispenser offered an empty tug, I scrubbed my hands long enough for Lisa to make her entrance.

"Hey, Jes." Lisa smiled, a sight that scared me more than Tosh's laugh. "I noticed your brace is gone. Is your wrist better?"

With a shudder, I gripped the wrist in question.

"I just wanted to apologize to you," she said.

Lisa's words held an edge that kept me on defense. "For what?"

"For the way Tosh treated you." She crossed to the wall of mirrors, tracking me in the reflection. "Tosh and I have always been friends, but sometimes she can be mean." Lisa smiled and stepped in front of me. "How does my eyeliner look? Is it even?"

"Yes." I moved closer to the door.

"I want to help you," she said, in reply to my silent question. "Tosh hates you and I know a way to change that. You need to make Tosh like you."

I stared in disbelief. "Tosh? Like me?"

"You can make Tosh like you, and I'll help. I'll make you cool."

"Cool?"

"Yes, Jes, even you could be cool." Lisa smiled like Bailey after a super sneaky plan. "Skip fourth block with me."

"Hello, my mom's a teacher."

"Don't be such a worrywart. There's a *fine* sub in your fourth block today." Lisa blinked and her voice returned from the faraway kingdom. "Anyway, he's not checking roll. When your third block is done, we can sneak out."

"To where?" I asked.

"My boyfriend Jarrod will pick us up by the band room and we'll take off. Just to Save Ali or something. We'll be back by the end of school, I promise. Your mom will never know."

'*No, no, no*,' screamed the voice inside my head.

"Everyone in school will think you're cool," she said, "even Pade."

As I pictured Tosh with Pade, something inside of me exploded. To hell with Pade. To hell with teachers giving big fat zeroes. To hell with rules.

"Okay." Saying the word exposed an odd sense of freedom, one that caused my skin to buzz and my head to float. Reality shifted inside as the sum of my problems changed from looming final exam to ten points extra credit. I felt in control of my life again.

"Great." Lisa headed for the door. "Meet me at the band room after third."

I washed my hands again, scrubbing until the tips of my nails were soft, translucent. Staring into the blue eyes, I shivered. The room was silent and cold. No one existed but me and the girl in the glass, and she was a stranger. I gasped, for my head spun and my lungs weren't working. Running for the door, I shoved it open and stumbled into the hall. Coughing, I fell forward, but someone caught my arm.

"Are you hurt?"

I squinted, but the man's face was out of focus.

With one hand still holding my arm, he bent down to the floor. He rose and placed something in my hand.

The metal was cool against my skin, and instantly I knew he'd found my glasses. With the glasses in place again, I stared at the man's green uniform, dragging the floor around his boots.

"That girl should not be trusted," he said.

"What girl?" I glanced around, but Lisa was nowhere in sight.

The man turned to his cart. "Stubborn like the other."

Only one sound filled the hall, the constant chatter of metal on tile. He didn't look back, and I watched his feet rise and fall, as if marching to a song no one else heard. His voice seemed familiar, and I thought of the day in Mrs. Pearson's room when the door opened itself.

Yes, the man she'd chewed out. He reached the end of the hall before I allowed myself to think of Lisa, of the afternoon looming, the excitement. I shook my head, pushing away the picture of him, and my strength surged. I'd face my parents if we got caught skipping school, no problem. If Lisa could live with the consequences, so could I.

* * * * *

I bragged about Lisa's offer during lunch. Angel and Rachelle seemed impressed, but Bailey frowned and didn't say a word. After lunch, she pulled me aside and insisted skipping school was a stupid idea, which only convinced me of her jealousy. Of course, Lisa had asked me. I watched my friend stomp off to fourth block before heading to the band room, some part of me satisfied she wasn't going.

Lisa was waiting with Jarrod at the edge of the road, facing away from the band room. Jarrod shifted the sputtering engine into drive as soon as I closed the door. The ragged seatbelt was a beacon to my right, but I hesitated to reach for the buckle since Lisa and Jarrod had passed.

"Hey, pull over at the next gas station and let me drive," Lisa said.

"You know I can't be seen with someone else driving. Dad would take the keys."

"But you let me drive before. I've got my learner's permit."

Jarrod glanced in the mirror. "Maybe when we leave the store."

He lit a cigarette and I cracked my window, leaning back against the seat. I sniffed my shirt as smoke filled the car. Ashes spiraled and landed on my face and arms, and the holey knees of my jeans. I closed my eyes and took small breaths, while adrenaline pumped a steady rhythm in my ears.

"Hey," Lisa said. "Didn't I tell you smoking is bad?"

My eyes flew open at Lisa's words.

"Who are you, my mother?" He laughed as Lisa stared out of the window.

"Just drive us to the store," she said.

I pulled out my phone and checked the time. We had exactly an hour and twenty minutes to get back before Mom started looking for me. In less than ten, Jarrod jerked us into the store's parking lot, forcing me to regret not putting on that seatbelt.

We walked the store for at least twenty minutes before Lisa led us to the jewelry department. She picked up several necklaces as her eyes zoomed in on the camera above. In one easy motion, she curved her fingers behind a display. Paper wrappers fell between two corners that meet with a gap. Lisa stuffed the treasures into her pocket.

I spun to Jarrod, who also stashed something in his pocket. "What are you guys doing?"

Jarrod looked around as Lisa whispered. "Haven't you seen anyone shoplift before?"

"Damn it you two, shut up," he hissed. "I'm not going to jail for no kindergarten crap."

Lisa looked at me. "You can be cool, right?" She turned back to Jarrod. "She can be cool. Go ahead Jes, it's your turn."

"My turn?" I thought of the folded twenty in my wallet, the one Dad always insisted I carry in case of an emergency.

"Show us how cool you can be." Her eyes glittered. "Trust me—you'll love the high."

I fingered a pair of earrings, sterling silver hoops I'd

probably never wear even if I got my ears pierced. Given the chance Lisa might be right, I slipped the plastic off the rack and ripped both labels. She finished a quick course in shoplifting, telling me how to keep away from the cameras, but not before Jarrod threw his hands in the air and left us standing by the jewelry counter.

"See you at the car," he mumbled.

She eased around a corner and glanced down the next isle. "Let's split up so we can make sure no one follows us."

I shivered. "Follows us?"

"They do that sometimes. You go to the grocery side and I'll go to the shoes. Then we'll meet back on the outside in fifteen minutes."

Even though the churning in my stomach was a different kind of sick from the night before, I headed for the bathroom. Just as I locked the stall, Lisa's voice blared.

"Yeah, she fell for it." A familiar set of crocs stopped at the sink. "Tosh, your plan is working perfect. Pade won't think so highly of her now. Why are you asking such a crazy question? Anyone can see he's hot for you. Who wouldn't be?" Lisa laughed. "I just wish I could see Jessica's face when she finds out we left her at Save All." She paused. "I don't care if her mom is a teacher. We parked away from the cameras. She'll be busted and there's no way she can prove she left school with me. Besides, she'll be too embarrassed to tell anyone. Hey, Jarrod's waiting for me out front. See you in a few."

The door slammed, sending a cold wave through my chest. Even with a vision of running for the checkouts, I knew I'd never catch her. Lisa was gone.

I reached the front of the store in time to see Lisa climb into Jarrod's car through sale-papered windows. I wanted to scream. I wanted to cry. I wanted back in fourth block.

The shock of being left alone faded alongside hope, only to be replaced by the realization I'd dropped my phone in Jarrod's car. For the next hour, dreary aisles passed with no plan for escape and no thought of earrings. All I could imagine was what my parents would say, when three hours before I didn't care.

In every face, I saw Tosh's smile, savoring my fall into her trap. When I thought about being totally alone, shivers spread all the way to my feet.

Was someone following me?

Around a corner, I spun as a figure darted into the next aisle. The guy was fast, but not fast enough to miss the back of his blond head, and the familiar glasses. Not to mention the new running shoes he'd showed off at lunch.

I raced to follow, but the entire aisle of drinks was empty. The main aisle extended the length of the store, with a group of women talking at the center, but no Chase. School had been out for at least an hour, maybe more. With my decision to call Mom, I shook away the weird feeling and headed for the front of the store. One of the last payphones in Credence hung just outside the entrance, but I never made it that far. Two guards stopped me at the door.

*****

I sat in one of two chairs in the small security office, head rested on my arms. Cold metal against my skin felt as uninviting as the single door that would soon open. My purse had been confiscated and one guard had Mom's number. Both stood outside.

After what seemed like hours, Mom came through the door. Moist red puffs hung under both eyes, a sight that made me regret getting into Jarrod's car all over again.

"Oh, Jes." She touched my hair, my ears, and my face. "Are you okay?"

"Yeah."

She released me and looked at the guards. "Why is she in here?"

"We caught your daughter shoplifting."

"Shoplifting?" Mom looked confused.

"The evidence is in her purse."

"You've seen this evidence?"

"We have her on camera. Her purse was taken, but we haven't opened it. I thought it best to allow you." He handed Mom my purse and she turned to the table. She ripped open the zipper and dumped the contents across the dull metal, sifting through makeup and folded notes from Bailey. The only part of my life not on display was a certain pair of earrings.

"What did she steal?"

The head guard looked to the other. "You were sure it would be here."

"She put the earrings in her purse. I followed her around the store and she never took them out."

His boss inspected the makeup and papers. "There are no earrings." He glanced at Mom. "I'm sorry for the mistake, Mrs. Delaney."

Mom extended an arm and replaced the contents of my purse with a wide sweep of the table. "Can we leave now?"

"Yes ma'am." He frowned at the younger guard. "I'll make sure he's more diligent in the future."

Mom grabbed my arm, hauling me out of the office. We crossed the front of the store and exited through the main doors, into an afternoon of sunshine. Freedom, I thought, except for the fact Mom still had my arm.

When we climbed into the van, I thought of the twins. Mom slammed her door and leaned back against the seat, closing her eyes.

People crossed in front of the van, some running and some caring about nothing more than the voices from their phones. A woman pushed a car-shaped buggy with two laughing toddlers and I envied the innocence of their world.

"Do you know how I felt when I got the call?"

I lowered my head. "You were probably mad."

"Mad?"

"And disappointed."

"Jessica Ray, you have no idea."

I sucked in my breath. She never used my middle name. "I came here with Lisa Johnson after third block—in her boyfriend Jarrod's car. They left me to get busted for skipping school."

"You came here with Lisa and her boyfriend?"

"If you ask, I'm sure she'll tell you the truth. She *is* one of your students."

"Honey…" My stomach sank as she hesitated. "Lisa and her boyfriend got in a wreck after they left the store."

My mind whirled like a tornado as I sputtered. "A car wreck?" Thoughts flew to a scene of someone tail ending us on the way home from school, leaving a web of scratches on Mom's bumper. "Are they okay?"

"Lisa and Jarrod are dead."

*****

My dreams that night made cartoons of the worst horror movies. Noises of people fighting awakened fears as the lights above dimmed and threatened to disappear. I gripped the arms around me, strong and familiar, as massive feet rose and fell on the rocks below us. Before I could scream, those arms shoved my body into a tiny space and closed a metal door. I tried to unfold my legs, but my head banged against the ceiling.

Hidden in darkness and alone, I begged for my father's return. My knuckles cracked and bled from a storm against the door. Smoke filled the air, causing my lungs to burn and tears to well in my eyes when I thought no more tears were possible. Minutes passed, maybe hours in my void of desperation. Finally, I collapsed and gave up on the prayer of hearing his voice again.

Just when I'd given up, a hand gripped my arm and pulled me into an open room. Voices argued around me. A burst of light flooded my eyes. I focused on a shiny object held by a man who glared, pointing the gun at me.

A shot split my ears and I landed on the floor. As my legs and arms coiled into a fetal position, a cry wedged in my throat. A woman screamed, but I couldn't make out her words. When the echo of the single bullet faded, strong arms again held me safe.

"Baby, it's okay. You had a bad dream, that's all," the voice said. "Just one horrible nightmare."

With a glance around the room, I realized Mom was

holding me back in New York, before the first move. "I saw him die."

"No, honey. No one died." Soothing words pushed me to a sound sleep, as she rocked me in the dark. "You're okay—I've got you."

When I opened my eyes again, sunshine drifted through my window in Credence.

CHAPTER TEN

Pain in Doses

I spent the morning after the wreck in bed, comforter thrown over my entire body. Numbness brought neither hot nor cold as Mom's words echoed in my head. '*Lisa and Jarrod are dead.*' Like a broken record, shivers skipped across my skin as the day replayed.

At some point, Mom knocked on the door. After no response from me, she tiptoed through my prison. The bed sagged as she crawled in. "Are you going to talk to me?"

Tears burned in my eyes. "I'm sorry." It took every bit of strength to force out those first two words.

"That's it?" Mom laid next to me, with the comforter forming a wall between us. "I called your father and told him what happened."

"Is he coming home?" Both dread and hope tugged my heart at the same time.

"Your dad can't leave simply because you got in

trouble. I know you didn't want him to go, but he has responsibilities."

"Are you sure he isn't sick again?"

"Don't you think we'd tell you the truth?"

"You didn't before."

"Oh, honey." Mom reached under the comforter and circled her arm through mine. "I can honestly tell you he's not sick again."

"Then why do you sound like the world's about to end? I haven't heard you this upset since his last radiation treatment."

"I'm worried about him traveling, but someday you'll see what his work means to so many people. Tokyo wasn't just a conference for his job. There's a study to determine the effectiveness of certain cancer treatments." She pressed her forehead to mine. "Tell me about yesterday."

"Lisa asked me to skip last block and go to Save All with her and Jarrod. No one ever asks me to hang out like that. I thought it might be exciting."

"And people would think you're cool?"

"I didn't think about what could happen."

"You probably didn't," she said. "And your cell phone?"

"I dropped it in Jarrod's car but I didn't notice until after they left me."

"You could've called from the store as soon as they left."

"I didn't want to see your face or make the call to Dad. For an hour, I paced the store, before walking to the front. That's where the guards caught me."

"You were really shoplifting?"

"Lisa dared me to put a pair of earrings in my purse.

She and Jarrod took some other stuff."

"What happened to the earrings?"

I closed my eyes, trying to picture the silver hoops, but all I saw was Chase. "When you looked in my purse, they were gone. I must have dropped them somehow."

"And then they left you."

"I heard Lisa on the phone with Tosh. They set me up to get busted for skipping school."

"Bailey explained the trouble you've been having with Tosh—all the mean things she's been doing to you. Why didn't you tell us?"

"Dad's always saying people should learn to deal with their own problems."

"He gives speeches to help adults deal with their problems. You're fifteen. You should be able to tell us when someone is hurting you." Mom stilled. "I'm glad you weren't in that car."

"Me too, Mom. Me too."

She hugged me close. "I'm sorry about what happened to Lisa and Jarrod. My heart aches for their mothers. My pain at the thought of you being gone is only a fraction of what theirs will be forever."

"What caused the wreck?"

"Jarrod's mom saw them leave Save All with Lisa driving. They ran a red light while trying to get away. An eighteen-wheeler crashed into their side." Mom's voice wrenched with emotion. "The police said they died instantly." She gripped me tighter. "Honey, they didn't suffer."

Another round of tears fell as we cried together. I pictured Lisa and Jarrod speeding down the street with me in the back, laughing and feeling the excitement. Instead, I was living the nightmare while they waited to get put in the ground.

"The police found your phone," she said.

"I don't care if I ever see that phone again."

* * * * *

Later that afternoon, I awoke to an empty room. Sunlight filtered through lacy curtains and made patterns of flowers across the far wall. With the sun resting at such a low angle, darkness would soon follow. I wiped away the grogginess of spending an entire day in bed. When a knock sounded, I hoped it wasn't Mom again, or Bailey ready for her shot at making me feel better. Nothing could make the headache go away.

The door opened, but neither Mom nor Bailey crossed the threshold. I expected Pade to drop into the beanbag, but he chose the edge of my bed. "Are you okay?"

Would he ever stop asking me that? "Yeah."

"I don't get it, Jes. What were you thinking leaving school like that? I mean, your mom's a teacher. Did you think she wouldn't find out?"

I shrugged.

Pade's eyes steeled. "That may work with Aunt Rainey, but I know you better."

I drew a breath, anxious for words to make him go away. "I thought it would be cool to leave with Lisa since everyone said I was no fun."

"No fun?" His eyes narrowed.

"You know, I was always lame." I fixed my eyes on the ceiling. Did I only imagine spots in the paint?

"Who is everyone?" he asked.

The spots began to merge. I blinked away the tears.

"Who is everyone?"

Still I laid in silence, comforter pulled to my chin.

"Are you talking 'Tosh' everyone?"

"She would never leave me alone."

"You seemed to deal with Tosh okay, even that night she tripped you."

My voice felt strange, as if someone else formed the words. "I was never 'okay' with anything she did to me." I laughed and faced Pade again, hating my weakness, hating he saw the tears.

He hesitated. "Do you know Tosh set you up?"

"I overheard Lisa on the phone with her at Save All. They planned to leave me without a way back to school, so I'd get busted for skipping."

"Tosh was bragging about it after last block. I heard her and went to Aunt Rainey."

My throat clenched. "You told my mom?"

"I was worried about you." Pade reached down and grabbed a pillow I'd kicked from the bed. "She sent Bailey to get the twins and I followed her to see Dr. Greene."

"Was Chase with her?"

A frown creased his forehead. "I haven't seen Chase since the night of the game. What does he have to do with this?"

"I just figured he was with Bailey."

"Bailey went to get the boys and Aunt Rainey called your phone. When you didn't answer, I tried myself, over and over. I couldn't think what else to do."

"I dropped my phone in Jarrod's car and didn't realize until after they were gone." I swallowed the guilt. "Mom must have been freaking out."

"She was and then Dr. Greene got the call about

Lisa and Jarrod. The last time she tried your phone, a state trooper answered."

I closed my eyes as a tear slipped down each cheek. Pade wiped the drops with his thumb, a gesture that only distorted my feelings further. I shrank away from his hand.

"What's wrong?" Pade's voice was barely more than a whisper.

"Nothing."

He grabbed my hands. "Damn it Jes, look at me."

As I remembered Tosh say the same words, my eyes opened. "I saw you in the locker room."

The lump in his throat bobbed as he swallowed.

"With Tosh," I said, drawing back against the headboard.

"Tosh?" he choked.

"I came to find you after the game. When I walked into the locker room, I saw you with Tosh."

He stared down at his hands, which were fumbling with the edge of the pillow again. "You were in the locker room?"

Some combination of his worry and obvious guilt set my anger on fire. "You were kissing her."

"I… I…" Pade said. "I'm sorry, Jes, I… never meant for you to see that."

The clock ticked to eternity and the light on my wall faded. When Pade spoke again, he was at the bottom of an avalanche. "Is that why you left with Lisa? Is everything my fault?"

"I'm the one who got in the car."

"I knew you were upset after the game, but I couldn't figure out why. If only you'd told me."

I shook my head as the anger fizzled. "It's okay."

He laughed without humor. "Just like that, you're gone again."

"What do you mean?"

"Every time I get close, you pull back and hide. Maybe it's pain, maybe it's love, but it doesn't matter. For a moment, you were mad. It was like you flipped a switch and became the same girl you were that first day. You weren't hiding then. That night at the movies you hardly noticed me."

Hardly noticed him? I wanted to tell Pade how nervous he made me on our date, how I felt electrified when he touched my hand. I wanted to relive our kiss, despite Tosh, but only two painful words emerged. "I'm sorry."

He stood and headed for the door. "If you're pissed, next time tell me."

"Pade?"

For ten steps, I thought he would ignore my plea. Pade opened the door and hesitated, but he didn't turn.

"Can we be friends?" I asked. "Real friends?"

"I thought you had Chase now."

Pade taking notice of Chase wiped away some of the shame. "He's not you."

"We'll be just like before." He stepped outside and pulled the door shut behind him. His feet whispered along the hall and beyond my tears, beyond my pleas for the door to reopen. Each creaking stair left me trapped with the tingle from his hands touching mine, and no meaning of 'before.'

* * * * *

The beep played again through the darkness. Even in

sleep I heard the two-toned nightmare. Three times. Four.

After climbing from the bed, I managed weightless steps down the stairs. On the bar rested my phone, as I feared. The battery was dying slowly and taking my soul along. Pushing the button was the easy part, unlike stilling the sound in my head. The phone found a new home in a drawer below the counter.

No.

I pulled the drawer back out and lifted the phone, squeezing without success. I slid open the keypad and flexed the phone until plastic cracked.

No more sound.

I choked a silent breath that wouldn't pass my throat, pounding my forehead with a balled hand, desperate for the pain. Any pain. The numbness made me dead inside. Dead, as if nothingness could be a feeling. Lisa was gone. Jarrod was gone. I could have been gone, like the sound.

I stumbled into the kitchen, eyes straining under the moonlight. Beams reflected on the oven's door, marking a path across the floor. Next to the oven stood a wooden block, securing Mom's special knives. I slid a hand along the black handles and snatched at random. Maybe not so secure.

Mom used the knife when she made bread. The length had always intimidated me, forced me to avoid the jagged edge. Fear became pointless as an unfeeling thumb glided across the peaks and valleys of the blade. At the tip, I pressed and a red drop appeared just above my nail.

Yes, it would be too easy.

I brought the knife across my wrist gently,

wondering how it would feel with more pressure. A fine white line appeared over my blue veins, but the memory of Mom's face stopped me. Her pain had been real—the pain I had caused and was about to cause again.

I sank to the floor, dropping the knife, while a tear slipped down my cheek. "I'm sorry," I said, as if making a solemn promise to Lisa, to myself. I'd fight the demons inside.

At least the pain had returned.

CHAPTER ELEVEN

Powers

The next day, October fourteenth, was one I planned to spend alone.

When the phone rang, Dad's usual call while getting ready for bed, I pulled the comforter over my head. Mom crossed the room, without knocking, and laid the phone near my ear.

"Jes," he said and I reluctantly lifted the phone. He asked how I'd slept and gave his usual dose of advice. When I asked how things were going in Tokyo, he said "fine," though fine felt like more than just a checkup visit to the dentist. He figured at least a month still before he'd be home.

About an hour later, Mom knocked on my door, even though the door stood wide open. I squeezed my eyes shut and she kept banging, until the bottom edge of the door bounced off the doorstop.

"Can't I sleep a little longer?" I asked.

"No reason to be antisocial, especially when you've

got company."

"Tell Bailey to come on up."

"It's not Bailey or Pade."

Chase sat at the kitchen table, across from the boys, listening as they described another video game. When I slid into the chair next to him, he made a half-wave in my direction. His eyes never left the boys.

Mom placed a steaming plate of biscuits and gravy in front of me. "If you could choose anything for us to do today, what would it be?"

To leave me alone. "Anything as in mall or movies?"

"Anything as in your heart's desire. We can even invite Chase. Come on, this will be your day. What adventure can you imagine?"

Having had more adventure than my head could wrap around, I had to find a way back to the safety of my room. "Fishing."

Mom's hand jerked, tipping her glass and spreading milk across the table. "Fishing, as in pole and hook?"

"And water," I said. "You and Aunt Charlie always talk about how your dad took you fishing."

Chase's eyes grew to the size of his plate.

My face was rigid, though every molecule inside of me felt ready to explode. It was the way her eyes moved about the room that bothered me. Her hands flexed in a tense calculation of how to stop me.

Mom leaned her head to the side, smiling weakly. "Fishing it is."

* * * * *

The dirt road narrowed across a bridge that was no more

than a couple of wooden planks and a rusted side-rail. Mom slowed the van to a crawl across the bridge, assuring us that she could drive to the property with her eyes closed if need be. Chase looked straight ahead through the windshield, away from the creek that flowed on each side of the wooden planks, as well as in-between.

"Don't worry," Bailey yelled from the backseat, between me and Pade. "That water's only about a foot deep. Pade and I used to follow those rocks all the way to a waterfall near the old mill."

The dirt was smooth up ahead, untouched to a clearing where a blue house stood. Branches littered the roof with pinecones. Pine needles piled up until the metal was no longer visible. Windows covered by boards made me mourn the house. The blue was not shiny but faded in the sun and peeling. A satellite dish, probably as heavy as the van and still on its metal pedestal, engulfed a corner of the front yard, with grass circling the legs. To the right of the house stood a barn, its roof half caved-in.

Mom parked the van, twisting to face the boys. "This was my home when I was your age."

"Wow," Danny said.

Collin pointed to a trail as he jumped from the sliding door. "Where does that go?"

"To the lake," Mom said.

Outside the van, I tugged at my collar in the intense heat. Were Octobers in Alabama always this hot? Chase was laughable at my side with his long sleeves and long pants. Like me, he'd covered almost every inch of skin. I wondered about his decision to wear a wide brimmed hat, until I remembered how he hated the sun. At least the extra fabric I wore kept Mom from suggesting another pound of oozy sunscreen.

Sun dazzled across the dark waves, sparkling light in all directions. Each breath was a taste of fish cased in the air's warmth. The edge of my own hat shaded my head, leaving dark sunglasses to take care of the rest—another prescription pair I'd managed to hang onto, thankfully.

Mom led our way down the hillside with the twins trailing, each carrying a white tub of worms. I muffled a laugh as Chase attempted to match Pade's stride while they carried the tackle boxes and buckets of minnows. Since Mom had the cooler, Bailey and I carried the poles.

"Showtime," Mom said, when we reached the rocks that lined the bank. She pulled a minnow from one of the buckets and slid a small hook below the back fin. "You don't want to kill it. The minnow swims and the fish grab it like a burger and fries."

Pade lifted his pole and a tub of worms and walked down the bank.

"Don't play in the worms," Mom screeched as the boys laughed. Half of the black soil, speckled with white, surrounded their feet. Even I enjoyed fishing my fingers through the dirt in an effort to capture the wiggle motion of the worms. She cast each of their lines, making two small splashes beyond the bank.

"Where did you learn to fish?" Chase asked, as Mom took his pole and tossed the line.

"I grew up here, on this farm and seven-acre lake. Daddy made fishing a treat for almost every weekend, sometimes even after school." She laughed. "He wanted a son, but instead had only girls. I think that's why he raised us like boys. After my mom died, it was just the three of us. My older sister Charlene—"

"My mother," Bailey said.

Mom nodded. "Charlie would've been here, but one of her coworkers caught the flu and she had to go in."

"I'm sorry I didn't get to see her," Chase said.

"Oh, there will be plenty of time." Mom looked down at me, irony thick in her voice. "If you practice, by our next fishing trip you'll probably be an expert. For now, you can start with standing closer to the water."

He eyed the water. "How close?"

Mom gave Chase a gentle nudge, but his feet were rooted in the bank. "Is there a problem?" she asked, studying his face. "Is it the water?" When Chase swallowed, eyes still on the waves, she circled an arm around his shoulders. "There's nothing wrong with being afraid of water."

"Why would you be afraid of water?" I asked.

Mom tightened her grip on Chase. "Everyone has fears. You were once afraid of water."

I rolled my eyes. "I've told you before—I can't remember being afraid of water."

"I can remember a time when you wouldn't go near the tub without me being there."

"I almost drowned once," Chase whispered, shrinking away.

"Don't worry," Mom said. "I'm an excellent swimmer. I'll be close if anything happens." She took Chase's pole and reeled in the line. "Here."

Chase took the pole and stepped closer to the water. He tossed the line, ending with two splashes, one for the hook and another for the minnow. Try after try, he flung each minnow off before his hook hit the water. On his fourth try, Mom insisted he practice before rebaiting. After help from Mom and encouragement from Bailey, his hook landed with a soft splash, minnow still attached. He smiled while Mom praised his good throw.

Bailey leaned against a nearby rock, tipping up her ball cap. "Chase, why don't you come over and sit by me?"

I glanced to where Pade sat. Concentration tightened his face as he gazed across the water, watching for any movement of his line, in the zone like when he played football.

Easing down the bank, I threw out my line and stole the other half of his rock. Water beat against the shore, reaching for our feet as a fish splashed halfway across the lake.

"Bailey really likes Chase, doesn't she?"

"Yeah," I said.

He sighed. "Is there anything she doesn't tell you? Bailey and I used to talk about everything before you moved to Credence."

I shifted on the fiery stone, wishing for a seat down by Mom.

"I know it's not your fault," Pade said. "I just miss my sister, that's all. You don't know how it feels to be that close to someone and have them taken away. I… what did I say wrong?"

My eyes stayed on the infinite rise and fall of waves. "I'm sorry you feel like I'm taking your sister away."

Pade found his voice, fast. "I didn't mean to put you down. I just thought we could talk. Like friends," he added, with an emphasis on 'friends.' Pade looked back at the water. "Remember, you wanted this."

I touched his arm. "Thanks."

He stared at me strangely. "For what?"

"For being you." I smiled.

As tension drained from Pade's arm, I fought the memory of his lips on mine. My head clouded with reasons to snatch my hand back and run, but beyond the mockery of knowing he kissed Tosh remained the guilty weakness of my heart. Instead of listening to reason, I leaned closer.

Pade's eyes widened in anticipation, before cutting to our audience down the bank.

With a sigh, I pulled back, but found some comfort in the thought Dad would be proud of my milestone. I'd found the right words to make things okay between us.

* * * * *

The lunch Mom packed consisted of ham and cheese subs, chips, and cokes. Chase held his can as if the sweet liquid might burn his flesh.

"Don't you like sodas?" Mom asked.

Chase cringed. "My mom says they're bad for you."

"Your mom is right, but I let the kids drink them on special occasions. There's water in the cooler if you'd like. Water is better for you, especially in the heat."

"No, this is fine. Thank you."

After lunch, we decided on a hike through the woods. Luckily, Mom turned down the boys' pleas to tag along. She laid out towels in the shade as we headed for a trail that would take us on a tour of the family land. "You four be careful and watch for snakes."

"Snakes?" Chase choked out, as if her hands were closing around his neck.

Pade snorted. "Yeah, man, snakes. We'll be in the

woods and snakes hang out near water."

"I hope we don't see any water moccasins." Bailey looked at Chase. "Those snakes will follow you out of the water and won't stop at the bank."

Chase glanced up and down the edge of the lake, probably wondering how close we might have been to a snake earlier.

"Come on." Pade walked ahead, leading us through briars that claimed a majority of the trail. As Bailey followed close behind, Chase planted himself by my side, fighting the stickers and branches at my pace. It wasn't long before Pade and Bailey were out of sight.

Chase scanned the ground around us. "Are there really snakes?"

"This is my first time here, remember? My dad has always said snakes are 'more afraid of you than you are of them.' We need to make lots of noise."

"Where is your dad? Doesn't he like to fish?"

Unsure if Dad had ever touched a fishing pole, I shrugged. "He had to go to Tokyo for his job."

"Tokyo is a long way from Credence. Do you ever travel with him?"

"Not since we've been living in Credence. We moved a lot before…"

"Before what?"

I shrugged. "Before we came here."

When we reached the edge of the woods, a wooden fence separated us from a green field that stretched as far as I could see. I swung a leg over the fence. "I bet you can't run faster." Before his hands touched the wood, I grinned and took off.

Each pounding foot drove anxiety like the wings of an eagle skyward. After what seemed like a marathon of steps, I dropped to my knees and collapsed on a blanket of grass. I laid back, arms crossed under my head. The sun was a purple ring, floating in the darkness of my sunglasses.

Chase joined me on the ground. "I thought... you... would never... stop."

I coughed to release the fire in my chest. "But... it felt... amazing."

He stretched across the grass, leaning back to stare at the sky. "For you maybe."

"This is how I deal with issues."

"Like Friday?" he asked.

"Friday was a nightmare."

"What did my mom say to you after second block?"

"She gave me an 'F' for missing words on the vocab tests. A zero, actually."

"Ouch."

"It pissed me off. She is dramatic about trying your best, just like you said."

"That's Mom for you." Chase laughed. "We were arguing that morning, which explains her bad mood."

"What were you arguing about?"

A gentle breeze teased the grass and fell against my face while Chase stared at the white puffs of cotton trailing the sky above our heads. "Today's my birthday."

"What?"

"She wanted to do something special since I was turning sixteen, but I refused. I told her I was coming to your house on Sunday, and she flipped out."

"Why my house and how did you know where I live?"

"The you part was only to make her mad. I can't be alone with her, not when we're half a family. She gives me three times the love, and that's not really like it sounds. The where part Bailey took care of."

Of course, Bailey. "I can't believe you're sixteen today. My birthday isn't until January second."

He smiled, narrowing his eyes ever so slightly. "Are you sure?"

Something in his voice felt strange, almost like a challenge, but I pushed the thought away. "I want to ask you something. Please don't get mad."

"You can't possibly hurt my feelings."

I took off the sunglasses and locked his blue eyes with mine. "Were you at Save All on Friday?" A boiling cloud, gray underneath, choked the sun while I waited for humor, denial, or even a good excuse, but his silence spoke truth. "Why?"

Chase's eyes lifted back to the sky. "I followed to make sure you were okay."

The feeling from our first day returned, only it had a name. "You were worried about me? Why?"

"You won't believe unless I lie."

"I'll believe whatever you say is the truth."

"Maybe," he said, "but I can't always protect you."

The air chilled my skin in spite of the warmth pouring down on us. *Protect me from what?* Thoughts of similar words from Dad surfaced. "Tell me how you got to Save All. Tell me how you got Bailey's phone back in her bag. There's something crazy going on and you've got to tell me. Please, Chase. Tell me."

Sterling blue eyes merged with mine. "You really want to know?"

"I have to know."

Chase nodded and I expected another entry in his long list of deflections. Instead, he stood and reached for my hand, pulling me up to stand before him. "Don't let this freak you out."

Freak me out? I glanced around. We were alone in the field.

He closed his eyes and took a deep breath. Before I could blink again, the green around my feet disappeared, and I stood in front of Chase by the edge of the woods, separated from the field by the same wooden fence we had climbed.

"Now you know how I got to Save All." His voice was bitter, but he made no move to escape.

My hands shook as I glanced around. We were still alone. Somehow, Chase had zapped us back to the fence. "What just happened?"

"I'm not from around here. I've got the power to move anything with my mind."

I met his stare with wide eyes. "Did you take the earrings out of my purse?"

Chase was waiting for my scream, or perhaps for me to run back down the path as if snakes had appeared for our show. My heart beat fast, but not at a freakish speed, and I felt exhilarated. For the first time, my dreams seemed possible. Maybe I wasn't crazy. "Does your home address end with a zip code?"

His gaze never left mine. "We call it something different on my planet."

I slapped a hand over my mouth, stifling a laugh. Chase might think my action hysterical, but I wanted to show him this girl could handle the wild truth. Then I remembered the notebook. "Why are you living in Credence?"

"Everyone has to live somewhere." He wore a trench across the width of the path before speaking again. "Could you trust me when I say we're not here to turn the people of Earth into blood sucking zombies?"

"You mean vampires."

He stopped. "Vampires?"

"You said 'blood sucking zombies,' but vampires would more likely feed on blood. Besides, some vampires are actually cute."

"Okay, could you trust I'm not here to turn everyone into vampires?"

"*Could* you turn us into vampires?"

"Jes, this is reality. Can you trust me?"

"Have you ever hurt anyone? What else can you do? Can you see the future?"

"No. Large objects like cars and people I have to touch while thinking." His tired laugh hung between us as he hesitated. "I wish like crazy I could see the future. I would have known about Lisa and Jarrod, maybe even saved them." Regret shining through sad eyes told the ultimate truth about Chase.

"My dad always says you can't 'live your life in the past'."

"I feel guilty knowing I had the ability to help. But you're okay with everything I said?" His blond hair seemed absurdly far from bald green monster. He might not *be* human, but he sure *looked* human.

"After the last forty-eight hours, I think I could be okay with anything." Not to mention weeks of dreams and the longing to share with someone who might believe. I wanted to know the possibility of me being from another planet. But a dark chill stopped me. A voice inside urged me, pleaded with me, to remain quiet.

Chase's shoulders relaxed. "I've got something for you." In one outstretched hand appeared a box about the size of the case for my sunglasses. The box opened to reveal a pair of glasses with lenses that sparkled like a pink crystal and rims rounded with blue-gray metal. "I wanted you to see it can be cool to wear glasses."

I unfolded the glasses and slid them over my nose, then jumped when a mirror appeared in Chase's hand. Even I had to admire the girl in the glass. "I can't believe you did this for me." Chase brightened at my delight. "And you got the prescription perfect. How did you… never mind, I can probably guess." We both laughed. "I hate you got me a gift and I didn't get you one."

"What do you mean?" he asked.

"It's *your* birthday."

"That's okay. Don't mention it. I mean for real, don't mention it. To anyone."

"Our secret."

Regardless of his abilities, I felt thankful to have Chase as a friend.

CHAPTER TWELVE

Making Up

On Tuesday, I fled into the sunshine, desperate for any chance to get rid of the pain surrounding my heart. All eyes had followed me throughout the service, and I had no doubt my name touched every set of moving lips. The suffocation level dropped as I reached the back of the funeral home, at least until I noticed a woman staring across the expanse of headstones. I recognized Lisa's mom, eyes glossed with tears.

"You must be Jessica," she said.

"Yes ma'am." I froze from the chill of her stare. "Mrs. Johnson, I'm really sorry."

What did I expect from her? Not the arm taking mine, or the slow walk down a hill to the lake. Not the silent invitation to share a wooden bench. Before us, swans glided atop still water, clueless of the events around them. Children ran in the distance, playing at a nearby school. Golden rays stretched from the sky. The day would be perfect if…

Mrs. Johnson pulled a pack of cigarettes from her purse. Her hollow laugh split my heart as she lifted the brown end to her lips and lit the other. After a deep drag, she spoke again. "Lisa had been on me to quit smoking for years." She turned, looking at me as if realizing someone occupied the bench beside her. "What are you sorry for?"

My throat felt like sandpaper as I strained to speak. "For what happened."

She took more drags, pausing after each to knock the ashes loose. "That wasn't your fault."

"I wish…"

"You wish what? That you could have stopped her? That you could have been there?" She tossed what was left of her cigarette and lit another. "Jessica, let me tell you something your parents may not have."

Mrs. Johnson stared at me, taking in every angle of my face except for my eyes. "We all make choices in life: some good, some bad. Lisa made a very bad one." She puffed and leaned over to rest her forehead on a trembling hand. "I loved that girl with every breath in my body. She was my world, my entire life."

Tears slipped down my cheek, but I couldn't wipe the burning trails.

"My daughter made the decision to leave school."

"To take me to Save All."

She dropped the cigarette to the ground, crushing the half-smoked paper stick with her foot. "Guilt can swallow a person whole—I know because I carry enough for two lifetimes. I tried to do right by my daughter, but there's only so much a parent can do. Lisa was a good girl," she said, as a crack formed in her voice. "But even good girls are not spared from tragedy."

"I shouldn't have gone."

"She would have left with Jarrod, whether or not you were in the car. I've heard the story and I know what she tried to do to you." She covered my hand with hers and lifted her eyes, finally meeting mine. "I will miss my daughter every day God chooses to leave me on this Earth, but I will also thank God every day that she left you at that store."

Mrs. Johnson stood and wiped her tears. "Please remember the decisions you make now will shape the rest of your life. It's unfair for a teenager to have such huge responsibility. Sometimes even your parents can't keep you safe—that's entirely up to you. Please Jessica, remember Lisa's lesson."

Not prepared for a hug, I shied away from the pleading behind her words, convinced Lisa's mom would hate me forever. After she released me, we walked back up the hill in silence. The weight of her arm around my neck eased some of the pain.

At the entrance, she tossed her not so empty cigarette pack in a trashcan. "That was my last one."

I believed her.

* * * * *

School surrounded me with the stress of an E.R. for the rest of the week. Most people were nice, though a few of Lisa's friends avoided me as if the pain I carried topped the list of symptoms for strep throat. Bailey stayed quiet in the van and at lunch, making the week of silence a new record. Pade made commitments to clubs I'd never heard of, ready to share the glow of football fame with those less fortunate. Tosh bragged about an offer to change schools, forcing me to dwell on how pure evil might deal with the loss of a close friend. Despite the fact she set me up, I felt a pang in my chest each time those eyes stared beyond her audience and glazed with a dampness no one mocked.

When Friday arrived, I beat the first bell to English, desperate to see Chase and have a normal day. Mrs. Pearson called for book reports and gave us another Shakespeare assignment to read, this time *Macbeth*. She picked students to read the parts aloud, but I was spared.

The woman had shown me five days of niceness, the kind that made me want to puke. I thought about the secret Chase had confided and considered what my knowledge might mean to her. At the end of class, Mrs. Pearson passed out vocabulary tests. I stared at the questions, though I knew every word and definition by heart.

"Jessica?" she whispered, as I placed the paper on her desk.

"Yes ma'am?"

"See me after class."

My stomach churned with a painful urge to run to second block. I only needed to push my feet into a forward motion. Instead, I stood in the shadows next to a set of lockers until the last person finished. When I reached the door, Chase stood by her desk.

"Run along, Chase," Mrs. Pearson said. "Close the door behind you."

Their eyes met in silent combat, which raised my fear level. Chase left the room as I entered, stopping to close the door—only he didn't use his hands. I pretended not to notice while I took my usual seat.

"You must be wondering why I kept you." She

pulled my vocabulary test from the stack. "A perfect score." As she spoke, happiness painted a new layer of beauty on the cold face.

True to her words, a one-hundred headlined the test she handed down. Three digits also filled the inch above my book report, graded during the reading session. She wasn't even listening.

"Another perfect score. I was impressed with your sentence structure and explanation of the book." She dropped into Chase's desk and I found myself drawn to solve the mystery of her features. Mrs. Pearson became a sight for envy when she smiled, with styled hair and clothes cut from a magazine, even down to the heels she never failed to wear. Flaming amber eyes held not a speck of blue as I'd once imagined, but the candy color warmed me like hot chocolate on a windy day in February.

"I never underestimated you. I knew your report would be excellent, which is why I read it first." Her voice lowered. "Jessica, is everything okay with you?"

Shock grew inside of me as I realized my teacher, the one who Bailey had dubbed the Wicked Witch of English, was worried. Not to mention she wasn't human. With her nearness, I questioned my ability to think.

"I know what occurred last Friday, only hours after we talked. My intention was to teach you a lesson that day, but I forget sometimes what it felt like to be a teenager." Jeez, she was talking like my mom. "Maybe I should not have made the comment of praise over your first test. Is that why you purposely missed questions? Obscurity must be the Holy Grail for all teenagers; even my son has begun to reason without the help of sense."

Only for those with a secret past. I nodded, feeling ashamed and once again under her scrutiny. She reached out and touched my hand. Without thinking, I jerked away and her face twisted. For an instant, bone-deep guilt erased every hateful thought.

She stood and crossed to her desk, retrieving a book from under a pile of papers. Her tone was almost normal when she spoke. "I want you to read this for your next report." She placed a copy of *Pride and Prejudice* in my hands, the binding overgrown with ivy across a wooden trail. "This is my favorite book, and one I first read as a teenager. It is a long read at sixteen, but I believe this read will be worth your effort."

Sixteen? I opened the cover and scanned the first pages. Some had words filling the margins, printed by a much neater hand than mine. "What language are these notes in?"

"An old style of English. You will be unable to read the words in the near future, but maybe one day…" She smiled. "I picked up this copy during a visit to England. The edition is early and the pages somewhat brittle. Please be careful."

Okay, she'd peaked my interest. "This will be for November's report?"

"If I am thoroughly impressed, you may substitute the grade for your last vocabulary test."

I flipped through the remaining pages at random. Hundreds of yellow pages, but I felt determined to meet any challenge from her.

"Miss Delaney?" She retreated to her desk. "Do you not have a second block class?"

I left the room, allowing a reluctant crowd to filter in.

* * * * *

As the last bell rang, the realization that Jes Delaney actually skipped school dwarfed the surrounding buzz of Friday. While other students were filling their backpacks and running to buses, I was pacing aisles at Save All. One week was far short of the eternity that seemed to have gone by. Five sleepless nights had haunted me with issues that wouldn't go away. Most importantly, I wanted Bailey back.

After rehearsing an apology on my walk from fourth block, I spotted her at the locker, snatching books and jamming them into her bag. She slammed the door when I walked up.

"Hey," I said.

"Hey." Her eyes stayed on the locker.

"Can we talk?"

"Let's go outside." Bailey led our way to the same bench we sat on the day she got her phone back from Chase.

Our instant of truth came, begging for my speech, but all the practiced words hit a roadblock on the way to my mouth. "I'm sorry."

Bailey sat in silence, staring at the ground and kicking her feet back and forth.

"You were right about Lisa." I hoped to ease her anger, but more silence from Bailey crashed my hope. "I don't know what else to say. Please tell me how to make things right between us."

"I know why you left with her and I can't say one-hundred percent for sure I wouldn't have gone under the circumstances. That's not what's been bothering me."

"What then?"

"Pade told me about him and Tosh. How you saw them the night of the game."

Reliving that moment was a layer of skin off my knee and a bandage soaked in alcohol, but I'd welcome the burning a thousand times for Bailey. "I can't believe he told you."

"I can't believe you *didn't* tell me. I know you too well, Jessica Delaney." Her voice filled with emotion. "I know seeing them had to be tearing you apart."

"But he's your brother. That made the whole situation kind of hard to talk about."

"Pade's a real idiot and I made sure he knows, but you still should've told me. Is that why you didn't want me to spend the night?"

"I couldn't tell you, not after what you said at the game."

"Seeing that horror show had to be humiliating. I realize now you must really love Pade."

"Not anymore."

Bailey's smile was sad. "You can't fool your best friend, remember?"

'Thank you' was my silent prayer. I wrapped my arms around Bailey as frustration mixed with happiness and made tears for us both.

When she pulled back, her normal smile had returned. "I'm glad that's over."

"Yeah," I said, as the weight lightened. "All this time I thought you were mad at me for skipping school without you."

"I tried to be a good friend and talk you out of it. You've got to decide from there."

"Thanks for being a good friend—the best."

"No problem, I'm just sorry my own brother acted like such a guy." Bailey stood and I realized we had to get going. "Trust me, I've been making him sorry."

"It's okay, Bailey. I'll be okay."

"The worst part is he really likes you," she insisted, as I shook my head. "If only you could see how upset he's been over this whole mess. I don't think he planned to kiss Tosh. What guy would want her?"

Any guy. My voice leveled as I spoke, boosted by remaining dignity. "Please don't go there."

*****

On Saturday, I slept until the afternoon. Remembering the gift from Chase, I rose and retrieved the small box from my top dresser drawer. I pulled the beanbag to the window and sank down near the floor. I removed the contacts Mom had replaced before school on Monday. Unlike the phone she'd found in pieces yet refused to mention.

The first line of my new book showed crystal clear through the new lenses. 'It is a truth universally acknowledged that…' Ugh. I decided to read some of the notes, without success. Since I couldn't understand a single word, the notes were zero help. The second page looked equally intimidating, but no way would I give up. My eyes moved ahead line by line, slowly at first. The story was set when cars were just a fantasy, with the British kind of English phrases that reminded me of a foreign movie missing subtitles. Mrs. Pearson was right—it was a long read.

Before I realized, the sun dropped behind the trees, forcing me to switch on the lamp by my bed.

* * * * *

Reading ran late into the night, followed by a deep sleep, and the most bizarre dream yet.

My feet pounded along a dark hall while my eyes darted in search of an exit. An echo followed, getting closer, making my fear level spike. Click. Click. Click. Like heels. Someone was chasing me in heels?

A narrow flash caught my eye and I turned, desperate to reach the light. My fingers traced the outline of a door as light spilled between the door and wall. Thinking fast, I stood on my toes and felt for a handle. Nothing.

With alarm growing like the approaching sound, my hands scattered in search of anything to grasp. Relief flooded through me when my fingers grazed the square handle. Either the door was shorter than usual or I was standing at my normal height. I touched the handle and pushed the door. To my surprise, I stumbled into English class.

Students leaned over their desks in silence, seemingly hard at work on an exam. I scanned my desk and Chase's—both were empty. As my eyes circled the room in search of Chase, another series of clicks sounded behind me and I spun around.

Mrs. Pearson stared at me, hands on her hips. "Miss Delaney, find your desk."

My eyes shifted back to Chase's seat. "Where is he?"

"That is not your concern."

"Is Chase okay?"

Her hands fell at her side. "This planet is killing him."

I awoke, fear squeezing me like the hand of someone desperate to be saved. After rising from bed and tiptoeing to the dresser mirror, I wiped away tears that glistened in the moonlight.

Worry for Chase made further sleep impossible, as did a yearning to replay the dream. Her words repeated in my head, but I heard only sorrow and bitterness. The resignation in her eyes burned to my core, like a flare at the dreaded limits of my memory.

*****

It took me until the next afternoon to get up enough courage to ask Mom about my dreams. "Are you sure I'm from New York?" I asked as she started dinner.

Mom glanced up from the cutting board and laughed. "Where else would you be from? You've seen the adoption papers. You were there." She held a strainer of cabbage leaves under the faucet. "We'll talk when your father gets home. How about helping me with dinner?"

"Cabbage and sausage?" I asked.

"With homemade macaroni and cheese."

Hmmm. The only thing she made perfect, other than pizza. "Did you ever meet my real parents?"

"Wait here." Mom turned off the water. She lowered the strainer and left the room, her feet shuffling down the hall into her bedroom. When she returned, a faded shoebox hung under one arm. She removed the dusty blue lid to expose a stack of newspaper clippings, pictures, and official looking documents. She pulled out the stack and flipped through the pages, stopping on a stapled set she handed to me. "These are copies of your adoption papers. The Naples never came to the hearings. Your father's attorney believed they left town instead."

"They really didn't want me?"

"Oh, honey, why think such thoughts? Those people had real problems. We've told you the story many times. You were placed in foster care after you ran away."

"But why can't I remember?"

"The doctors seemed to think you faced some sort of trauma and blocked out everything. Sometimes the mind finds unusual ways to protect itself."

Sounded like something Aunt Charlie would say. "I just *forgot* everything? When will I remember?"

"When you're ready."

"Mom, that's not helpful."

"The doctors told us remembering would be a long process for you." She held my face with both of her hands. "Don't worry. When we adopted you, your father and I were fully prepared to love everything about you. We'll always be here to help." She released me and extended a hand to the fridge. "How about a soda?"

As she tugged on the black handle, I brushed my fingers over an article at the top of the yellowed newspapers. Familiar words framed a picture of me in the center, the same picture I'd pulled up online. My hands paused on a new headline. 'Four-Year-Old Runaway Leaves Home After Father Threatens Mother.'

"I thought we had some."

I scanned faster. There was a huge fight. He threatened his wife with a gun and fired. Jessica ran outside and down the dark sidewalk, alone… I jumped as a strong arm ripped the paper from my grasp.

"Don't read that," Mom cried.

"But it's about me."

She collected every piece of paper and jammed the stack into the box. "Sometimes the past should stay in the past."

"It's *my* past."

"And one day we'll have that talk. Just not today." She rummaged in a drawer beneath the counter, retrieving a band, as if a quarter inch of rubber could keep me out. "Why are you asking these questions now? Have you remembered something new?"

I swallowed hard. Would Mom freak if I told the truth? "I've been having really weird dreams."

Mom leaned against the counter and crossed her arms. "Everyone has weird dreams. But go on."

"I dreamed about my real parents arguing. About a gun. About running away. Now I know why."

Her shoulders sagged. "Jessica…" she said but looked away.

We stood in silence, a heavy fog around us. Voices flowed from the TV in the living room, with a round of clapping, followed by the twins' laughter.

Mom turned back and sighed. "Do you still want to help me with dinner?"

"Sure." At least she didn't think I was crazy. Good thing I left out the part about the spaceship.

* * * * *

On the following Saturday, Mom took the boys and me to the library. She said it was good for us to get away from the 'lonely without Dad' house.

As Danny and Collin disappeared between the

shelves, I headed for the young adult books. I thumbed through some of the newest paperbacks, finding two with a promise of welcomed escape. Seated near a wall of windows reaching from the floor to a two-story ceiling, I opened book number one.

After thirty minutes, I flipped to the last chapter. Yep, it ended just as I'd thought. Deciding to reshelf my disappointment, I grabbed the remaining title and my purse from the table. I passed two computers on my way to the index file, both ready for my search, but the wooden drawers called to me. The drawers had a familiar smell—a hint of the carved chest Mom had left in Atlanta.

I'd finished Mrs. Pearson's assignment in one week, a new record in the thick old books category. Pulling out the 'A' drawer, I flipped to *Persuasion.* That title, like all the others by Jane Austen, was missing from the shelf. Frustrated, I made another pass and lifted a book out of place. *A Tale of Two Cities* almost found its home in the 'D' aisle, but my newfound confidence made the length seem appealing. And the fact that book was also on Mrs. Pearson's list.

I considered reading the first page by the windows, but feared I'd be unable to stop. Instead, I decided to find the boys and speed up our progress to the doors.

Danny and Collin sat in the reading pit, an octagon bull's-eye in the center of the children's section. They smiled as I stole a spot between them.

"What do you think about this one?" Collin asked.

Danny grabbed my arm. "No, look at mine first."

I took *A to Z Amphibians* from Danny's hand and my breath caught as I remembered a man reading another book with gold trim. My eyes closed as the twins picked through a stack of books on the floor. Their argument faded and another male voice filled my head.

'Kay Ray,' the man said, before laughing and surrounding me with his arms. From my seat on his lap, I couldn't see his face.

Collin was hitting my shoulder.

My eyes opened, to the book in my hands, which were shaking. For the first time in eleven years, I'd remembered a *real* piece of my past. The experience felt nothing like the dreams haunting my nights for weeks.

For seconds that seemed to span hours, my real father had held me tight and read without anger or sadness. Only the long-forgotten nickname made sense. *Kay Ray.* The knowledge of him washed over me with the force of a tsunami. After the wave came a feeling of being loved unconditionally, the feeling I'd waited my whole life for. I knew, regardless of what happened between my real parents, my father had loved me.

I opened the cover and read the words, trying to block the voice in my head. Collin was demanding I look at his book. When I glanced up, both held a book in each hand, but I hesitated to release the one in mine. The room spun as their words brought thoughts of yet another, a voice from the past still beyond reach. My own heart betrayed me with a closeness that grew, covering my skin like a warm blanket, until I noticed Chase. He leaned against the doorway, watching us like the last thirty seconds of a season finale.

Chase approached the pit, eyes locked with mine. He reached the outer edge before Collin and Danny noticed him and scrambled to their feet. "Hey guys." The boys talked fast, but Chase nodded as if he'd heard a lifetime of twin talk. "Jes was helping you find a book?"

"Yeah," Collin yelled, despite the glare of a passing librarian.

Danny laughed. "Jes is the greatest sister."

Yeah right, I thought. Chase would never buy their act.

Chase smiled and tousled Danny's hair. "I bet she is."

Collin stared up at Chase. "Don't you wish you had a sister?"

For only a moment, I forget Chase once had a sister and smiled. The fading of his smile reminded me of the cold truth. My arms ached to reach around Chase, but in full view of the library and my younger brothers, hugging him seemed like a horribly embarrassing idea.

"Chase," Mrs. Pearson said from behind.

"Mom," Chase said. The room seemed to drop twenty degrees.

She smiled at me. "Hello Jessica."

I smiled back, but without enthusiasm.

She spoke at least two octaves above her strict classroom voice. "Who are these handsome young men?"

"Young men?" Danny laughed.

"Handsome? That's funny," Collin said, and Mrs. Pearson gave them a sideways look.

Mom approached the pit with a new cookbook in her hand. "What's so funny?"

"Did you hear what that lady called us?"

"Collin Delaney, don't ever let me hear you call someone 'that lady' again. This is Chase's mother, Mrs. Pearson." She turned to my teacher, face aghast. "I'm sorry."

"All is well, Mrs. Delaney. I can assure you of my tough exterior."

Mom put an arm around each boy. "Please, call me Lorraine. I know we've only managed brief meetings, but I feel that should change. Chase has become like part of our family."

Mrs. Pearson read the top title in my hand and lifted her eyes to study mine. The darkness in her face scared me, but I didn't look away. Her gaze returned to Mom. "You have nice boys, Mrs. Delaney."

Mom cringed at the mention of her name, or maybe it was the cold stress placed upon each syllable.

"I suppose they look like their father."

Mom's voice was soft. "Yes, they do."

I stared at the woman intruding on our family, and fear began to build. She must be powerful, like Chase. How could I ever tell Mom and make her believe?

Then I realized Mom's words bothered me more than Mrs. Pearson's. She said the boys looked like Dad. Adults were always saying stuff that drove me crazy and made me wonder if I looked like my real parents.

I glanced at the twins but couldn't see how they looked like Dad. Maybe a little. *Okay, more than a little.* Mom and Dad both had brown eyes and hair, not the same shade, but a small spin of the color wheel didn't lower my blood pressure, not when those were the very traits I'd been denied. I hated to admit how jealous I felt of Danny and Collin's connection to our parents. Their tie was blood.

"Come, Chase," Mrs. Pearson said. "We have work to do." As Chase walked away, she paused at my side. "You might enjoy that book, though probably after a struggle to begin. I assume you have finished the other?"

With ten seconds and no answer from me, she nodded and followed Chase.

A shiver crawled the length of my body as Mrs. Pearson's heels clicked away. I was torn between curiosity and hatred for the woman, the latter mainly in response to her treatment of Mom.

As if forgetting the last few minutes, Mom gathered the books Danny and Collin had pulled from what seemed like every shelf. Then came the argument over which five they'd each be allowed to check out. When Mom aimed them for the front desk, I fell in behind.

"Got everything?" She smiled, but I heard the faint tremor in her voice.

Did I imagine my teacher's eyes, narrow and unforgiving, as if determined to upset Mom?

CHAPTER THIRTEEN

Future Told

That afternoon, storms left three hours without power and no chance to escape the house. I grabbed a flashlight and read the first page of my new book several times before closing the cover, unable to focus on anything except for Mrs. Pearson. Downstairs, the boys begged me to play Monopoly. Their constant pestering should have angered me, but I couldn't hide a smile as their faces lit up after my 'yes.'

When evening came, the rain ended, and I tried everything short of a tantrum to get out of dinner at Aunt Charlie's. I wanted to stay home and be gloomy. Alone.

Following the click of our front door was my long-held sigh of relief. I considered Mom's words on her way out. "We'll be right next door if you need us." *Maybe they'll stay next door*, I thought as guilt filled me.

"Don't leave this house," she'd said, as if people were lining up to claim me. Where did she think I'd go?

After peeking through the blinds, I entered Mom and Dad's room in search of the box. My ears strained for any movement as I dug through the closet. Each item was ironed, placed in order of color, and every plastic container was evenly marked. I collapsed to my knees next to the bed, pulling up the flowered dust ruffle. Plush carpet spread before me, a garden of fibers smoothed in the same direction.

Like a kid who'd just received tofu instead of pudding, I returned to my bedroom and again tried the book. Fifteen pages of worry-free reading wasn't an extreme request, but a week of ACTs seemed easier.

I climbed into bed and pulled the comforter tight around my body. Darkness filled the air around me, except for light reaching through the seams. Cursing myself for leaving the light on, I considered rising, but a noise from downstairs froze every thought. Even thuds sounded across the floor below.

My first thought was of panic. A fear of someone breaking in had always haunted me, though crime in Credence was almost nonexistent. How could I face off against an intruder? I knew Dad kept a shotgun and exactly which corner it called home. He'd plainly said 'hands off' unless he was with me. Another sound below. Was that the fridge opening?

Alone. I was alone for the first time ever, at least for the first time since I'd lived with Mom and Dad. I hugged the comforter tighter while trying to convince myself Mom must have come back.

The steps crossed the floor again, then silence. I eased from the bed, tossing the comforter aside and nearly crawling down the stairs. The last of my fears dissolved as I stuck my head inside the kitchen, where every light was on.

"Hey," I called, expecting Mom's brown hair to rise above the fridge door, but it wasn't her eyes that met mine. "What are *you* doing?"

Chase grinned, reaching for a salad left from lunch. "Checking out your fridge. Is that not cool?" He looked up and the grin faded. "I thought we were friends."

"We are, but you can't zap yourself into my house. It's not cool to scare me like that."

"Come on, I wasn't trying to scare you."

"You could have called. Don't you have phones on Mars or wherever it is you're from?" My eyes swept the windows. "What if my family found you in here?" I turned for the stairs, throwing my hands in the air. "Leave the way you came."

He jumped in front of me, holding up both hands. "We don't have phones exactly and I'm not from Mars. And you're alone, so I can't get you in trouble. Your mom's next door with Danny and Collin."

"You've been watching me?" I remembered the day at Save All and cringed.

"I've been watching you since before the lights came back on. That's how I knew you were alone." He swallowed. "Your dad isn't here either."

"My dad's still in Tokyo." I fought a laugh with the image of Dad's face after a surprise entrance. "Don't you have stalkers where you're from?"

Chase smiled, though much more reserved. "I believe I understand." He followed me into the living room but didn't settle on the couch next to me. "Where are all the pictures? Humans always have pictures of themselves."

I considered the empty walls surrounding our living

room. Well, not exactly empty. There were paintings of a beach, bronze framed mirrors, and shelves lined with candles. "Mom has pictures, somewhere I'm sure. She buys our school pictures every spring and fall."

"But she doesn't hang them for people to see? Don't you think that's strange?"

"Maybe she's not into the whole picture thing." I tried to recall Mom hanging pictures in any of the places we stayed long enough to get unpacked. Had she even bothered to pack the pictures when we left? "How many pictures are hanging at your house?"

"None," he said.

"Then what's the big deal?"

"We're not human."

I rolled my eyes, wanting to argue, but unable to shake the feeling Chase had made an important observation. "Let's talk about something else."

Mischief formed in Chase's eyes. "Why don't we talk *somewhere* else?"

"I can't leave—I'm grounded. Mom would kill me."

"Not if she doesn't know."

"Oh, she'll know if I leave. That woman has some kind of radar on me. I thought it was bad before I skipped school."

"Obviously, she cares about you. Trust me, Jes, I'm an expert when it comes to moms. I have the strictest mom ever, but I still get away with sneaking out. I came prepared." He smiled as a glowing square appeared in his hand. "This will let us know when they return."

Chase planted the device at our front door and took my hand. "I have something to show you."

I closed my eyes and heard the rush of water. The breeze on my face felt like a cooler of ice had fallen from the sky and smothered my frustration. One breath. Two breaths. I opened my eyes to moonlight across the creek. "How did you know?"

Chase stood beside me, staring across the water. "From the drawing you made, I could tell this place is special for you."

With a smile, I spun, taking in glitter someone had spilled on the rocks, a whirlpool calling to my feet, and the scent of pine trees brimming like syrup on pancakes. "I thought you were scared of water."

"You notice I'm not standing close to the edge." He laughed weakly. "You *would* love a place with water. When Mom brought home the drawing, I spent half the night trying to find this place."

"I thought you were sick." Without thinking, I flung my arms around Chase's neck.

"I wasn't sick," Chase said, returning the pressure against his arms.

For the next half-hour, we explored the creek under the safety of our nightlight. Chase talked of his planet, mixing English with words and fancy names I tried to understand, mostly in vain, but I did get the fact there was no moon.

"Night is usually less than six hours of darkness. Golvern is half the size of Earth and covered with almost ninety percent water, but it turns slower. Most land is located opposite the glacial edge at what you might consider Earth's North Pole, though our planet is not polarized in the same way. The top always reaches for our suns—yeah we've got two—and people live in the warmth of summer all year."

"I don't know if I could live through a year of Alabama summers."

"Golvern is never as hot as Alabama or as cold as New York. Less land, less people, less darkness. What else?"

"You said six hours of darkness, but how long is a day?"

"Same as yours," he said.

"I find it hard to believe that two random planets have the same number of hours in a day."

"Not just the same day, but the same number of days in a year."

"You're all about science. Explain how that can possibly make sense."

"Easy. Your planet copied ours, which is why the timing doesn't work exactly. You still have to add a day every four years. Now, ask me a hard one."

"I remember you don't like the sun."

"The radiation from Golvern's suns combined is weaker than Earth's."

"Then our sun is harmful to you?" I asked.

"It's deadly to me."

"But if the sun is tragic bad, why come here?"

"Yeah, it's tough. No one from our planet can survive on Earth more than a few years without going home for treatment."

Would he ignore my question? "How many years?"

"I don't know, maybe three."

"You're sure?"

He nodded and looked back at the water, eyes glossy in the moonlight.

No way could I let Chase know how this new information unsettled me. With memories of living on Earth for at least eleven years, any chance of being from Chase's planet shifted to impossible. I remembered Mrs.

Pearson's words about the planet 'killing him', words that existed only in a dream. Then I thought of the day Chase missed school. He'd never said anything about Earth hurting him before, but now I understood his fear from the day we stood in the sun. "What happens when you go home?"

"There's a treatment for the radiation," he said. "It's called regeneration."

"That sounds freaky."

"Regeneration pulls the radiation from our skin."

"Why not get treated on Earth?"

Chase shrugged. "I guess we could, but it's safer on Golvern. Recovery is ten days of darkness. Besides, Mom has to go back. Lots of people depend on her."

"Don't tell me she teaches there too."

His lips formed a small, secret smile. "Not exactly."

After silence from Chase, I turned the conversation to intense convincing, and he took us to the top of a rock formation marking the highest point of the creek. Below us, water crashed on smooth rocks and split in all directions. Clouds began to move across the moon, causing a disappearing act for the sparkles along the water's surface.

"I told you it would be awesome up here," I said.

"It doesn't feel awesome. What if we fall? I've never been able to swim."

"Why are you afraid with all of your powers?"

"I don't have all the power you think. And when I'm scared, my powers don't always work."

"Don't worry, I'm not afraid of the water." I took his hand in mine, tight to stop the shaking.

He fell silent again and I shivered. Jumping from the rocks flashed in my head and I wondered just how deep the water below might be. Did nerve form the thought, or was it unhappiness with my life rushing back in a flood? The power from knowing I could jump with no one to stop me felt confusing. At the same time, I was powerless to change the storm of heartache surrounding me.

Chase placed his other hand over mine, sandwiching my fingers between his. "Tell me what's wrong. I'll promise to keep your secrets."

"I have days when I love my life and days when I hate it."

"What could be so bad about your life?" he asked.

"Sometimes I feel like I don't belong here."

"Here on this planet or here in this town… or here with me?"

Did I imagine he asked the last part carefully, as if afraid I might say yes? "I guess I've never felt right anywhere for long."

"When was the last time you were happy?"

I thought hard for a truthful answer. "Probably the night I went to the fair."

"Fair?" he asked.

"You know, rides and games and stuff."

"I know, but you surprised me. How could the fair make you happy?"

Pade, I wanted to say. "Haven't you ever been?"

Chase laughed, this time amused. "We don't have fairs back home."

Okay, let him laugh. "Maybe you should."

"Maybe." Chase stood, confidence showing in his smile for the first time that night. "Yes, I think maybe we should." He held out a hand and helped me to my feet. "How about now?"

I gave a muffled laugh. "I hate to tell you this, but the fair only comes to Credence once a year."

"Then we'll just have to find it."

* * * * *

The excitement of the fair felt exactly as I remembered, even in another state. After zapping us to South Carolina, Chase convinced me to ride *every* ride, a feat no one else had accomplished. Music and food flowed through the air as we walked the midway. We were hundreds of miles from home. No one was watching. No one was judging. I wanted to run as fast as I could and scream.

"You feel it too?" he asked.

The excitement crashed as heat burned in my cheeks. "What?"

"You don't have to be embarrassed. I can feel the rush of this place. I know why you wanted to come here."

"I've never been away from everyone I know like this. My parents would freak if they could see me."

"Mom wouldn't be happy either, not with all the danger you…" he began but hit the brakes fast.

"Danger?" I asked.

"Don't worry about me," he said, in full reverse.

"But you said…"

"Sorry, it's just that Mom is… well, she worries a lot."

I summoned all of my courage. "Why are you and your mom in Credence?"

"We're here to find someone."

A certain list of names flashed in my head. "Who?"

He looked away. "I've already said more than I should."

"Why Credence?"

"Because we failed in New York. Next you'll ask why New York and I'll say that's where the trail ended."

I decided to take a chance. "You couldn't find her."

"No," Chase said. "That is..." His eyes lit up. "How did you know?"

"I guessed."

"Oh." The excitement disappeared from his voice. "I thought maybe you had a reason."

My mind was running about a dozen scenarios, but none quite fit. "What about your friend in New York?"

"Lauren?"

"Is she from your planet?" I asked.

"No, I just thought she was..."

"Thought she was who?"

Chase sighed. "Do you really have no idea who I am?"

"Your name isn't Chase?"

"Actually, it's Chadsworth."

"I can see why you want to be called Chase."

"Mom hates calling me Chase."

We continued our walk down the midway in silence, passing row after row of games. I wanted to ask Chase more questions than days I'd been late for the semester, but none seemed right.

"We'll be leaving soon. How do..." Chase grabbed my arm, forcing me to stop. "How do you feel about going home with me?"

"Credence *is* my home."

"But not always. I bet you even lived in New York."

"Yeah, but only for a little while."

"I knew it." He released my arm and spun, throwing his arms into the air. "She was lost in New York."

"Chase, my real parents abandoned me."

He stopped celebrating and grabbed my shoulders, pulling my face close to his. "How can you be sure? Do you remember them?"

"I don't remember anything before my adoption." The words felt like a lie, but the dreams seemed more like scenes from a movie I watched long ago.

"Come back with me and I'll help you remember."

Wrenching free, I pushed him away. "I can't just leave—my parents would freak." So would the twins and Bailey, maybe even Pade.

"They're not your real parents."

"But they're my family." After saying the words, I felt the gravity of a connection strong enough to keep my feet on Earth. My head was swimming, ready to explode. Fortunately, we had reached an end to the lights and noises.

Chase was the first to notice a small shack set apart from the last row of games. "What is that?"

"Our fortuneteller," said a passing man with a spider's web of tattoos down both arms, who reeked of the night's heat.

"Come on," Chase said. "Let's check it out."

"I don't believe in any of that stuff. Seeing the future is crazy. Even you said it wasn't possible."

"It's not possible for me, but there are people with that power on Golvern."

I rolled my eyes. "You've heard someone tell the future and what they said came true?"

"I hope so." His voice was sharp. "We call them Olsandyols."

"In English, please."

"Olsandyol is made of three words."

"The first part is old?" I waited for his nod. "Old as in more than one hundred?"

"Old as in wise. Sand as in the particles that flow through an hourglass. Dial as in the controller of time. All three words can be found in English but were connected with our language through visits to Earth made more than a thousand years ago."

"And you believe what this old sand person said?"

"Did you believe people could move things with their minds before we met?"

"I never even thought about meeting someone from another planet, forget being zapped around. What's your point?"

"My point is you've got to hear your future before you'll believe. What's the harm in us checking out Earth's version of an Olsandyol?"

The shack sagged to the right, as if drawn by a magnet to the little pond. Dark wood, weathered with splinters, held up the rusted metal roof. Plastic had been forced into the gap where the wood didn't quite reach the roof, a continuous flow of balled-up grocery bags. I expected a red sign flashing danger, or the words 'fall hazard' in huge letters. Instead, a board above the door reading 'Super Swami Mike' loomed as if outlined in crayon.

"Bill," a woman said as she pushed through the door, "I've heard enough rubbish for one night. Imagine it—I'll be rich beyond my wildest dreams. That's almost as bad as me getting married to some pervert. Did I really pay twenty dollars to hear that unoriginal nonsense?"

The man behind her nodded and pressed his lips into a lazy smile. As we passed, his eyes met mine and worked the slow length of my body. Chills shot down my spine as I realized the man was checking me out. An urge to cough up a polish sausage and half a funnel cake followed the chills when I considered his age had to be approaching Dad's.

We entered the dark room, hazy with purple smoke that had no odor. I expected wrinkled hands brooding over a crystal ball. Instead, a man held up one finger, insisting we wait. He finished checking his phone before waving us to the round table. Candles illuminated our path, each glowing at a glass tip. I lowered into one of two cracked wooden chairs, afraid of finding myself on the floor.

He waved away smoke that drifted between us. "I am Super Swami Mike, here to tell your future."

As Mike peered into my eyes, I failed entirely at holding back a smile. "You are searching for someone," he boomed.

Too bad he picked me for that line and not Chase. "I don't believe anyone can see the future." I turned to Chase. "I'm sorry, but this isn't working for me."

Before Chase could reply, Mike laughed. Chase met my eyes, both as wide as his, and we stared at the man across from us. He removed a hat modeled from *Alice and Wonderland,* along with a beard fifty years in the making. As he leaned back, face smooth and wrinkle free, I realized Super Swami Mike wasn't much older than me. He smiled wide and the metal lining his teeth forced me to laugh. Our fortuneteller had braces.

"Most don't believe. I'm not here to impress people, just entertain them."

Chase frowned. "Then you can't really see the future."

Mike ran a bony hand through his hair, short on top but below his shoulders in the back. He searched Chase's eyes and his smile disappeared. "You *are* a believer."

Chase squirmed and I bit my lip, wanting to say 'I told you so' on many levels.

Mike lowered his head. "A few years ago, I dreamed about getting in a car wreck with some friends from school. For an entire week, the scene played out in my head each night. From the backseat, I saw the tree flying at us, felt that screeching stop. The song 'Lightning Crashes' drummed in my ears. On the following Friday, I watched us hit the tree for real, and when it was all over, that song played. Half the engine was in the front seat, but the radio still worked."

I swallowed hard while Chase stared, eyes glued on Mike.

"Most people never make a connection between what they feel will happen and what actually does happen. I can either tell people what they want to hear or the truth, but most won't believe the truth." He pointed beyond us. "They'll walk right out that door and dismiss what I've said because they already know what'll happen and refuse to face it."

"Because it's bad," I said.

"It doesn't matter, good or bad. People don't want to know their future is already written."

Mike glanced from me to Chase, his expression melting into a smile. "Sorry you guys. Didn't mean to get all gloom and doom on you. I'm just a southern boy from a small town in South Carolina, not far from here.

I'm big on trucks, the bigger the better. That's how I got the nickname Super Swamper Mike. When I got this job, I thought the 'swami' part fit perfect."

Chase's eyebrows rose. "What does a swamp have to do with a truck?"

"He's not from around here," I said.

"I can tell." Mike reached across the table. "Give me your hand and I'll tell you what you want to know."

"The future?" I asked.

"If that's really what you want to hear."

I eased a hand across the table and Mike laid his over mine, gently gripping my sweating skin.

Music filled the air, rumblings from a faraway fair. He closed his eyes. "You are important to many people. They are searching for you, some good and some not so good."

My stomach churned.

"You should beware of the not so good. Not everything is as it seems. You will be fooled by those around you."

"What do you mean fooled?"

"Your gifts will keep you safe. Your heart will save those who need you. Remember where you've come from." His eyes pressed tighter. "You're also searching for someone."

"My real parents."

"One of them is closer than you realize."

I held my breath, desperate for more.

Mike released my hand and opened his eyes, leaning back again. "One day you'll be on the run and traveling through South Carolina. Don't look so worried—you can't change what'll happen. It's fate."

I thought of Mom. "Fate?"

"Look it up when you get the chance. How do you think I can see the future?" Mike waved his hand in a motion meant to silence my questions. "We don't have much time. Just remember to stop at a small diner about mile marker ninety-five off the interstate. You'll know when you see the sign. My mom works there as a waitress and she'll help you. Her name is Faith—just don't forget to mention mine." He nodded at the door as a deep-throated man entered and said our time was up. "Never give up the fight only you can win."

I tried clinging to the chair, but Chase dragged me out the door.

"That was cool," he said, but his words didn't mesh well with the anxious tone of his voice.

We walked back to the midway in silence, despite the air of noise and electricity that surrounded us. As we rounded the last row of games, I noticed Bill forking over several dollars for a shooting game. His lady was at the other end of the tent, eyes fixed on a TV blaring the local news. I started in her direction and Chase followed, eyes averted.

A man was on the screen, pointing as white balls bounced inside a plastic cage. The balls began to fall and he lifted a microphone. "Tonight's jackpot is two hundred and fifty million dollars." He called a series of six numbered balls. With each number, the lady's excitement grew. After the last, she ran to Bill and grabbed his arm.

"Hey," he whined. "You made me miss my shot."

"Bill, I just won the lottery."

"Chase," I said, but he was pulling a device from his pocket that flashed with a tic-tac-toe board of lights. "Is that a phone?"

"If you choose tool eighty-three it is. Looks like your mom's home."

In less time than it normally took Mom to crank the van, I was back in my room, surrounded by the safety of four walls in Alabama.

CHAPTER FOURTEEN

Homecoming

On Monday, Chase and I were the first to find our seats at the back of Mrs. Pearson's class. We whispered about Saturday night until after the bell rang, and neither of us noticed Mrs. Pearson until she stopped by my side.

Chase was silent while she laid composition books in front of us.

"You two are getting along well," she said.

Since no judging entered her voice, I wondered how much of our conversation she overheard as I slid my fingers along the ridges of the black-marble cover.

"The formula for your final grades has changed," she said, from the front of the room. "From now until the end of the semester, everyone will keep a journal."

A series of groans sounded around the room and she turned to the board. "I planned for this assignment to comprise five percent of your grades. Would you like to make it twenty-five?" No surprise, all groaning stopped.

When class was over, I approached her desk. "Mrs. Pearson, I'm not sure how to do this assignment."

"I have enjoyed the privilege of viewing your art. With the level of narrative on display in your drawings, this assignment should seem like a book report written for fun."

"But drawing is easy. I don't think about what to draw, I just draw."

She leaned back with an expression that bordered a smile. "Drawing is only one way to express the world around you. Writing can also be used to convey your thoughts."

Students began to file in for their second block and my voice clashed with the rising noise level. "What should I write about?"

"Start with what you know and the rest should fall a step behind breathing." Mrs. Pearson dismissed me with a wave.

Outside, Skip Greene called from across the sea of voices. "Can I walk you to second block?"

Despite a stumble comically timed with 'walk,' I recovered with a small "okay."

"How's it going?" he asked when he reached my side.

"Okay," I said again, though my hands flexed with the raw need to hit something.

His voice lowered. "I was wondering if you're going to the dance on Friday. I thought, that is if you aren't going with anyone…" He coughed. "It's just that I thought maybe we could go together."

I walked faster. "You don't have a date?"

"Yeah, maybe if you would slow down."

Something felt wrong. He should be asking Angel.

"There's no one else in first block, no one—?"

He grabbed my arm, spinning me around. "I promise, there's no one else."

Mr. Larson's class was up ahead. The bell would ring at any moment. "I guess that would be cool."

"Thanks," he said, launching down the hall before I could change my mind.

* * * * *

The cafeteria was full by the time I reached the table with my tray of food. Angel and Rachelle sat to one side laughing, with Bailey and Chase directly across. I took the empty seat next to Bailey and shoveled something resembling spaghetti into my mouth.

Bailey leaned close. "Chase just asked me to the dance."

Angel laughed. "You don't have to whisper about it. Everyone in school will know by fourth block."

"Probably by the middle of third," Rachelle said. "It won't take long with the way Bailey is spreading the news."

"Jealous?" Bailey drummed her fingers on the table as her cheeks reddened. "Admit it, you'd all be spreading the news. Especially Angel."

Rachelle grinned. "Yeah, when Skip gets around to asking her."

I dropped my fork. "Skip?"

Bailey sighed, disgust on her face. "You really shouldn't eat so fast. One day you'll choke and I'm not giving you mouth-to-mouth."

"You mean CPR," Rachelle said, watching me closely. "You were saying about Skip?"

Chase's eyes were on me. "Weren't you talking to Skip after first block?"

Lips moved at every table in the room, but I only heard silence until Angel spoke. "I was late this morning. He asked you, didn't he?"

"Yeah," I whispered.

Angel stood, throwing her backpack and purse over her shoulder. She pulled a pair of sunglasses from her purse. Her hands shook while she lifted the dark shades to her face. "Later," she said, but the voice wasn't hers. Each step Angel took toward the doors was faster than the last, and she stumbled twice.

Bailey turned to Rachelle. "Aren't you going to follow her? Check and make sure she's alright?"

Rachelle's eyes locked with mine. "No."

"Well, then," Bailey said, rising, "I guess I've got this."

Chase stared at me, both eyes wide, and jumped when Rachelle slammed the table with her fist.

"Chase, you need to go." Though her voice was calm, chills danced across my skin.

I nodded to Chase and he stood. Without a word, he lifted his bag and left the table.

"You're going to the dance with Skip?" Rachelle asked.

I looked down at my hands. "He asked me after first block."

"Do you ever think about anyone but Jes Delaney? Poor, pitiful, adopted Jes whose real parents didn't want her? Don't you ever notice how the people around you feel?" She shook her head and dragged a hand down one side of her face. "How long have you known Angel likes Skip?"

"Angel has liked Skip since I've been in Credence, but that doesn't mean… he asked me. I didn't ask him."

"Now I have my answer." Rachelle gathered her books and circled the end of the table, dropping into Bailey's seat. "I bet you haven't heard about Pade. He's taking Mia." She laughed. "From the look on your face, I'm glad I got to tell you."

"I'll tell Skip no."

"But you can't. If you back out, he'll know something's up and there's no way we're telling him about Angel. She's liked Skip since sixth grade and I'm not messing up any chance she has."

"All this time, I figured if Angel had been interested in Skip, they would have gone out."

Rachelle's voice softened. "The way you should have gone out with Pade?"

"You knew?" I shook my head. "That's why you enjoyed telling me about Mia. Maybe if I stay home Friday…"

"No." She stood once more. "Go to the dance with Skip. Just watch your back when it's break time."

* * * * *

The hall was empty when I stopped at the locker after school, or so I thought. As I concentrated on the door Bailey would soon rush through, two hands slammed me back against the lockers.

"Delaney," Tosh said.

I winced and closed my eyes as pain shot across the back of my skull.

"Hey Lamo." She grabbed my arms. "I'm talking to you."

We both jumped when someone threw open the next locker. "Hey Jes, what's up?"

Tosh's eyes were wide. "How… how did you do that?"

Chase's voice was guilt free. "Do what?"

She released my arms, glaring at Chase. "Are you here to back *her* up?"

"Do I need to back her up?" he asked.

She laughed and I almost pitied her. Before Tosh could grab me again, Chase glanced up and down the empty hall. He punched the locker door with his hand. With a loud crash came the opening of every locker, top and bottom, from one end of the hall to the other. Mountains of books spilled to the floor, sending Tosh stumbling back. She looked at me, rare fear shining in her eyes. Tosh first walked, then ran out the closest door.

With glowing satisfaction, I turned to my rescuer and smiled.

His eyes were blazing. "How long are you going to let Tosh talk to you like that?"

I sank to my knees as satisfaction drained with my strength. "I figured she'd eventually get tired of messing with me." I yanked the tie from my head and ran my hand through my hair. "My dad always says 'fighting isn't the answer'."

Chase slid a strand of hair from my eyes. "My father always said 'sometimes fighting is the only answer'."

His fingers, meant to console, brought a smile to my lips, though swirling emotions drove me to push Chase away. Eventually he'd leave, like almost everyone else in my life had. It was time to kill the attachment I'd grown for him. I needed to escape the pain that threatened our horizon, though a part of me would never let go. Anguish forced my eyes shut as I leaned back against the lockers.

"Your hair is a strange color," he said.

The statement sounded weird coming from his not-so-human mouth, but I knew the brown had grown out considerably since the last time Mom brought home a box of hair dye, as usual matched perfectly to her own true brown. I felt as if all the energy had drained from my body. "My roots are beginning to show."

"You dye your hair too?"

"I'm such a fake. Sometimes I think nothing about me is real." I sighed, but Chase remained quiet. "I think I'll ask Mom to color it again before the dance."

"You're going to the dance?"

My eyes shot open as I realized the sound didn't match Chase's voice. Above me stood Pade, smiling.

I scrambled to my feet so fast my head swam. The hall was empty to either side of us. No books. No open lockers. No Chase.

"Well?"

I knelt and wiped a hand over the mirror hanging from my locker door, the only locker still open. My eyes were glossy, but my face looked almost normal. I grabbed two books at random and stood.

"Let me help with those," he said.

Pade wanted to carry my books? Chase had disappeared? I pulled the books to my chest, desperate to grip something not breakable. "I've got them. But thanks." Looking down the hall again, Bailey was nowhere in sight.

"I thought I heard you mention the dance. Who were you talking to?"

"No one, I was just thinking. But yeah, I'm going."

Pade flashed a smile that no longer made my stomach flip. "I was hoping you'd go with Bailey. She's been talking about Homecoming for the last two weeks."

Yes, Bailey. No wonder she was late to the locker. "Bailey's going with Chase."

Pade's smile died. "When did she say that?"

"He asked her at lunch. I'm sure she wasn't keeping it from you."

"Yeah, right." His face soured. "How do you feel about being left out?"

"She's not leaving me out."

He laughed sardonically. "Yeah, Jes, keep on believing that. What are you going to do, tag along?"

"For your information, I'm not 'tagging along' with anyone. I have a date."

Pade's laughter stopped. "With who?"

"Skip."

"Skip?" He stared at me. "You're going to the dance with Skip, the Jolly Greene Giant?"

"So what? He's really tall to me, but you've only got about three inches to call him by that stupid nickname."

"You know he should be in eleventh grade, but his mom held him back."

"Why are you being mean to Skip? I thought he was your friend."

"He is, but he knows that I…" Pade sighed. "What did you expect me to say?"

"Uh, maybe good for *you,* Jes. Landing a date who can actually take me to Homecoming is better than going alone, but what would you know about that?" I gave a big, fake smile. "You're taking Mia Stevens."

"I'm meeting her there." He leaned against the locker next to me, head lowered. "Mia asked me, and I owe her a favor. Plus, you've already turned me down once. What's so great about Skip?"

"He's a nice guy."

"Nice is boring."

"You probably think so."

Pade's head rose, his voice melting into anger faster than I could take back my words. "What do you mean?" I shrugged and he shouted. "What do you mean?"

Anger burst from my mouth. "I mean Skip and I will have an awesome time at the dance. I'm sure he'll treat me well."

"You want to go with Skip because you think he'll treat you *well*?"

"I'm sure I won't catch him kissing anyone in the bathroom."

Pade slammed a fist against the locker to my side. "Thanks a lot, Delaney."

I pressed my lips as he walked away, not bothering to look back.

*****

Bailey and I skipped the game on Friday and only showed up for the dance.

When Mom dropped us off by the office, I touched my lips, just to be sure the smile had not faltered. "Thank goodness she didn't volunteer to chaperone," I whispered to Bailey.

At the doors, Skip led our way inside. "You look really pretty."

"Thanks." In his words, I felt nothing. I asked Skip

about the tattered suit, faded as if someone had sliced two pairs of jeans and sewn the ends together, but his reply was lost to the guilt. Others passed, dressed as if Credence High had a makeover to nightclub. I burst into laughter, certain I looked appalling in my layers of pink lace. Why had I let Mom talk me into dressing like a princess from a hundred years ago?

My smile never dimmed until I saw Pade.

Watching Pade from across the room made me cherish memories from our night at the fair. For one night, I stood by his side, equal in every way. Tonight, he wore a tuxedo, blacker than the hair against his ears, which brought a smile to my face at the same time I fought tears. Seeing him dance with seniors and cheerleaders blurred all the reasons 'we' could have been, along with my eyes.

Even if I hadn't pushed Pade away, the knowledge I'd never fit into his world remained between us. He stood next to Mia during the crowning ceremony, while I looked on as no more than a tenth-grader, wide-eyed and dreaming. Beyond being family to him, a fact I preferred he could forget, I was nothing.

As if drama demanded another appearance for the night, Terrance had asked Tosh. Around every corner, someone gushed about the cutest couples. I wanted to puke.

At one of the later DJ breaks, I pushed open the bathroom door and froze with the sounds of Tosh shouting. She and Mia stood before the mirror, surrounded by the lies and accusations Tosh spit into the air. For a moment, I considered turning and running from the bathroom, but then Chase's words gave an encore performance in my head.

Sometimes fighting is the only answer.

I passed Tosh, her eyes following me in the mirror. She stopped screaming and formed a smile that curled in true nastiness. When I approached the sinks, she turned to Mia.

"Do you know Jes actually thought Pade liked her too?"

Mia finished a layer of lipstick. "Maybe he does."

Tosh snatched the crown from Mia's head and threw the nest of glimmering stones. The metal skipped across the floor and clanked against the far wall.

Without a sound, Mia crossed the floor and lifted the crown. Tosh put both hands on her hips and stared down at me. Our eyes met in a fury, but I didn't cringe or look away.

"What now, Lame-o? Will you run like always?" she screamed and shoved my shoulders.

I stumbled but got back in her face.

"How could you possibly think Pade ever liked you? How? *How*? So, you want to fight me? You're not going to turn and run this time, Delaney. Not after what you pulled with Lisa." Her voice bled pain and guilt as my own guilt threatened to drown me.

"Leave her alone," Mia said. "It wouldn't be a fair fight. This is between us."

"You're right—I'll deal with you first. Then I'll teach Jes a lesson she'll remember every time she steps through that door." Tosh's laugh engulfed the room, conflicting with a steady beat from the cafeteria. She stepped to my right and reached for Mia's hair.

Mia ducked and forced an elbow into Tosh's ribs.

Tosh grabbed again for Mia's hair, this time catching her shoulder as both lost their footing and landed in a ruffled heap on the bathroom floor.

They thrashed, rolling across the floor with talons bared. Tosh broke away and climbed to her feet, but she slid on water that had pooled under one of the sinks. She steadied her feet by grabbing the porcelain and looked up as my palm crashed into her cheek. Sputtering a sentence where my name was the only word not etched across the bathroom walls, she raised both fists and I fired at her other cheek, sending my enemy back to the tile.

Tosh stared at Mia, who had inched away and now stood by the stalls, and once again pulled herself up.

"I'm still waiting for my lesson." I took a step forward. "Well?" Tosh was out the door before I could take a second.

Mia reset her crown in the mirror. "Thanks." She beamed with the kind of smile that begged for another. "I thought you were amazing." Reaching for my hair, she pulled some of the pins from the side of my head, which allowed a few soft curls to fall.

When I looked in the mirror, I struggled to recognize the face, my face, lit by a new radiance—the glow of being back on top of the world.

"*I'm* not surprised," Mia said. "Tosh can be real nasty, but she's not so tough inside. You've put up with her for a long time, much longer than I could have. She seemed really jealous of you and Pade."

"Don't you mean *you* and Pade?"

"Do I?" Mia grinned and circled an arm around my neck. "Thanks again. You saved me from… breaking any nails."

We laughed and headed back to the cafeteria, to where Pade leaned against the entrance. His eyebrows knotted into a 'V' when he caught sight of Mia's arm, still attached to my neck.

"We were starting to wonder," he said.

"Worried about us?" Mia shot me a secret look. "I guess a lot can happen in the girls' bathroom."

Pade straightened. "What happened?"

"Oh, just a little Tosh trouble." Mia rolled her eyes. "But it was nothing Jes couldn't handle."

Terrance stopped next to Mia and handed her a drink. "Jes?"

"Yes," Mia drawled, "Jes. Let's just say I don't think Tosh will be bothering her anytime soon." She turned to me. "You'll have to teach me that move of yours." Her excitement amplified each word. "I'll never forget the sight of you knocking Tosh Henley to the floor of the bathroom in building one." Mia tossed her hair and looked at Terrance. "Sorry about your date."

Terrance balled his fist. "We're not being nice to that girl anymore. I know you're on this mission to save the world, but Tosh is a lost cause."

"Agreed." Mia put an arm through his. "I was right about Jes, but I can't be right about everyone."

"I guess not." Terrance smiled. "But I'm glad you try."

Terrance escorted Mia through the door, leaving Pade as my only company for the walk inside.

"Was Skip in on this too?"

"No," Pade said. "He overheard Mia's plans to trick Tosh into acting normal, as if that were possible. He asked you out before I could explain what was going on, which made things weird with Angel. That's why I was standing at the door. Rachelle got Skip and Angel together, and I promised to keep you occupied until they were dancing." He pulled the door open and followed me inside.

"Have you seen Bailey?" I yelled.

"She was dancing with Chase before the last break."

I slapped a hand over my mouth, forcing back laughter.

"What is it?" Pade asked.

"I was just thinking how every girl in this room must be waiting for a dance. You might have to play offense if I get tackled."

He grinned. "Not even Tosh is that brave."

"But I'm sure you don't want to disappoint anyone." I glanced around the room, but no sign of Bailey. My eyes landed on Skip and Angel dancing, about the time Pade spotted them.

He reached for my arm. "Let's dance."

Pade led me to the center of a room filled by half the school and a song about Romeo and Juliet. The beat was swift, in rhythm with my heart, while his hands glided along my palms. With motions borrowed from a stage, he spun me as if the music played the tune of our lives and nothing else.

There I was in glitter and lace, with my prince crowned, no more than a breath away and ready to steal forever. Nothing could have filled the moment with more magic until the last verse of the song. As his head lowered, I wavered between growing hunger and a sad dose of reality.

With Pade's lips almost to mine, I tilted my head from the path to freedom of emotions. Away from the feeling my soul cried for, the ache only Pade Sanders could bring.

Pade stepped back and found my eyes, his own

cloudy. "What's wrong?"

The tremor in his voice brought the same kind of hurt to my heart. "I just didn't want you to."

His eyes shifted down. "I thought maybe you changed your mind about us."

"No," I said, fighting to keep my words firm. "We can either be friends or nothing at all."

Pade studied my face. "That's really what you want? A friend?"

"Tonight it's what I need."

I pictured him running from the center of our stage. His face was a window for a spectrum of feelings, from anger to denial, and then a tight smile.

Pade slid both arms around me, bringing his head next to mine. "I'll give a year of tonights if you ask, but at some point, tomorrow will follow."

* * * * *

Since Bailey wasn't clinging to Chase anywhere on the dance floor, I escaped into the courtyard, able to get away from Pade without complaint. As I rubbed the prickles on my arms, the glow from a window in building five caught my attention.

The hall was darkness except for light filtering through a crack in the door to our first block class. Bailey stood near the door, one ear tilted to the conversation inside. Two people were talking; their faces took form through the crack as I approached. Thoughts of what Bailey had already heard Chase and Mrs. Pearson say raced through my head, before I realized our teacher's words made no sense.

"No," Chase said. "I'll only speak English here."

Mrs. Pearson sighed as he paced in front of the desks. "I do not know how much longer you can… are you listening to me?"

He shifted from one foot to the other. "Yes, ma'am."

"Do not say that word. You sound like them."

Chase lowered his eyes and I felt his discomfort as if she lectured me.

"For months, you have been free from the many responsibilities and hardships my position on Golvern has forced upon you. I have given your fantasies of 'normal' considerable latitude, but I believe we must leave Earth soon."

"I miss home, despite how they treat us, but I feel leaving here now would be a mistake."

"We have finished our research, but the facts seem to stand against your friend. I know how bad you wanted it to *be* her this time."

"But she's adopted."

"As are many people on this planet."

"She dyes her eyes and hair."

"You have visited Earth long enough to realize humans hate themselves. They always want to be someone different."

"What about her parents?" he asked.

"Lorraine Delaney attended this school with Dr. Greene."

"How can you be sure they're human?"

"No other answer makes sense. Only her abductors would know the truth, and Lorraine Delaney does not fit the profile."

"I never found pictures of her dad. When I searched their house the day I missed school, I couldn't find *any* pictures. Health Made Simple does exist, but there's no public information. I haven't been able to crack the encryption on their servers. We should wait and meet him."

"The question of her father's illness has been prevalent in all of our minds." Mrs. Pearson lifted a red folder from her desk. "I obtained Justin Delaney's medical records, which I might add date back more than thirty years." She nodded as her son straightened. "For once I ignored the rules regarding the privacy of this world's inhabitants. Learning his past seemed crucial.

"He was born in Colorado and almost died of pneumonia at age five. At thirteen, he broke both bones in his lower right arm and at fifteen cracked several ribs. He was diagnosed with skin cancer a year ago and underwent radiation therapy." She smiled weakly. "You know such a treatment would be fatal to any of us. The fact Mr. Delaney has spent a lifetime on Earth should at least prove he is human." Her voice fell to a whisper. "And that she is too."

"It has to be her," Chase said. "I won't accept she's gone. I won't stop believing we'll find her, but I don't want to be wrong like before."

"If you truly believe, Jessica will be on the ship tonight."

"I need more time."

"I will take the blame if you are wrong."

"Don't you think Jes will hate us?"

She extended the folder to Chase. "This is a picture of Mr. Delaney, taken while he attended college in Denver. Do you think the boys look like him?"

"You saw them at the library."

"Your opinion is important."

Chase stared at the picture for a long moment, before closing the folder and handing it back. "Will my answer change your decision?"

She swallowed. "Yes or no."

His eyes met hers. "Yes."

Mrs. Pearson faced the board.

"Are we taking her back to Golvern?"

Her voice was hollow. "Any chance… we have no choice."

I stumbled back and autopilot took over, allowing me to retreat past the empty rooms. Away from Mrs. Pearson and the implications of her words. Away from the offer of adventure Chase was prepared to make good on. My heart skipped with excitement while an earthquake shook the flesh beneath my skin. Not until I reached the safety of cafeteria lights was breathing possible, and I still jumped like a caged animal when someone touched my arm.

"Am I going crazy?" Bailey swung me around. "I wanted to find Chase, but they were talking all weird. Please tell me I'm not freaking out. Mom is always saying I'm going to end up on the first floor of the hospital. You know, the psych ward!" She paced the narrow sidewalk. "I'm freaking out and my boyfriend is some psycho lunatic loose from who knows where. And his mother is el primo psycho of the year."

"Let's get back to the dance," I said, my drama scale pegged for the night.

Bailey checked her phone. "It's almost time for my mom." Her eyes met mine with a flash of concern. "We didn't see anything."

"Anything like what?"

"My thoughts exactly."

*****

Aunt Charlie parked in her driveway and I walked the path to my back door, with no other thoughts but Pade. Only the absence of a single kitchen light brought me back to Credence. I crept toward sounds flowing from the living room. Dad was talking with Mom, though I couldn't make out their words. Hearing his voice brought relief, but their voices stopped when the floor creaked beneath my feet.

Dad turned, his eyes shining like the sparkles on my dress under the lone lamp. "You look lovely."

I threw my arms around him. "I'm so glad you came home early." After inhaling the familiar scent of his aftershave, a memory of my real father replayed in my head. Again, I heard the man reading and felt his arms around me. '*Kay Ray*' he called me. But he wasn't the one who'd been there for me. How could I hug Dad and think of some other man? I cringed and Dad pulled away.

With light shadowing his face, he looked tired, and old. "I'm glad to be home. It's been a long journey for me."

"From Tokyo?" I asked.

"I'll tell you about it one day."

I wanted to tell Dad the truth. As he hugged me again, I almost convinced myself to disclose every amazing detail about Chase and Mrs. Pearson. Dad would believe me, even in a frantic state. I would make him believe me, somehow.

Instead, I climbed the stairs.

CHAPTER FIFTEEN

Lauren

I awoke the next morning, amazed I ever got to sleep. My mind reeled with events from the night before. Hitting Tosh. Dancing with Pade. Seeing the truth about Chase.

Bailey lounged in a chair beside the rose bushes, facing a square of awkward grass lighter than the rest of her backyard. Her eyes were closed, but she wasn't trying to get a tan under the dreary sky.

I tore a leaf from one of the bushes. "Are you still sad about the pool?"

"You're stalling," she said. "Tell me what you know about Chase."

Bailey was quiet while I talked about Chase, starting from the first day we met. When I finished, she opened her eyes. "You didn't think I should know? I thought you were my friend."

"I promised Chase I'd keep his secret."

"And you told me." Sarcasm dripped from her

voice. "A little late, don't you think?"

"You deserve the truth, promise or no promise."

"I finally meet the perfect guy and he turns out to be from another planet. The worst part is, he seemed to really like me. Why is this happening? Uhh!" She jumped from the seat and threw her hands into the air. "Why did Chase tell you? Why are you so special?"

Though I'd never considered the question, Bailey made it seem like an obvious one. "I guess we made a connection with the whole outcast thing."

"You're not an outcast—you're adopted. I can't imagine you having anything in common with an alien."

At Bailey's mention of the 'A' word, I giggled. She'd get angry, I knew, but the giggles soon became full-blown, rolling-on-the-ground laughter.

"Have you lost your mind? Did you not hear what Mrs. Pearson is planning to do to you?"

Bailey's words had the effect of dampening my laughter. In fact, the world around me sobered fast.

* * * * *

Bailey grabbed a seat at my kitchen table as I made us drinks, insisting I tell her more about Chase. "Did last night have something to do with the list of names from Chase's notebook?"

"They're looking for a missing girl." I dropped into a seat across from Bailey. "That's why Chase and his mom are in Credence."

She stared at the drink I'd placed in front of her. "You think they're looking for you?"

"I tried to get the truth out of Chase, but he never told me the whole story."

"So, he *didn't* tell you everything."

"He acted like a CIA agent over the girl they're searching for, but Chase said his people can't stay on Earth more than three years without going back. Our sun is deadly for them."

"Which is why Mrs. Pearson decided you can't be her. But why did she say they had no choice?"

"It doesn't make any sense," I said.

Bailey leaned back in her chair. "We've got to find out more about this Lauren girl. I bet she knows what all of this is about. Didn't you say Chase was looking at her picture online?"

"Yeah, but I didn't see her last name."

As Bailey's fingers slid along the edge of the table, her eyes shadowed the beginning of a plan. "We'll look online until we find her."

"Can we use your computer?"

"Pade was playing some game on the Internet when I left, and he hasn't done that since our father called. He never said a word, even after I pounded every stair on my way down."

I fought an image of the night before. "We can't use the computer here. Right now, I don't need a mob scene over whether or not aliens exist."

"Uncle Justin would probably freak or think we're crazy."

"What are our options?"

She chewed her lip, before her eyes lit up. "Let's go to the library."

"Aren't you forgetting something?"

"Like what?"

"Like transportation."

Bailey smiled. "My mom will be home from work in

an hour. She'll be happy to take me to the library."

We laughed together, knowing Bailey would never ask to go to the library for fun.

* * * * *

Since the library was empty, choosing a computer in a lonely corner was a breeze. After sorting through only a small portion of the world of Laurens, however, we still had found zilch. When Bailey went to the bathroom, I typed 'Lauren' and 'New York' in the search window. Thousands of hits appeared, mostly about clothes.

I leaned back and shook my head. What else? She wasn't from Chase's planet, but he thought she was. He was wrong. She was the before. Chase must have taken Lauren back to Golvern. It was the only way he'd know for sure. After York, I typed 'kidnapped by aliens.' Again, thousands of hits appeared, but this time most of the articles were about Lauren McCall. Bailey retuned just in time to read the headlines.

'Teenager Disappears Under Incredible Circumstances', 'Parents Seek Information on Kidnapped Daughter', and 'Girl Returned to Family Unharmed' were some of the titles. With each story about Lauren McCall, the connection between us grew.

The McCalls were a rich family in New York City, and a political force from the sound of the articles. Their only daughter, also adopted, disappeared and then returned home three months later. 'Friends' of the family insinuated everything from her running away from an abusive home to her being kidnapped by aliens. The tabloids were like starving lions to those people. After once having a newsworthy name myself, I understood the pain they must have felt. Not only at losing their daughter, but also at seeing their lives made into a reality show before the entire country.

Bailey's eyes were wide. "Could you imagine being that famous?"

Yes. "No."

"It would be too weird."

"Yeah." And no one could ever pay me enough to be famous again.

"Wow," Bailey said, as we opened Lauren's page. "She's pretty."

A twinge of jealousy bugged me from imagining how close Lauren must be to Chase, how she left Earth to visit his planet.

"Do you…" Bailey lowered her voice. "Do you think Chase likes her?"

I shook my head, focusing on Lauren's profile. Her 'out of this world experience' grabbed my attention as if shielded by a cobweb. She never actually posted that she visited Chase's home, but the description of Golvern probably made more sense to me than most of cyberspace. Lauren even gave a shout out to her 'long lost friend.'

Bailey snatched the mouse. "We should send Lauren a message. She's online."

I leaned back. "And say what?"

"Whatever it takes to find out what she knows about Chase."

"Okay, but don't forget we're logged in under my name."

"You might be Jessica, but this account says you're twenty-five and live in South Dakota. No one will know who you are."

I typed 'I know ur friend—chase.'

"Hey," Bailey said, grabbing my arm. "Don't tell her everything yet."

I backed over 'chase' and 'friend,' typing 'long lost friend' instead. My heart raced when 'whatz his name?' appeared on the screen.

"We got her attention," Bailey cried. "Go ahead and tell her."

I typed 'chase.'

The page hovered, long enough for my doubts to grow into fear we'd made a mistake even an escape button couldn't fix.

'hey jes'

I almost fell from the chair after Lauren's response, except for Bailey's grip on my arm. My breath became shallow as I scrambled for a reply.

'still there?' came across the screen.

'yeah,' I typed. 'how do u know my name?'

'ur profile silly.'

Okay, fair enough. 'y did u call me jes?'

She paused. 'chase callz u jes.'

Bailey sniffed. "He told her about you? I wonder why."

Then Lauren typed the words that almost made my heart stop. 'tell him I said hey when he finds you tonight. Have fun when u go—I did.'

Bailey's irritation vanished. "She thinks you're going to his planet."

I looked around the room, but no one glanced our way. The sinking feeling churned in my stomach again.

Bailey leaned closer, concern in her eyes. "Are you okay?"

I typed 'thanx' before closing the page. I rested my

head on my hands, only seconds from tears.

"We should leave." Bailey reached for her phone. "I'll call my mom." As she dialed, the phone vibrated in her hand. "Damn it, Chase is texting. He wants to hang out this evening." She looked up, indecision on her face.

"Your mom won't let you go to the Fun Connection tonight."

"No, but there'll be all kinds of people at the mall on Saturday night. Chase won't make any moves in a public place and we'll finally get some answers." She grinned. "We won't let him leave without the truth."

"I think it's a bad idea."

"What happened to the girl brave enough to skip fourth block without her best friend? How often does something crazy happen to two normal people like us?"

* * * * *

"Let's go to the food court," I said after forty-five minutes of walking in and out of the mall's stores. The smell of pizza drifted from the restaurants nearby and Chase still hadn't bothered to show his face.

"How can you think about food? Chase said he'd be in front of the shoe store by six." She checked her phone. "Whoa, it's five after six already. He must have changed his mind."

"He'll find us at the food court."

"Ten more minutes." Bailey pointed to a pair of red running shoes. "Check out the zebra laces. I could try out for cheerleader in these."

Moving behind the store's glass window, I flipped over the tag. "You'd make a serious contender."

"That's exactly what I mean. I should throw the

shoes away and wear the tag around my ankle. Oh well, while we're in here…"

I followed Bailey between the rows of shelves. "I don't think Aunt Charlie would buy any of these."

"But my father would. Money is love to him, and his pockets weigh more than his heart. Maybe I'll start a list so after Christmas I can act like the new rich bitch."

"Does anybody work here?" shouted a familiar voice.

I eased around the last section of shoes, though I'd pictured the face already.

Sarah Beth was standing at the counter. As the cashier raced for a spot before the register, she shoved a pair of shoes across. "Don't you have these in size eight anywhere other than on the top shelf?"

"See," Bailey said. "I told you she's not as nice as people think."

The cashier stepped back. "I'll check the stock."

Sarah Beth looked away and smiled. "Forget it. I think my boyfriend found a pair."

Bailey grumbled. "Unbelievable. I wonder who fell for the act this time."

We followed Sarah Beth's dreamy gaze to see… Pade walking in her direction.

"Here you go, size eight." He returned her smile. "No reason to bother anyone."

Bailey pushed me aside. "I'm gonna kill him."

"Not with me here," I said.

She fought my grip, but her foot caught on a pair of boots left in the aisle. Instead of balancing the tug of my arm, Bailey fell against me and we both landed with a bone-jarring thud on carpet no thicker than a tablecloth.

"What the hell?" asked another familiar voice.

"Pade, you've got to see these girls making out."

Bailey rolled onto the floor, allowing me to breathe again. I opened my eyes to the glare of lights behind a vision of Terrance and Mia upside down.

Pade circled the register. "What are you yelling about?"

"Oh, man." Terrance laughed. "You missed the show. Good thing since you'd have nightmares 'til graduation."

"Shut up," Mia hissed and punched his arm.

The laughter died when Bailey climbed from her knees to her feet in one motion. "I can't believe you're here with *her*," she screamed and shoved a trembling finger at Sarah Beth. She glared as Pade crossed the floor. "What about yesterday? Before the dance, you said you'd do anything to get Jes back. You said she meant *everything* and that you wouldn't leave until she danced with you!"

Pade looked down as Sarah Beth's face turned a deep shade of red. Terrance cleared his throat but failed to cut the tension. I held my breath as the revelation hung in the air, begging to be grabbed as I stood.

Only Mia's calm voice broke the silence. "But they did dance."

"Jes would've told me if they danced." Bailey turned to me. "Right?" When I hesitated, she snorted. "*Right?*"

I struggled for words, any words she might understand. "Pade danced with me, before I found you looking for Chase."

"Why didn't you tell me?"

Mia stood solemn next to Terrance, but I couldn't bring my eyes to Pade's. About the time pain rose beyond worry of embarrassment, a light flashed in

Bailey's eyes. She looked back to Pade and the anger became a sigh. "She turned you down, didn't she?"

Pade didn't have to answer, and probably couldn't have after our eyes met. We were one, two souls sharing the same painful bond.

Poor Bailey didn't know if she should hug her brother or reach for me. I left the store, racing for the food court, which no longer offered calm for my stomach.

"What happened?" called a voice from behind, just as I reached the main artery of the mall.

I froze, staring at the hand that grabbed my arm. "Please don't make me tell the story. It hurts too much."

"I thought you really liked him," Bailey said.

"I did. I mean I do. Oh god, I don't know what's happening to me. I want to take every sonnet from our English book and burn the word love. I want to pull my own hair out. Most of all, I want to throw my arms around him, but I can't."

"Why not? That should be the easy part."

"He tears me up inside and I don't…" I choked on a laugh of pure agony. "I don't think I can survive one more moment of Pade Sanders."

"It's okay." Bailey folded me into her embrace. "I wanted you guys to work out more than me and Chase. I dreamed about us being sisters, but you have to realize we'll always be friends, no matter what. If my brother makes you this unhappy, we're all better off knowing now."

"Can we not talk about Pade?"

We didn't speak on the way to the food court or while in line. Or while finding a table, which was nearly impossible in the crowded room. I dropped into a chair across from Bailey and inhaled a plate of pizza faster than she could open a box of chicken nuggets. "We should get out of here. I feel like puking, but that's not an option since I still plan to be in school on Monday morning. Call your mom or I'll call mine."

"You want to leave?" She choked on her first bite of chicken. "Now?"

"I don't want to wait around and find out what Chase is planning for us."

Bailey leaned over the table, voice lowered to a whisper. "You don't actually think he'll hurt us, do you?"

"I don't know."

As Bailey looked away, I reached for her phone. Before my fingers connected with the hot pink case, it disappeared.

"You really don't know?" Chase stood next to our table with his hands in his pockets. "How could you think I'd hurt you?" Pain glimmered in his eyes.

Instead of answering, I cleared a spot to my right. The table seated four and there was no reason he couldn't sit with us, especially with half of Credence enjoying dinner. We were safe, for the moment.

Bailey closed the nuggets and pushed away the box. "We overheard you and your mother talking last night, in case you didn't know."

I shook my head at Bailey, but she merely tossed her hair. "That's right," she said. "We heard it all."

Chase straddled the chair and leaned toward my face. "Is that why you contacted Lauren?"

I felt as if the entire crust of pizza had lodged in my throat. I met Chase's eyes, deep blue and searching. What did he want from me? It couldn't be just friendship, not when he'd had that for weeks.

"I'll tell you why," Bailey said.

Chase's eyes never left mine. "You tell me."

"Lauren is your friend," I choked. "We wanted to find out more about you."

"You watched me look her up in the library that day." His eyes narrowed. "You were spying on me. Why?"

"I wasn't spying on you. I didn't even see Lauren's last name." As soon as the words were out, I threw my hands over my mouth.

"There must be hundreds of Laurens online," he said.

"Thousands, actually," Bailey said.

Chase glanced at Bailey, but turned back to me.

"I searched for Lauren and New York."

"Smart idea. Now you know everything." His words caused my skin to prickle like I'd just begun to sweat off a fever. Chase relaxed in his chair and appeared to send a message from his phone.

Bailey shoved the nugget box and empty bag from the table, her voice rising. "Where's my phone?"

"You won't need it anymore," Chase said.

Bailey's eyes found mine as adrenaline kicked in. She motioned to the nearest exit. "I've gotta go to the bathroom." Snatching her purse from the table, she jumped to her feet.

"Sit back down," he said.

"Come on, Jes, you know I can't go alone."

A man caught my attention, looping through the crowd with a plate of Chinese noodles. As he passed, I closed my eyes in silent prayer, every thought in my head focused on the red tray in his hands.

The tray landed on Chase and I grabbed Bailey's

hand, launching us into motion across the food court. We reached a bathroom near the entrance of the mall, with Chase nowhere in sight. I pulled Bailey ahead of several women who shouted but lacked the speed to stop us. We squeezed into a stall and I locked the door, ready to suck in every molecule of oxygen from the surrounding air.

"What happened?" Bailey asked, dazed like people on TV after some big disaster.

I rested a hand on her shoulder. "We've got to get out of this mall."

"Chase…" Bailey covered her face with her hands.

I wished the situation could disappear, that we could somehow zap ourselves home, but we had no power to fight Chase. "We've got to call Mom and Dad."

"What if…" Her voice shook like her hands. "What if Chase hurts them?"

Closing my eyes, I fought the horrible thought. "I can't let that happen."

The stall door slammed open as she pushed me aside. I followed, the length of floor between us growing. Around a corner and back through the center of the mall, I spotted her near the main entrance about the time I noticed Chase. Two security guards caught Bailey's arms, keeping her from the doors.

"Help," I screamed. "Someone is trying to hurt us."

One guard raised a hand and another guard appeared to my right. Bailey fought her captors with strength akin to sumo wrestling, punching and kicking anything close enough to reach. I lurched forward in time to see Chase signal the guards.

Bailey broke free and ran for the door. I bypassed

the captors who scrambled to regain control. A couple of women approached the door, and Bailey crashed past them on the sidewalk. Their bags flailed and landed at their feet. I escaped into the night, dodging the bags, and nearly tripped over a purse. Rain pelted my face as my feet splashed on gaps in the concrete, the cold shock awakening my senses.

She stepped off the sidewalk and slipped between the rows of cars. I glanced at the lights, hanging above on long poles, a halo of moisture making a ring against the dark sky. "No," I muttered, as Bailey ran toward a vacant section of the parking lot. I followed, desperate to catch her.

Someone yelled from behind and two of the guards were at her side. As a third appeared and reached for my arm, the guard to her right drew a weapon…

"Bailey," I screamed.

The guard held his weapon at arm's length and fired. Bailey fell to the ground in a crumpled heap. I threw my hands over my face and dropped to my knees. There was my friend, soaking wet and not moving, with the guards reaching down for her. *Oh God,* I prayed, *please let her be okay*. "Bailey," I cried against the rain as a gust of wind howled, carrying my voice away.

"She's not hurt," Chase said.

I shivered and stared into his blue eyes, feeling the connection as strong as the day we met. He cupped my face in his hands, and my arms ached to reach around him, to pull him close.

With another gust of wind came reality, and I recognized the heavy drops of rain, for a moment lost to the darkness. In the end, he'd betrayed me. When Chase asked me to return with him at the fair, I'd felt a special thrill. Faced with no choice in leaving, terror swallowed every thought.

"I'm sorry" was all he could say.

Water soaked through my jeans and climbed my legs. My toes were cold, bent painfully under my rear, and I coughed, fire burning in my chest. Tears flowed down my face. I looked behind me, at a family crossing the parking lot. Children ran, sloshing in the rain, while their parents demanded they slow down.

Seeing a split-second chance, my feet spiraled into motion. I ran in a dance, from one foot to the other as if dodging bullets, and screamed for help with all the force my lungs could give. I extended my hand but a slap from behind silenced every muscle. The ground rushed to my face until I hovered about an inch above the pavement. Hands appeared and held my arms, the same hands that flipped me skyward.

In my head, I fought their grip, but in reality, no part of my body responded. Chase's worry creased his face. He spoke clearly, though I wanted to drown out his words with tears.

"You were shot with a paralyzer but you're okay. Don't worry—it's only temporary. You won't be able to feel again for at least an hour."

We were no longer in the rain or the darkness held at bay by the lighted parking lot. Visions of the sky changed to a smooth-as-glass ceiling with no reflection. Down a long hall, I drifted, ending in a room that smelled of freshly dried sheets.

Alone, with no sound, I stared at the glass above, imagining the strain I felt, holding my face like a clenched fist. Itching urges spiked in my bones but nothing I could think of would overcome Chase's paralyzer.

Emotions swirled inside, threatening to break out of my body. My pulse sped as fear grew in my throat, which threatened the only movement possible—the shallow rise and fall of my lungs. Faster, faster, the heartbeat drummed in my ears. The rhythm quickened beyond what I could count and I felt sick, though my stomach never moved. A beeping split the air, piercing my ears, and a face appeared at the corner of my sight with what looked like a needle. Blackness trickled through my eyes as warmth filled my veins, a happy sticky sludge that radiated to my toes.

When I awoke, a padded surface stretched beneath me. Glass still loomed above, no echo on its surface, but my body no longer shrank away in response. I felt numb inside, as if the air didn't really smell of fresh laundry, like my own brain had betrayed me and fled to Chase's side. The guards led me down a hall enclosed with the same smooth glass. At the end of the hall, Chase waited, head held high before a plain door. He advanced, speaking to the guards in their language. They released me but hovered at a safe distance.

Chase squeezed my arm and I jerked away. His eyes took on the same weariness from the day at the lake. "Bailey is fine. The weapon was for retaining purposes only. Our doctor has checked her out." He touched a square handle to the right of the door and it opened, revealing a brightly lit room. Flashing control panels lined the outer edges of the room, with blackened glass rising in the space above.

A table sat at the room's center, with Mrs. Pearson standing to the side.

She crossed the floor with lightning speed, concern

in her eyes. "Is she intact?"

One guard answered calmly. I recognized the janitor's voice. "She put up a fight and we restrained her."

Mrs. Pearson's eyes gauged the length of me, her face less than a foot from mine. "You should have given them your cooperation."

I couldn't speak as fear paralyzed me all over again.

She pushed the hair from my face, still damp and clinging to my skin. "Do you know who you are?"

I nodded and tried to swallow, but my throat tightened.

"What is your name?" she asked.

Although I needed my words to sound defiant, I managed only weak and scared. "Jessica Delaney."

"That is not your real name," she said.

"It is now."

"I know you are adopted. Jessica, I believe we finally know the truth. Your real mother is…" Uncertainty forced her eyes from mine. "A woman of great importance."

"You know Marsha?"

"Marsha?" She looked up, forgetting the doubt. "Who is Marsha?"

I laughed as the irony of our situation became clear. Some woman was searching for her daughter and they had it all wrong. "Marsha is my real mother."

CHAPTER SIXTEEN

Secrets Revealed

"Most people *know* I was adopted, but few know who my real parents were. As much as I'd love to hear you say I've got a real mother who wants me back, it's not possible."

"Tell me about them," Mrs. Pearson said.

Tears formed at the corners of my eyes, hot tears that threatened to trail down my face. I didn't need them, I never had. To look back and regret the fact they didn't need me shredded my heart like confetti. Though I'd promised myself never to regret them, the feeling had returned so quickly my head spun. Now I must tell the whole story without freaking.

"Frank and Marsha Naples," I said.

No one said a word as I turned for a full view of their blank faces. "They lived in New York City, on a bad side of town. My dad was taking a shortcut and it was snowing."

I pushed down the sobs in my throat. "My real

parents fought that night and I ran away. They reported my disappearance to the police and, because of blood found in the house, became the primary suspects. Four days later, and about five miles from their house, Dad found me in the middle of a dark highway. He had to slam on brakes and barely missed hitting me. He said I wouldn't tell him my name or where I lived. Knowing the area's reputation, he decided to take me home with him and call the police. They put me in a 'safe' house and assigned a social worker. Her name was Lorraine Conners."

Calculating eyes pierced the air between us. "The woman you call mom?"

"She'd just transferred to New York. Through the investigation and court hearings, Dad came to see me every day. My real parents were cleared of any foul play in my disappearance, although Frank had been involved in a bank robbery. Dad proposed to Mom and they decided to adopt me. They petitioned the court and my custody hearing was in December, a week before Christmas. Frank and Marsha never showed."

Chase shook his head. "You're wrong."

Mrs. Pearson waved a hand to silence him. "You remember these events?"

"I was four years old. I don't remember much of anything from back then."

"You have no memory of your real parents, only what you were told."

It was the moment for me to tell this woman all about my dreams and make her story more than just plausible. Chase would say 'I told you so' and they'd whisk me back to their planet. I'd travel beyond the hazy dome of air surrounding Earth, wave goodbye to the moon, and see the stars up close. Mom would cry every night and Dad would… "I remember meeting Lorraine. I remember Dad visiting me, and the day he promised we'd be a family. They took me home for good on Christmas Eve." The memory brought strength to my voice and I raised my head. Someone had wanted me, and from that point on, I'd always been taken care of.

"Why are you sure of this?" she asked. "You have no memory of the time before you were found."

"It's not like this was a secret or anything. Every news reporter knew my name, as did half the country. Jessica Naples, 'the four-year-old runaway.' Just search for the name online and see what you get."

Chase typed quick strokes on a keypad. Only moments ago, his eyes expressed complete disbelief of my story. "I've found an article," he said, as Mrs. Pearson joined him in front of the screen. "Frank and Marsha Naples do exist, and this story reads just as Jes said. How did we miss—?"

She gripped his shoulder and Chase looked up at her, neither saying a word for what seemed like an eternity. Finally, she motioned me forward.

In the center of the screen glowed a black and white picture of me at four, one I wanted to reach for and run from in the same instant.

"This is you." Her words were more of a statement than a question, and her voice held more curiosity than accusation.

Chase pushed back from the keypad. "Your parents never hid this from you?"

"What's the point? Dad always said I should know where I came from. That way I can decide where I'm going."

Her voice held a touch of compassion. "You are lucky to have a family who loves you, even if they were not the first."

"I just wish…" I stopped after realizing I almost gave up my feelings to her moment of compassion.

Her eyes bored into me. "We have no plans to cause harm."

"Can you read my mind?" I asked.

"No, my dear, but fear is evident from your expression. We did not come here to make you uncomfortable. We came to complete a mission."

"Mom," Chase said.

She held up a hand. "We have been on a crucial mission for the last six years. Maybe if you understood our purpose here, you would feel more at ease."

"You're from another planet." I watched my words reflect in her face. "Aren't you?" For a few crazy seconds, I imagined being wrong.

Mrs. Pearson smiled, amusement gleaming in her eyes. "Will you be scared if my answer is yes? From my experience, human children are much better equipped to accept the unknown than their parents. Do you agree with me? Are you open minded, Jessica?"

"Are you going to hurt me or Bailey?"

"As I said before, we are not on this planet to cause harm."

I sighed. "Why are you keeping us here?"

"You have told us your story. Now I would like to tell you ours."

She offered me a seat at the table in the room's center. She dismissed the guards and the room emptied except for the two of us and Chase, who took a seat along the far wall. Mrs. Pearson sat opposite me, hands rested on the table. She stared into my eyes until I looked down.

"We have been on a mission for six years. You could say we are here to reunite a child with her mother."

"And you think I'm her."

"This girl was lost eleven years ago, kidnapped by her own father. He died in a horrible accident shortly after and many people believed she died with him. About six years ago, we found information that led us to quite the opposite conclusion. This information came from a reliable source and I decided to take up the cause. We followed through on multiple leads, all of which ended with no connection to her. Finally, we found evidence that led us to Earth.

"I know you must be thinking, why Earth? Many of our people have traveled to this planet over the last thousand years. The two worlds are similar in atmosphere and Earth can support our lives in much the same way as it supports human lives. Even our language structures are comparable.

"For the past year, our team has made Earth a home in the search for her. Unfortunately, there is one staggering difference between our planet and yours. The radiation from your sun causes changes to our bodies, down to our genetic codes. Certain abilities are inherent to my people and months of exposure to your sun will cause us to become much like those born on Earth. Years of exposure will kill us. I am sure you can see how this creates a problem."

Lights dotting each side of the room seemed to spin, or maybe only my head took flight. The woman wielding power with a story filled by space in the cage made of glass was accessory to a dream, not a memory. One point lodged itself firmly in my brain: the girl's father kidnapped her. No way had my real father kidnapped me.

"You have questions, though I am sorry to say I have no good answers. What I can tell you is we are out of time."

"What does time have to do with me?"

"We came to this planet to find a girl and the plan is for us to return with one. Our abilities have already started to fade. The ship's doctor believes even a week more on this planet could cause permanent damage." Her voice lowered. "I am worried for Chase. He feels the effects more than I do."

Chase sighed. "I keep telling you not to worry."

Mrs. Pearson studied her son as if she expected welts to explode from his skin, and then sighed, exactly as Mom did when she decided not to argue with me. "My son does not realize the magnitude of our situation or the potential harm to himself. At sixteen, how can I expect him to?"

A deep groan flowed from a panel along the wall. She waved a hand and the noise stopped. "You are angry with me," she said, without accusation. "I can see the fire in your eyes."

I considered what to say next, glaring at the unblinking pair of eyes opposite mine. I remembered knocking Tosh to the floor. Had it happened only yesterday? The thought started me laughing. It began with the corners of my mouth curling up. My hands flew to cover my face, shielding the giggles ready to burst from my mouth. Classes flashed before me—all the times I hated school. My parents hugging me, the twins causing trouble, Bailey…

How would I get out of this? How could I get my life back? Dad's words repeated in my head, '*Be careful what you wish for.*' I felt cheated by fate and my real parents. They left me and eleven years later, I was still in pain. "I want to know how you could hurt your son like this. Why did he have to come here?"

Mrs. Pearson's face softened. "You are angry about how I have hurt Chase. Interesting."

"I know how it feels to be hurt by family."

"You know nothing of what family means. You know two random people shared your blood and hurt you, which causes you to feel a kinship with my son. What about the people who raised you? What if they made choices meant to protect the well-being of others? What if those choices put your life in jeopardy?"

"What do you mean by 'the well-being of others'?"

Mrs. Pearson sat back, pursing her lips as if she'd said too much. "Just to put events in perspective for you, I, as Chase's mother, do feel guilt for bringing him here."

He opened his mouth, but again she held up a hand.

"Chase has a special gift needed to find the girl in question. We have traveled tirelessly in search of her, and the trail has ended here in Credence. He has ruled out every prospect except for you."

"Can't you just do a DNA test?"

She smiled. "Remember what I told you about Earth's sun?"

"You said something about radiation."

"Radiation changes our genetic code. Long-term exposure renders your DNA analysis useless, which is why I have decided to take you back with us."

The articles about Lauren's disappearance filled my head. "I can't leave."

"It would be a new experience for you, and maybe even your friend. Yes, we will take Miss Sanders as your companion. We can restore you both to this planet once your skin has been regenerated and a proper analysis of your genetic makeup has ruled you out."

Did they tell Lauren the same story? "What if I am this girl?"

"That would be… a unique situation." Her face filled with a glimpse of hope.

"What are the chances of me actually being her?"

Mrs. Pearson eyed the black glass. "Based on the information you have given us, I see the possibility as lost to the realm of faith. Fortunately, a thorough analysis will provide us with the answer we seek."

I closed my eyes and lowered my head.

"It's not bad where we're going," Chase said. "I can finally show you my home. Please agree to come back with us."

His statement from the night of the fair jumped into my head. *'You could leave if you want to.'* I opened my eyes to the boy seated beside me. "Agree?"

"Chase!" Mrs. Pearson said.

"Agree?" I asked again, staring at Chase. "You mean I have to agree before you can take me?" The ground below my feet began to solidify. Tears disappeared as a surge of strength replaced my anger.

She sighed. "We have laws on our world, just as humans have laws. We cannot interfere with the natural inhabitants of another planet unless they allow us to. That is why you are here, why I am asking you to come with us. This mission cannot be completed on Earth. Do you understand?"

"I don't understand any of this." I stared into my hands as a vacuum drew our situation to the point of no return. The woman needed me in a way no small words could change, but I had the knowledge to keep me safe.

"I thought maybe you could sympathize with our intentions. Somewhere on this planet is a girl whose mother has spent years seeking her tearful return. Nothing would bring me more pleasure than seeing them reunited."

The truth in her words filtered through me. She wanted this reunion, wished to see the tears with all of her heart, and the longing in her eyes nearly choked me. My hand ached to reach for hers, but I had to stay strong. "The possibility of me being this girl is almost nonexistent. Isn't there anything you can check here?" The voice rang in my ears, but someone else must have made the screeching sound. "You could let me go and I'll forget all of this. If I can forget my real parents, I could certainly forget you."

She smiled, this time as if to humor a child throwing a tantrum. "Jessica, we are out of time."

"Why is this girl so important to you?"

"When you remember, you will know."

"I don't get why you think she's still alive." I looked to Chase. "You said this planet kills your people. You said *no one* from your planet has lived here more than three years without returning home. I think I'd remember leaving Earth in the last three years."

"An Olsandyol said I would find her," he offered, with quiet hope. "On Earth, before her sixteenth birthday."

"In Credence? This town doesn't even qualify for a

big dot on the map. Plus, I'm not sixteen yet."

"She was lost in New York, just like you. At first, I thought she was Lauren, but when we took Lauren to Golvern and regenerated her skin, the new cells didn't match. We'd almost given up, until the Olsandyol said go to the first state and never stop believing." He smiled. "Credence means belief. After returning Lauren to her adopted parents, we spent months in Delaware."

"The first state," I said, breathless.

"One day, when the chance of finding her had become a dying star, we stopped at a gas station. As Mom paid the cashier, I picked up an atlas with every state listed in alphabetical order. Alabama came first."

I looked to Mrs. Pearson. "But after so many years?"

She nodded. "We have no choice but to continue in our belief she is alive. Her sixteenth birthday has already passed."

"My birthday is in January."

"Maybe it's not," Chase said. "Maybe when we met you were fifteen and now you're sixteen."

I shook my head. "I'm not going back with you, but I'll do anything else to help."

"I know you are frightened," she said. "But you have to realize any possibility of you being her is worth our efforts. Would you not want to know your mother has spent years searching for you?"

Okay, maybe diplomacy wouldn't work. "My real mother left and there's no way she's ever given me a second thought. I've got all the family I need with me here." Her wince delivered some satisfaction, but not as I'd wished. "I hate her, even if she is my mother. You say she wants me back. She wants to take me away from everyone I know and love. What loving mother would torture her child like that?"

"What are a few weeks of your life when you could be helping others?"

"Don't turn a selfish mother into a plea to help others. I don't believe you, and I don't believe you'll be taking me back."

Mrs. Pearson was stunned, maybe even speechless, but her eyes still held strength.

I thought of Pade, felt the irony of love and hate in the same breath. "Please don't ruin this for me."

"Ruin what?" she asked.

"My life. There might be a small chance I'm this girl, but Mom and Dad love me. *They* adopted me. *They* are the reason I'm not in foster care or worse. If you make me leave, you'll screw up everything." My voice rose to the breaking point. "They might not want me back."

Desperate words hung in the air as she considered. Mrs. Pearson pushed a button to her left and spoke in a shaky voice. A moment later, the door opened and a serious-looking man entered. His trail across the floor zigzagged from one flat heel to a three-inch boost that caused the white coat to hang at an angle, but I'd know a doctor anywhere. I met enough of them when Dad was sick.

"We talked of a method to test her here," she said. "What have you come up with?"

"Instead of regeneration, I believe there is another way. Her skin has been damaged from years of exposure to the sun in this system, but, if my calculations are correct, the inner tissues of her bones carry residues of her true genetic code. If we take samples, we can complete an analysis upon our return." He looked at me, as if to satisfy his curiosity.

Mrs. Pearson followed his gaze. She stood, head rising with decision. "If you agree to provide us with a sample, we will return without you."

Chase's face twisted with shock.

"You'll really leave me? And Bailey?" I held my breath.

"As I said before, we have no intention of harming you. Most likely there will be no match. In that truth, you will never feel the fear of our company again."

Still looking at Chase, I nodded. Maybe giving them a sample wouldn't be the smartest thing I'd done, but I believed it would settle the question in all of their minds. I almost felt sorry knowing they'd return home empty handed.

Almost.

* * * * *

The next morning my eyes opened to sunshine, bright and warm and inviting. Then I remembered the night before. Chase. Bailey. The mall.

Bailey and I returned to the mall just before the van pulled up at the front entrance. Mom noticed Bailey wasn't her usual talkative self, no surprise since she was still groggy from being rendered unconscious. I offered no help with the gaps. On the way home, I decided Mom would never hear about that night.

Mrs. Pearson and Chase had delivered us, minus all the guards. Despite a flood of relief when they turned to leave, confusion tore at my insides like someone had demanded my big toe.

"Chase," I yelled and he turned back, eyes filled

with tears. I ran to Chase, throwing my arms around his neck and pulling him close. Pain tightened my chest as I realized no amount of kidnapping could erase our closeness.

He clung tight enough to make me wonder if he'd ever let go. "I'm sorry for leaving you here," he whispered and finally pulled away. "I promise to come back for you. One day you'll agree to return because you want to. Then I'll show you a world where you don't have to worry about people being mean to you, a place where you don't have to feel weird all the time."

"I'll never feel weird with you." I hugged him again and closed my eyes. When I opened them, Mrs. Pearson stood nearby with tears in hers. In that moment, I knew I'd never truly understand the woman.

"Are you really going to leave her here?" Chase asked.

She spoke slowly, her strength a dam for raw emotions. "We must go home to complete our mission. One day you will understand what it means to follow through, at any cost."

"I think this sucks," he said.

"We are fighting for a cause greater than any of us, and that cause must remain our primary concern."

"We should tell her the truth."

"We will not know the truth until the data is analyzed. Our analysis will take some time and no doubt require resources not available on this planet." She paused and a sliver of thoughtfulness entered her voice. "You are still sure?"

Chase crossed his arms. "The facts fooled us in the beginning, but I've known the truth since the day I met her." He turned back to me, but this time the closeness made my skin crawl. "We were born on the same day. We were together the night you disappeared."

Mrs. Pearson gripped his shoulder, pulling him away. "The Olsandyol said she must remember on her own."

His eyes prodded mine while I dredged the crevices of my memory. Voices flashed in my head as my parents argued. The spaceship loomed before me after the long hall. Booming sounds. People fighting. The man with a gun. Air that smelled of smoke and a woman's scream. Something about her voice stirred deep inside me, but I shoved the feeling even deeper.

"Remember I had a sister? Kayden was her name—is her name."

"No," I said. "You've got it wrong."

"You're lying. You remember something. Is it that night? You remember getting on that platform. The ship was about to leave."

"No," I whispered, taking two steps back.

Tears filled his eyes, tears of anger. "Why did you leave me?"

"I don't remember you," I screamed. "Please, Chase. Please go."

He recoiled as if I'd slapped him. Chase hesitated long enough for Mrs. Pearson to wave her hand and they disappeared.

I stole a glance at the clock by my bed. Seven-thirty seemed early to be wide-awake on a Sunday. A year of Mondays loomed ahead and many nights to pass before I could free my mind of Chase Pearson. How would I fill the gash Chase had carved into my life, knowing my view at night would always be different from his?

The first step would be breakfast.

When I entered the kitchen, the table filled with steaming bowls made me realize I wasn't a freak or crazy. Maybe my life had bordered normal more than once. I inhaled and smiled, marveling at how wonderful eggs could smell.

"You're in a good mood this morning," Dad said.

My face beamed as the twins made their way to the table. "It's going to be a great day."

Dad lowered his paper. "I'm glad to see you stop and smell the coffee for once, or in your case, the eggs. Most people don't understand how wonderful something is until they almost lose it."

If Dad only knew I was almost stolen away on a spaceship. Finally, I understood how he felt about dying. "I'll try to keep that in mind."

When the twins finished eating and climbed the stairs, I rose.

"There's a matter we need to discuss," Mom said, in her serious voice. "I got a call this morning from Dr. Greene."

I rubbed the sore spot on my upper leg.

"Last night your English teacher left town with Chase. Apparently, his father passed away."

"That…" I said, "is awful." Yeah, right his father died!

"This has to be hard on Chase. I know the two of you are close and I don't want you to be upset."

"Why would I be upset?"

Dad covered my hand with his. "It's okay for you to be upset. I just want you to know we're here if you need to talk."

"I'm sorry to hear about his father," I said. "Too bad Chase had to go home for such a horrible reason."

Mom stood and kissed my forehead. "Don't worry, honey. I'm sure Chase will be okay eventually. You know I was twelve when my mom passed away, so I do understand how he feels. Mrs. Pearson took a leave of absence to travel to California and Dr. Greene has no indication of when they'll return."

"Mom, I really am okay."

"Jes," Dad said, "I know you and you don't look okay."

"I just need some space."

"Space?" He laughed softly. "I guess we all need space, probably more so at fifteen. Just promise not to grow up too fast."

Just promise not to get sick again. "No problem," I said, smiling.

I reached the first stair but froze when Dad spoke from the doorway. "I'm sorry I never got the chance to meet Chase. Your mother says he's a nice young man. Too bad things didn't work out."

"You do know I wasn't dating Chase? We were just good friends."

Dad laughed again, his eyes twinkling. "Always remember how important good friends are."

I smiled, for there wasn't a single line around his eyes. "I'm sure Chase and I will always be friends, even if we are from two different worlds."

Dad raised an eyebrow. "Different worlds? Jessica Ray, you have to quit watching so much television. No one can be that melodramatic."

His voice translated to safety and love inside my head, but I barely heard the meaning above a replay of *'Kay Ray'*. "Has my middle name always been Ray?"

"Okay, maybe *you* can have that much drama. How

many of your classmates will ever have the chance to ask such a question?"

I couldn't help but laugh. "Asking is a waste if you never answer."

His laughter stomped out all teasing. "I never thought you'd catch me with words. With the Naples, your middle name was Lynn, so your answer is no. You once insisted we call you Jessica Ray. Actually, Jessica was too long and you pronounced it Kay Ray. Don't you remember?" His eyes met mine with gentle pleading, as if somehow my remembering the past might one day be welcome. "You and I even made a game of it once upon a time."

I shrugged, concealing surprise and anger. Was he now inviting me to remember the past, when he had warned me so many times?

Dad's smile faded. "Lorraine told me about your phone."

I'd *almost* forgotten. "What about it?"

He cleared his throat. "She mentioned you need a new one."

I shook my head and started up the stairs.

"You really don't want a new phone?" he yelled, as I reached the top. "I'm taking the boys to the mall. You can come along and pick out whatever you want."

"Not today."

"Are you *sure* you're okay?"

"I'm fine, just not ready to go there yet."

Dad left me to the empty room and thoughts of Chase. If only he'd pushed harder. A few more questions and I might have spilled.

From my bedroom window, I watched him pull out of the driveway with the twins, grateful I still could.

CHAPTER SEVENTEEN

Alone

For ten nights I watched the stars, sure I'd never see Chase again. At the same time, a part of me waited, and on the darkest days even hoped.

When school ended for the second week after Chase left, I realized he wasn't coming back. Since Bailey was heartbroken enough for us both, I buried my feelings and listened as every sentence started with 'if only' and 'I can't believe.'

Even worse, she started talking about her father again. Mr. Sanders planned to drive from Colorado a few days before Christmas. Aunt Charlie swore he would come, though Bailey vented her doubt during first block and lunch. The new English teacher didn't seem to care that she'd pulled a desk next to mine and decided to stay for the remainder of the semester. Every statement became 'My father said…', or 'My father promised…', and I wasn't sure if she planned to accept his gifts or slap his face when he showed up in her driveway.

Since Pade had become an expert at keeping his distance, I had no idea how he felt about his father's return.

The weekend after Thanksgiving brought Bailey's birthday. Mom took us to the Fun Connection, no pleading necessary. I ate a mega-bucket of popcorn, down to the kernels, while Bailey talked about Chase.

"He's cuter than that guy in the nacho line," she said. "He would love the last preview." Even before the lights dimmed, she'd already said his name a dozen times, though not once did she mention the night Chase left.

"I don't think I want to see another movie," Bailey said when the credits finished.

That made two of us. I slurped the last sip from my drink. "Never?"

"Never ever," she said. "They're coming in to clean."

Bailey followed as I left the theater, walking straight for the main exit. She spotted Skip and Angel buying popcorn for the next movie. "At least someone's happy after all of this."

"Yeah," I said, smiling.

As Angel crossed the floor, Bailey fought a smile, but lost. "This is awful. I've sworn to stay depressed at least until Christmas. How can anyone see her face and not imagine birds singing and little mice sewing a dress like in Snow White?"

"I think that was Cinderella." Angel put an arm around Bailey. "How are you doing?"

Bailey shrugged her off. "Not as good as you, but I guess that's okay."

The light in Angel's face dissolved. "Sorry, I didn't

mean—"

"We were just leaving," I said.

"Have you seen *Zombies Never Die*? Stay and watch it with us. My uncle's working today—he can get you guys back in for free."

"You decide," I said to Bailey. "I'm going to the bathroom." Maybe Bailey would want to stay or maybe not, I really didn't care. At the bathroom door, I heard a familiar voice and stopped.

"You're not my father."

I felt a wave of guilt remembering the same words I said to Dad. Near the door to the men's bathroom stood Tosh, along with a bald man in a leather jacket.

The man grabbed her chin. "I'm close enough." The veins in his neck bulged as his face approached hers. "You'll keep doing whatever I ask, just like your mother." With his other hand, he twisted her arm.

The bathroom door slammed against my back as a huge woman pushed her way out, half-black, half-silver hair netted around her ears. "In or out, hon, but you can't be both." She noticed the scene before me. "Hey," she hollered. "Get your hands off that girl."

"Mind your own business," he said, but other people had taken notice. Glares surrounded him and he released Tosh. Her eyes were fixed on the floor.

I ducked into the bathroom before Tosh could see me. All the stalls were empty and I chose one with the light out overhead. I thought of the man's hand, gripping Tosh's arm, and the tears in her eyes at a Saturday afternoon movie. Those eyes had screamed of innocence, the kind only a child could know. A child hurt by her parents. Like me, she'd probably been tortured by the truth for years, hers physical in addition to the head-case I'd become. Wetness fell, forming splotches on the knees of my jeans until I slapped my face, refusing to pity her.

The bathroom door opened and closed at least twenty times before I left the stall. My tears had dried, but I felt weird inside. I washed my hands and sounds of the water faded, replaced by gentle sobs.

Towels covered the counter and I pushed each crinkled brown piece of paper into the trash. I washed my hands again. The sobs were louder.

Pools of water surrounded the two sinks, splashed behind the faucets and onto the mirror. The bathroom door was silent while I grabbed more paper towels. Sounds of snot and tears filled the room as I soaked up every drop. Tossing away the towels, I thought of Mom, of how I'd sworn to never end up so anal about cleaning.

Only one stall door remained closed. I stared into the mirror. Why had I not already escaped?

I walked to the stall and shoved open the door. "You need to tell someone. That man will never stop hurting you."

Tosh stared up from the tiled floor. "Why do you care?"

"Maybe I don't. Maybe I can't stand him either." My voice rose. "Maybe I've been bullied for too long."

"That's why you're being nice to me?" She sniffled. "Because I've treated you like crap?"

"I finally realized you only treated me like crap because I let you. I should've turned you in that first day."

She made a choking sound. "It's a little late now."

"It's never too late to make things right."

Tosh wiped her eyes and smiled. "Get the hell out, Delaney."

* * * * *

We celebrated Pade's seventeenth birthday as a family on December fourth. He chose an Italian restaurant and I imagined the two of us seated in a corner of the dim room, enjoying a candlelit dinner. The thought faded as Mom insisted he blow out the candles, over a cake she'd managed to form into the shape of a football.

On Christmas Eve, we gathered around the table for a game of cards. As Pade dealt, Aunt Charlie rushed into the kitchen, excitement on her face. "What do you want most for Christmas?"

Bailey rolled her eyes. "A new pool."

Dad choked on his glass of wine. "Pool?"

"To replace the one we had before Jes came to town."

"Bailey," Aunt Charlie said, "that's not fair."

"She's not even afraid of water. You should see us swimming in the creek."

My eyes widened. "What are you talking about?"

"Come on," she said. "Admit it, you love to swim."

Aunt Charlie crossed the kitchen and grabbed Bailey's arm. "You're not doing this tonight. We don't need any more drama in this family, especially on Christmas Eve."

As Bailey argued, I backed away from the table, escaping for my room. Before I reached the stairs, she was behind me.

"Some friend you are. You should've had my back."

I spun around, but Pade stepped between us.

"Leave her alone," he whispered.

She snickered. "What will you care after next week?"

"Next week?" I stared at Pade. "What happens next week?"

"Dad asked Pade to move to Colorado and he's going."

Pade's eyes were sad as he backed away from Bailey. "You promised to let me tell her."

My face was numb. "It doesn't matter." I ran upstairs and threw the pillow over my head like a scared child, abandoned yet again. Beneath the comforter, I cried for hours, until the door opened and a pair of pink fur-trimmed shoes stole across the floor.

Bailey's voice was soft. "I'm sorry about earlier."

I sniffled and wiped my nose. "Please, just leave me alone."

"We have to talk."

I pushed away the comforter. "I know why you were so mad."

She frowned. "Those things I said, I didn't mean to—"

"It's fine, whatever."

"No, I caused a scene about you when everyone was looking at me." Bailey approached the bed and I noticed her eyes were swollen like mine. "I told them I was lying about the creek. Are you okay?"

"I'll be fine. I'm over Pade."

Bailey crawled in, forcing me over. She took my hand under the comforter and squeezed. "Jessica Delaney, I know you better than that. You've always liked Pade and that hasn't changed."

Tears streamed down my face. "How can he be

leaving us like this?" I gulped between the sobs. "How can he be leaving you?"

"I'm going with him."

"What?"

She looked away, her voice shrinking. "Dad wants us to move to Colorado and complete the second semester. It's only 'til summer." Her last sentence spilled out in a rush, as if to cover the one before.

I stared at the ceiling. The lamp at my bedside cast strange shadows above us. "Just like that, you're moving to another state." My tears dwindled and dried a path to my chin before Bailey replied.

"You of all people should understand. I haven't seen my dad in two years."

"So, he shows up and you just go?"

"I want the chance to know him." Her voice cracked. "Do you think you're the only one who's wondered about your real dad? About why he didn't stay around?"

"No." Faced with the ugly truth, how I was only one of many kids hurt by their real parents, I laughed.

"What's so funny?"

"You made me feel normal."

She shifted on the bed. "Dad wants me and Pade to come to Colorado and live with him. We can finally get answers."

I pulled my hand away from hers. "Good luck."

Her voice rose. "Can't you be happy for me?"

"Does it have to be for the whole semester?"

"Mom's staying here while we go. I know it sounds strange, but she has her job at the hospital." Bailey sighed. "Dad promised to bring us back when summer comes."

"How can you forgive him, like he only sent you to your room?"

"He's my dad."

"So, now you call him dad?"

"He's always been my dad. Don't be jealous because yours isn't here." Her words filled the air around us, buzzing in my ears until I wanted to scream. I covered my ears, desperate for an end to the sound, to lie alone in bed, for the room to be dark. The lamp glowed from my bedside.

"Jes, I…"

"We'll talk about it tomorrow," I said, through clenched teeth. In one sentence, Bailey had cut to my deepest feelings and my worst fear. Rolling over, I reached for the lamp, but never felt the switch. My fingers grazed the spot where I should have touched it, at the same time a crash sounded. The room flooded with darkness.

Bailey and I fell asleep in silence, and neither of us mentioned the lamp.

* * * * *

On New Year's Day, I slumped into my normal seat at the table. Mom served collard greens and black-eyed peas, both of which I refused. "Good luck," she said and filled me in on the old southern tradition, but I'd given up on luck.

When I headed for the stairs, no one seemed to notice how much food lingered on my plate. The air outside my bedroom window was warm enough for shorts. I stared through the screen as Pade knocked on the door.

"I think we should talk before I go," he said.

I shivered, focused on a line of clouds above the trees.

"Nothing to say?"

"I've heard Colorado Springs is not so bad."

He opened the door and crossed the floor, quiet until he stood behind me. "You want me out of here, admit it."

My face flamed and I turned. "Say anything you want. Find a way to cover the guilt, no matter how bad I feel."

He laughed and shook his head. "Except for the last five minutes, you haven't said more than hi or bye to me in weeks."

"I never realized we'd run out of time."

"I didn't know about Dad taking us back until the week after my birthday."

"Does it really matter now?"

"Look, Jes, I've stayed away because I knew how upset you were about Chase leaving. Bailey told me everything."

I collapsed into the beanbag and lowered my head.

"No one can help that Chase isn't coming back, but I'll be back after school is out." He held out a box. "Happy birthday."

The paper loomed before me, stripes of yellow against dark green. I thought of the glasses Chase gave me, in a similar box, on his birthday. "I won't be sixteen until tomorrow."

Pade pushed the box into my hand. "You know we're leaving tonight."

My fingers trembled as I ripped through the paper and opened the lid. White silk lined the box, a soft bed for the gold chain that shined from the center. "It's beautiful."

"You don't sound impressed."

"I'm tired, that's all."

"You know I'm coming back." A storm began in his eyes. "I promise."

When he reached for my hand, I retreated, toppling from the beanbag. With a stumble, I dropped the box and stood, back against the wall.

"Why are you so afraid to touch me? It can't be that silliness about our parents, not when we're alone."

I took a long breath. "No."

"My parents don't have to know. Your parents…" His voice lowered. "Do you know how much I care about you?"

"Don't," I whispered.

His face neared mine, until his breath tickled my cheek. "Say the words and I'll stay."

"You've promised your dad and Aunt Charlie. I won't make you choose between them and me."

"But it was okay for Bailey to choose?"

"That was different."

He sighed. "It was never Tosh. That night in the locker room, it was only you. I had to kiss someone to know I wasn't going crazy. You can't understand, but I think I love you, and it's the insane kind of lose-my-head love that scares me." He gave a bitter laugh. "The worst part is, I've never believed people could fall in love. Just look at my parents—see how that turned out?"

I stared at Pade, my heart racing. "I don't believe in love either."

"Then it sounds like maybe I am crazy. You don't feel the same and you've been telling me all along, haven't you?"

How could I tell him the truth? He was leaving no matter what I said. In that moment, I realized I'd tarnished him, cursed our chances just like Jessica Naples was born to do. Anger burned inside me. I slammed my fist against his chest.

Pade put a hand to his ribs, his face twisting. "Do you hate me that much?" He placed his other hand under my chin, gently forcing my eyes to his.

I wanted to cry. Instead, I screamed.

Before Pade could figure out what to do next, Mom and Aunt Charlie rushed through the door, planting themselves between us.

"What's going on in here?" Mom grabbed my arms.

Pade's voice transformed to cool and calm. "Jes was upset about Bailey leaving. I was trying to cheer her up."

"Is that true?" Mom asked, releasing me.

I looked out the window, but never saw beyond the metal lace. "Yes ma'am."

Aunt Charlie whirled me around to face her. "Are you sure you're okay?"

"Like he said, I was upset. Everyone is leaving."

Mom hugged me. "Pade and Bailey will be back before you know it. And your dad and I will never leave."

Aunt Charlie rubbed my arm. "The kids might come home for spring break. That's only two months away."

I smiled as a robot might if a computer could translate desolation. "Thanks."

Mom hugged me again and pushed Aunt Charlie toward the door. "We'll be in the kitchen if you need us."

"Maybe Pade should come with us," Aunt Charlie said.

"I'll be down in a minute," he said quickly. "I just need to talk to Jes about Bailey, to make sure she's okay."

"Fine," Mom said. "Five minutes."

Pade exhaled as the door closed, his eyes darting back to mine. "That was close."

"Get out."

His eyes widened.

"You asked me to say the words. I never want to see you again."

His face paled. Pade took a step in my direction, hands outstretched.

I shoved him away and ran from the room, locking myself in the bathroom. Footsteps stopped outside the door. A shadow fell across my feet.

Pade didn't jiggle the handle or threaten to break down the door. A soft thud sounded against the door, about where his head would have touched the wood. "Goodbye, Jes," he whispered.

I sat before the toilet and stared at the dome light above my head, until my eyes burned. The pain in his voice was enough to make me cry for most of the night. Sometime, maybe hours later, I climbed to my feet and opened the door. Something gleamed on the door and I reached down.

A gold chain hung from the handle.

* * * * *

When I finally slept, I dreamed again of the spaceship. Fear followed me down the long hall and onto the platform. At the end, I gripped the metal rail along the bridge that separated me from the ship. I closed my eyes and picturing myself on the ledge that protruded from beneath a lighted door. With a deep breath, I opened my eyes to the door six inches away and a gold mesh of metal at my feet. Swirls of wind weaved my hair as I touched a keypad and the door split. Before I could step inside, the voice thundered again.

"Chadsworth!"

I spun, catching sight of a boy on the bridge below, back against the rail. Beneath him stirred water, strong circular currents made by wind from the ship's engine. When he turned, blue eyes cut through the wind as my heart and head met in sudden agreement. "Come on," I screamed, extending a hand.

His hands rose in desperation, only seconds before a patchwork of cloth covered his entire body. Great arms lifted the mass like a rag doll. The hooded figure glared up at me, but I saw only the amber eyes, alive with hatred. In one calculated move, my brother was lifted over the rail and into the water. One hand flailed from under the blanket, fingers that were last to disappear from sight.

The whistle of a door closing sent me stumbling backward. I jumped through the gap, falling against black glass as the ground plunged beneath me. I lowered my head and poured out a decade of tears.

It was never me in the water. It wasn't my fear, but his. Seeing him over and over had me shaking again. My brother was dead. No one could survive beneath the surface of that dark water. But somehow Chase had.

When sunlight finally silenced darkness, a lifetime of regret and loss had passed. My birthday had arrived, but the day meant nothing. Voices filled the floor below, those once marked by a daily offer to rise and join the family. Now the invitation felt hollow.

Until that morning, my sixteenth January second, I never understood losing the closest person in the world. Chase was my brother, I knew with every part of me, every beat of my heart. He would have come for me already, if he could have. I felt the fear, the evil eyes that watched me, stole him away while I stood on that platform. One memory, one night was all I had. A thousand questions flowed through my head, but none mattered. Once again, Chase was gone.

I pulled out Mrs. Pearson's lingering assignment, the black marbled journal, and penned the first page. Had the woman been my mother all along? Or was she his captor? The only way to know was to remember, so I started with the beginning. Every word from Chase became a clue to the mystery of my past and every detail of her another step to remembering. Soon, I found that writing flowed easier than drawing.

Eventually thoughts of Chase gave way to Pade and I closed my eyes, seeing only an image of him pacing the length of his front yard like a tide refusing to give up the beach. The smell of his cologne, the feel of his fingers touching mine bombarded my senses. His lips were moving, maybe he argued with Sarah Beth or Tosh on the other end of the phone he gripped, and I tried to convince myself it no longer mattered. He no longer mattered.

What a joke when I was the one who sent him away. The only guy I'd ever loved, and he would never know the truth. Maybe I wasn't Jessica Naples, but at least I could ensure he never made the mistake of loving me again. Pade was gone like Chase. Like Bailey, leaving me alone as I'd always feared. Only my parents remained, but at what point would they burn the bridge out of Credence in an effort to escape me?

I opened the porch door with care, each exhale a fog of crystals as I snuck onto the porch. Pulling the jacket close, I laughed bitterly, for even the seasons had changed overnight. Dad reclined in a padded iron chair along the banister.

"When were you going to tell me Frank and Marsha weren't my real parents?"

His eyes remained closed until I stepped back, bitter about wasting all that nerve.

"When you remembered they weren't," he said, his words almost fading into the breeze.

"All this time you and Mom lied to me."

"We did what was required to protect you."

"Protect me from what? For the last eleven years, I thought my real parents abandoned me. Isn't that bad enough?"

"Jessica Naples disappeared the same week you appeared."

"But why lie and say I was her? Of all people?"

His eyes flew open. "You still don't get it. You have no name, no parents, no background waiting for you to discover. According to New York State, you never existed before the night I found you."

"How is that possible?"

"The doctors said to wait, that you would remember eventually. You had to remember on your own for it to be real, for you to feel safe."

"I don't understand."

"You were terrified. From the fear in your eyes to

the distorted words you cried out in the night, you witnessed someone die and you wouldn't go near water. You spent most of the first month hiding under your bed, but we couldn't let you go. Lorraine and I couldn't let them take you away from us. It made sense to tell the world you were Jessica Naples. Otherwise, I never would have gotten you out of New York."

"But what about the real Jessica Naples?"

"I'm sorry to say she's most likely dead. She was my only regret in all of this. Claiming you were her prevented the police from arresting those horrible people."

"What really happened to them?"

"I can only assume they were smart enough to disappear before someone found out the truth."

Did I ever tell him about Chase? "What about my fear of water?"

"Honestly, I'm not sure why you feared water. Whatever happened to you was before that night in New York." He leaned forward, taking my hand. "This is great, really. We can finally talk about what happened back then without doing this little dance around the pins and needles."

"*Her* birthday was January second, not mine. So much for Sweet Sixteen. Today means nothing to me now."

"Since you couldn't tell us when you were actually born, I didn't think keeping hers would break your heart after all these years."

"But I know now. It's October fourteenth."

Dad released my hand. "How do you know for sure?"

I thought of Chase, of the day at the lake, one of

the happiest in memory. He owned that day as I did, and I couldn't betray him again. "I can't explain. It's in my head, like a date I've known forever but just now remembered."

"What else have you remembered?"

"My real name was Kayden."

"And?"

Two pillars of my past and he wanted more? "That's about it so far."

His lips pressed together in the faintest of smiles. "Now we know where the name Kay Ray came from."

I hadn't made the connection. "Now that I know, what should I do?"

"We find more doctors, better doctors who can help you remember." He touched the side of my face. "We find a way to jog that fuzzy head of yours."

"We?" I asked, holding my breath.

"You're still my daughter. We're still a family. Whatever it takes, however long it takes, we fight this one together."

I fell into Dad's open arms, for the first time thanking fate.

* * * * *

Please look for *Secrets Return*, Book #2 in the Leftover Girl Series.

Acknowledgements

I want to thank everyone who has read this book and especially those who are willing to give a few minutes of their time for an honest review. It means more to me than you can imagine.

Thanks to Sherri—my sister, my friend. She helped make this dream real.

Thanks to my parents for teaching me the only way to truly fail is to give up.

Thanks to Louise for her detailed eye. Her help and encouragement brought me to the turning point where I realized publishing could really happen.

Thanks to Christie at EbookEditingPro. Her editing insights made our time wonderfully constructive. Also, thanks for the cover design that nearly brought me to tears.

Thanks to Jacquie Flynn—her words of encouragement kept me writing in the darkest hours.

Thanks to my husband for realizing I can't exist without dreaming, or dream without writing.

About The Author

C.C. Bolick grew up in south Alabama, where she's happy to still reside. She's an engineer by day and a writer by night—too bad she could never do one without the other.

Camping, fishing… she loves the outdoors and the warm Alabama weather. For years she thought up stories to write and finally started putting them on paper back in 2006. If you hear her talking with no one to answer, don't think she's crazy. Since talking through her stories works best, a library is her worst place to write… even though it's her favorite!

C.C. loves to mix sci-fi and paranormal—throw in a little romance and adventure and you've got her kind of story. She's written eight books including the Leftover Girl Series and The Agency Series.

Please visit her website at www.ccbolick.com for updates on future releases.

Made in the USA
Columbia, SC
24 May 2020

98292687R00167